Taming Riki

Volume II: A World Divided
Part 1

Taming Riki

Volume II: A World Divided
Part 1

By Kira Takenouchi

ARIK ENTERPRISES

Paris London Tokyo Reykjavik

ISBN-13: 978-1517320416
ISBN-10: 1517320410

Chapter 1 ~
A Blondie's Authority

FOR AMOI'S YOUTH—ELITES AND MONGRELS alike—the days following Jupiter's Appearance were celebrated with great enthusiasm, the streets of Midas and Tanagura teeming with drunken youths glad for any occasion to use as an excuse for revelry.

But for the older Elites, Jupiter's proclamation was greeted with less festivity and far more criticism. It was a time of intense debate and discussion; Jupiter's potential admission of mongrels into Amoian society was a concept so surprising and distasteful to many that it was almost unfathomable. It went against everything they had been taught, and because of this, many felt the need to discuss it.

And of course, this was not all the Elites talked about. High on the list of favorite topics was the subversion and conspiracy of Iason Mink, Raoul Am, Omaki Ghan, Heiku Quiahtenon, Xian Sami, and Megala Chi. Surprisingly, the status of these Blondies only increased after their failed insurrection, partly because, without exception, all six Blondies retreated from society, declining the numerous invitations that poured in for parties, cotillions, and debates. They were admired, talked about, and eagerly sought out, but for days afterwards none of them were seen. Omaki remained hidden in the Taming Tower, Heiku was on self-imposed "indefinite" leave from Tanagura Medical, Xian was thought to have retreated to his villa, and Megala, Raoul, and Iason remained secluded in the Eos tower.

But, though invitations to cotillions and gatherings might be ignored, Headmaster Konami's summons that they meet weekly to endure his lectures could not be, and so, arriving with exaggerated reluctance, the Blondies converged at Iason's penthouse every Jupiter's Eve, for dinner, followed by an evening of lectures on the General Code.

"OF COURSE IT'S RAINING," HEIKU GRUMBLED, as Toma led him into Iason's penthouse.

Heiku was the first to arrive that evening, their third meeting with Headmaster Konami, and though he pretended to deplore the weekly gatherings, he in fact quite looked forward to dinner at the penthouse, for he believed Tai to be the best chef in the Quadrant. But rain made his bionic prosthesis ache at the point of insertion, and so that particular evening he was rather out of sorts.

"Welcome, Heiku. Can I get you a drink?" Iason purred from his chair, where he sat studying the General Code.

"Don't get up. I'll get it," he answered, heading for the bar. "Blasted arm."

"It's bothering you again, is it? From the rain, I assume?"

"Yes," the Blondie growled. "I'm about ready to detach it and throw it out the window."

Once it became clear that his Master was getting his drink himself, Sarius eagerly followed Toma into the kitchen to escape Heiku's foul mood, which he had, unfortunately, been forced to endure the entire day. He had come to dread rainy days more than the Blondie, who was completely insufferable when his arm tormented him.

Mathias, Heiku's new pet, waited for a few moments in the foyer, but upon receiving no further instruction, made his way over to one of the bedrolls Iason had laid out in the great hall, for the pets that would be accompanying their Masters to the penthouse. He curled up there on the thick, soft cushions, waiting for the others to arrive.

"You look as though you're in pain, too," Heiku remarked. "Are those spectacles helping your headaches at all?"

"A bit," Iason answered, closing his book with a sigh. He removed the spectacles and rubbed his eyes, dreading the evening's lecture.

"Hmmm." Lord Quiahtenon strolled over to the chair nearest him, making himself comfortable by the fire, a glass of cognac in hand. "I must say, dinner smells glorious. What is it, this time?"

"It's roasted pheasant with mashed bungu roots smothered in cream sauce," Iason answered. "And Tai has something special planned for dessert."

"I spy fresh-baked sweet buns," Heiku announced, eyeing the warming dome on the table. "I do love those."

"I know you do," Lord Mink replied, smiling.

"At least we have your marvelous dinners to look forward to. Though I'm sure we must be quite an intrusion, each week."

"Not at all," Iason replied, as always nothing but the most gracious host. Privately, however, he found the weekly gatherings a bit taxing, and wondered how many more they would be forced to endure.

"Lord Am has arrived," Askel announced, over the intercom.

Raoul entered the penthouse, looking extraordinarily grumpy.

"Ah, Raoul. Did you enjoy memorizing the Code?" Heiku teased. "All *three* sections?"

"I did *not*," Raoul replied, scowling. "I'll be lucky if I can remember one section, let alone all three. Damn that Konami, anyway." He poured himself a drink and joined them.

Yui slipped into the kitchen to see if he could be of any assistance there, while Regiland, Raoul's new pet, joined Mathias in the great hall.

"He *is* rather annoying," Heiku agreed. "And I really don't see what the point is, to memorize the Code. I mean, it's not like we didn't know, more or less, what was in the Code."

"He's punishing us," Lord Am answered. "He knows we hate it."

"Lord Ghan," Askel announced, as Omaki strode into the hall, followed by Ru and Enyu.

"Damn it all!" Omaki cursed, dripping wet.

"Where's your umbrella, Omi?" Heiku asked, laughing.

"It got turned inside out and blew away. Blast!"

"Why didn't you park in my reserved area?" Iason asked.

"I did, but I wanted to run down to the pavilion and then I got caught in this mess."

Toma rushed into the hall to greet Omaki. "Lord Ghan! I'll...get some towels for you."

"You'll need more than that," Iason said, rising. "Your clothes are soaked through. I'll find something for you to wear."

"I'm grateful for that," Lord Ghan answered, shaking his head. "What a start to a lovely evening."

"Did you see Yousi?" Heiku asked.

"Yes. I asked if he was coming, but he told me he had too many new paddles to count."

Raoul smiled at this. "Perhaps he's not as slow as we all thought. I know I wouldn't be here, if it wasn't required."

Ru took the towels Toma offered upon returning to the foyer and helped dry his Master's hair, as Omaki shivered.

"Come over here by the fire," Lord Quiahtenon suggested. "You'll catch your death of cold."

"Is it rain or snow?" Lord Am asked, looking out the window.

"Both. I don't know," Omaki answered, taking the towel from Ru and moving over to the fire. "It's a mess. And it's windy."

"Good. Let's hope Konami gets into an accident and we can all go home."

"Raoul," Iason scolded, as he returned with dry clothes for Omaki. "Surely you don't mean the Headmaster to come to any *real* harm." He nodded to Enyu, who was making his way over to the area where the other pets had gathered. Enyu smiled, pleased to have been acknowledged by his former Master.

"Oh, yes I do," Raoul replied. "Though, to be fair, I'd prefer to tie him up and beat him with a stick."

Omaki smiled at this. "As would I. Although I wouldn't mind doing other things, as well. His breeches can hardly contain those muscles of his. I'd love to see him sprawled out, completely naked, on my bed."

Lord Am put his gloved hands over his ears. "Stop, I beg you."

The Blondie laughed and proceeded to strip off his wet clothes.

"Thanks for the free strip show, Omi," Heiku remarked, wryly.

Raoul nodded in agreement. "Yes, Omaki, for heaven's sake. Have a little decency."

"You know you like it," Lord Ghan answered, now completely naked.

"Lord Chi has arrived," Freyn announced.

Megala walked in nervously, stopping in his tracks when he saw Omaki standing naked by the fire.

"Come on in, Megala," Heiku beckoned. "Don't mind Omi, here. He's just in a kinky mood."

The others smiled at this, though Megala continued to stand, looking decidedly uncertain.

"Yes, yes. That's right, Megala. We're just playing a little game. Spin the penis." Omaki took hold of his cock and began to spin it in a circle, much to Heiku's delight, who nearly fell off his chair laughing.

"Oh, for crying out loud," Raoul muttered, shaking his head.

"I don't want to play," Megala announced hopefully.

"What? You must play!" Heiku insisted, pointing to an empty chair. "Now, get your ass over here. Raoul's next. You want to see Raoul spin the penis, don't you?"

"Well," Megala began, glancing at Lord Am, whose face turned beet-red.

"Lord Sami," Askel announced.

"Oh! Help me," Heiku gasped, laughing so hard that his stomach began to hurt.

Xian stepped into the hall, and upon observing Omaki in full disrobe, had no reaction whatsoever, stepping over to the bar to make himself a drink as though nothing were out of the ordinary.

"Hey, get me a drink while you're over there, Xixi," Omaki demanded. "Just whatever. Surprise me."

Juthian stood awkwardly for a moment before he finally followed Toma to the kitchen, where the other attendants had all gathered.

"Juthian," Yui nodded, smiling, as the flustered attendant stepped into the kitchen. Then he frowned, studying him. "What's wrong?"

"Master brought that stupid pet, Enshu," Juthian replied.

Yui nodded sympathetically. "Yes. Master Raoul brought Puki, too."

The others all snickered at Yui's nickname for Regiland.

"I hate Enshu," Juthian grumbled.

"And I hate Puki," Yui agreed. "He's exceedingly annoying. He expects me to wait on him hand and foot."

"Well, you *are* his attendant, Yui," Toma pointed out, smiling.

"I wish I wasn't."

"I've been looking forward to this all week," Sarius announced. "Master Heiku has been insufferable all day. I guess his arm is bothering him, but still. He's been a royal pain in the ass. I can't wait to see Lord Sung chew him out."

"My Master couldn't memorize his sections," Nomi giggled. "I think he's in trouble."

Yui smiled. "Mine, too."

"Tai, do you need any help?" Ru asked, feeling a bit guilty to be standing around talking while the panicked Aristian rushed around the kitchen.

"Um, can someone set the table? I haven't had a chance," Tai replied a little breathlessly. "And oh! The flowers! What did I do with those?"

"You mean these, Tai?" Toma asked, pointing to the vases of fully-blown yellow and orange roses that were lined up on one of the counters.

"Yes, yes. I'm losing my mind. Can you put those on the table, too?"

"Oh, those are beautiful," Juthian exclaimed, bending forward to smell them. "And they smell wonderful."

"They're from our garden, I think," Toma replied, feeling a bit proud.

"Lord Mink really does have incredible gardens," Sarius remarked. "It's amazing that they're all indoors."

Yui nodded. "Master Raoul says Iason has even more amazing gardens at his villa."

"Which dishes should we use?" Ru asked, staring at the immense hutch full of expensive porcelain. "The ones with the silver trim?"

"Um, this time use the ones with the scalloped edging," Tai directed.

"Dinner smells amazing," Sarius announced, sniffing the air. "I'm really hungry, too."

"Is that dessert?" Nomi squealed, pointing to a five-layer cake covered with frosting and caramel.

"Yes," Tai replied, smiling.

"I can't wait!" Ru whispered, eagerly, as he retrieved dishes from the hutch to set the table.

"Where's Riki, Toma?" Juthian asked. "I didn't see him."

Toma shook his head. "He went out again. He loves that new car Master Iason bought him."

"Shouldn't he be back by now?"

"Probably."

"He was out late last week, too," Yui remarked. "Seems like he gets away with almost anything these days."

"Well, he should," Sarius pointed out. "I mean, after what he went through?"

"He's still a pet, though," Nomi argued. "He can't do anything he wants. No other pet has their own vehicle and gets to go scalavanting around at all hours of the night."

"Scalavanting? What's scalavanting?" Sarius laughed.

"You know what I mean," Nomi protested.

"He means gallivanting," Yui corrected, with a smile.

"I think Master Iason is getting a bit fed up with Riki," Toma said, thoughtfully. "I'm just waiting for a big confrontation."

6

The conversation broke up as the attendants all helped Ru set the table, immediately falling silent when they went out into the great hall, where the Blondies were discussing the weather.

"What are the roads like?" Iason asked.

"Seems like it's starting to get a bit nasty," Xian answered. "On the Channel they're predicting a huge late season ice-storm."

At this, Iason frowned and pulled out his phone, flipping it open and sending an outgoing beacon to Riki.

The mongrel picked up, sounding impatient. "Yeah?"

"Come home," Iason ordered.

"But I'm in the middle of a game! And I'm winning!"

"Riki, I told you to be home before sundown. We're about to start dinner."

"I'm not hungry," Riki argued.

"It's raining out. The roads are getting slick."

"All the more reason for me to wait until it blows over."

"The roads will only get worse after dark."

"So? I'll use hover-mode."

"You don't have a pilot's license yet, Riki. You heard me. I want you home NOW."

"But—"

"Riki! This is not open for discussion! Come home this instant!" Exasperated, Iason had risen from his chair, and now moved over to the window, frowning out at the rain, which looked to have turned into sleet.

There was a slight pause on the line. Riki was furious, as he had been enjoying a game of billiards with some new friends at Depravities. Since Jupiter's proclamation, Riki had become a living legend, a sort of hero among the mongrels. Now he stood, his face flushing red with anger and embarrassment as the mongrels looked on, exchanging knowing looks. It was not the first time Riki had been called away by his Blondie Master, and while they did not find it surprising, Riki felt humiliated.

Though he had enjoyed increased privileges since the day Iason had offered him his freedom, there were times, like this, that he began to resent Iason's demands. He found it irritating that the Blondie still treated him as a pet. He had expected more equality in their relationship, and yet Iason still had the same expectations as before. He still told him what to do, still scolded him if he did not immediately obey. Though he had far greater freedom and movement than previously, he still had to ask permission to do almost anything. It was annoying and humiliating.

"Iason," he began, his voice lowering to a pleading tone.

"Riki. You heard me. I want you home. NOW."

"But, can't I just finish—"

"Riki! Shall I come and fetch you?" Iason demanded, his exasperation evident by his tone of voice.

"You don't have to yell. Sheesh."

"I expect you to be here within half an hour."

"But, I'm all the way over in Midas. You don't want me to speed, do you?"

"No," Iason replied, frowning. "Very well. Be here within the hour. Drive safely."

Riki sighed loudly and dramatically, hanging up without another word.

Annoyed, Iason stood for a moment, staring out the window, then returned to his chair, brooding.

"Having a little pet trouble, Iason?" Heiku asked.

The others all smiled at this; it was not the first time Riki had delayed coming home on Jupiter's Eve. The mongrel seemed to realize that Iason would not truly be at liberty to "fetch him" while Headmaster Konami was at the penthouse, and he took advantage of it. Although Iason had been a bit more lenient on previous occasions, now he was worried about the weather, and more than just a little irritated with Riki for arguing with him.

Lord Mink shook his head, his eyes to the heavens. "That boy knows how to push my buttons."

"Well, at least he obeys you eventually. I'm still furious with Ima. Do you know, she refused to tell me who got her pregnant?"

"What did you do with her, Heiku?" Omaki asked.

"I sent her back to the Academy. They'll do some genetic profiling to determine the father. Actually I expected the results by now, but apparently there was some mishap with the sample, and they're running a second profile."

"You haven't any idea who it might be?" Raoul asked, curious.

Lord Quiahtenon shook his head. "Whoever he is, I'll be paying his Master a visit, and I guarantee you, it won't be a social call." He was still annoyed with the embarrassment of Ima's pregnancy, which he perceived to seriously compromise his reputation. On that point he might have been correct at any other time, for Elites viewed unsanctioned pairings as a reflection of a Master's authority, or lack thereof, more precisely. Any other Elite might have suffered for it, but

Heiku, being one of the six Blondie rebels who had dared to challenge Jupiter, did not seriously lose status, even when news of Ima's condition reached the gossip network.

"What's this?" Omaki asked, as Xian handed him an unfamiliar-looking drink.

"Try it," Lord Sami answered, smiling mysteriously.

Lord Ghan shrugged, taking a sip. "Hmmm. It's quite interesting, actually. What is it?" The Blondie stood casually by the fire, as though not in the least concerned that he was stark naked.

"It's a new drink. See if you can guess the ingredients."

"Omaki, for crying out loud! Put some clothes on already!" Raoul chided.

Heiku smiled. "Yes, Omi. We've had enough of a show for one night."

At this, the Blondie turned around and wiggled his bare ass in defiance. Raoul and Heiku both leapt up and immediately proceeded to smack his bottom.

"Ouch!" Omaki laughed, turning back around. "All right, all right!" He put on the pair of silk pants and tunic that Iason had offered him. "My. This is very comfortable. Is this Aristian silk?"

"Yes," Iason replied.

"Hey! Get out of my chair!" Lord Quiahtenon demanded, when he saw that Xian had quietly taken his seat.

"It's not *your* chair," Lord Sami clarified. "And anyway, no one was sitting here."

"I was sitting there," Heiku retorted, "as you know perfectly well. So get your ass out of it!"

"No."

Now Lord Quiahtenon appealed to the other Blondies. "Do you not all see that he just took my seat?"

Raoul groaned, letting his head fall back against his chair. "I hate Jupiter's Eve."

"Children," Omaki scolded, "play nicely or some *real* punishment may be in order."

"Don't make me use my arm," Heiku threatened, spinning his bionic fingers around in a disconcerting manner in front of Xian's face.

"Oh, fine. I suppose if Heiku *must* have his way," Lord Sami sighed with exaggerated annoyance, moving to another chair.

"I give up," Omaki announced, raising his glass. "What's in the drink? I can't guess."

"There are six ingredients," Xian hinted with a smile.

"I just told you I couldn't guess them, it doesn't particularly matter if there are six or six trillion. Although whatever it is, it must be pretty strong. My head is spinning already."

"It's cognac, kuluna, fire kiss, jujufizz, yint, and gold stinger. It's a new drink called Blonde Rebellion, and it was created in honor of us."

"Are you joking?" Omaki asked.

"Actually I'm not. It's all the rage in Midas, apparently."

"Hey, let me have a taste of that, Omi," Heiku demanded, snapping his fingers.

Lord Ghan held his drink protectively. "Get your own drink."

Frowning, Lord Quiahtenon turned to Xian. "Make me one, Xi."

"Do I look like your attendant?" Lord Sami replied, crossing his legs languidly.

"Oh, come on. If there's a drink in my honor I want to know what it tastes like."

"I wouldn't mind having a taste myself," Raoul remarked.

"I'll make you the drink, if you let me have the chair," Xian bargained.

"Oh, all right," Heiku sighed, looking extraordinarily grumpy.

Triumphant on securing the coveted chair—though mostly because he knew the Blondie physician preferred it—Xian rose and went back over the bar. "Iason, would you like to try it as well?"

"If I must. I don't care much for fire kiss."

"I bet you'd have a different view, if you tried *my* fire kiss," Lord Ghan announced, with a mischievous smile.

"Omaki, do you ever *not* think about sex?" Heiku demanded.

"Only when I look at *you*," he replied, without missing a beat.

Lord Quiahtenon rolled his eyes, making himself as comfortable as he could in Xian's chair.

"Megala? What about you?" Lord Sami called.

"Yes, please," Lord Chi answered.

"We were just discussing what we would do to Konami, if we could, when you arrived, Megala," Heiku remarked. "Raoul votes for beating him with a stick, and of course, Omaki wants to violate him sexually."

"I think we should torture him," Xian answered. "I don't care how we do it, as long as it takes forever."

"I must protest," Iason said, frowning. "I'll not have the Headmaster talked about in such a manner."

10

"Iason has a crush on Konami," Omaki explained, "and wants him all to himself."

"Nothing of the sort. But he deserves our respect, surely."

"Of course *you* take that view," Raoul argued. "You were always his favorite, Iason."

Lord Mink made no reply to this, though he smiled slightly.

"I had trouble memorizing the Code," Megala confessed, nervously.

"That's my point exactly," Raoul replied. "It's ridiculous! No one can memorize three sections of the Code in one week!"

"Heiku, are you going to claim Ima's offspring as your pet?" Omaki asked, curious.

"That depends who the father is."

"I can't imagine what sort of pet could be disobedient enough to pair with another pet without authorization," Megala mused.

At this remark, all heads turned to Iason, who frowned. "Well, it can't have been Riki," he asserted.

Heiku smiled. "No, of course not."

"And why not, may I ask?" Omaki pressed.

"Because," Iason replied, clearly annoyed, "he cannot ejaculate unless I remove the restriction on his ring. Besides, he's hardly been out of my sight since he came to Eos, until very recently."

"Yes, we noticed," Xian teased. "We're all waiting to see him pair, you know."

"You can wait as long as you like. I'm not showing him," Lord Mink replied, firmly.

"Why not, Iason?" Megala asked. "Isn't that what pets are for?"

The other Blondies all smiled at this, knowing perfectly well why Iason refused to show his pet.

"He already has a pairing partner," Omaki said, arching a brow. "Isn't that right, Iason?"

The Blondie made no reply, lost in thought. He looked at the clock and wondered when Riki would arrive. The sun had set and it seemed to be raining harder, which worried him. Even though he knew Riki was a fairly good driver, he had chided him, more than once, for driving a bit too fast. It occurred to him that he should have programmed the vehicle with a maximum speed limit to prevent him from driving recklessly. He would have to remember to do that.

He also felt annoyed that, yet again, Riki had talked him out of having a bodyguard with him, realizing now that Odi would have ensured that Riki return home by sundown. He sat brooding, completely unaware of the conversation that went on around him.

Meanwhile, at Depravities, Riki had been so angry after speaking with Iason that he'd flung his phone across the room.

"I guess this means the game's off?" Maiko teased, smiling. Maiko was one of Riki's newest friends, a mongrel that Riki only vaguely remembered from the Orphanage, with a beautiful smile and twinkling eyes. He always seemed to be in a good mood, and his laugh was infectious. Riki learned from Maiko that the remaining members of Bison, his old gang, had been arrested again, and this time had been sent to the prison in Urus for a year after a failed robbery attempt of an Elite's condominium in Apatia.

To Riki, this news had come as a huge relief. He didn't know whether they knew about Guy, or Kei, but he wasn't looking forward to meeting up with any of them again. That was all ancient history; Bison was dead to him now. Besides, Maiko had turned out to be a lot of fun to hang with.

"Hell no," Riki replied, tossing his head. "Iason can go fuck himself. We're finishing this game."

Maiko laughed. "After this, you wanna watch some pets? I'd like to see a pairing."

"Sure, why not?" Riki shrugged, grinning. Though he knew it would have been a lot more fun without his ring restriction, he was having a blast. Depravities had expanded to become an open club, with a new viewing room and stage for pet pairings. He liked Maiko, and Maiko's friends. And everyone, it seemed, liked him. It was hard to leave when he was having such a good time. It had been so long since he'd had a real social life, and now that he'd become such a celebrity in Ceres, he truly enjoyed spending time there again.

Even though he knew Iason wanted him home, it was simply too tempting to ignore him, especially when he felt certain there would be no *real* consequences to his delaying. Iason would fuss at him, no doubt, just as he always did, but surely that would be it. So, he soon forgot the Blondie's mandate, distracted, first, by his game—which he won, of course—and then by a pet pairing show afterwards, which he watched with his new friends.

Back at the penthouse, dinner was announced and the Blondies moved over to the dining table as the attendants brought in the food. As if by unspoken consensus, everyone sat down together at the table, Blondies, pets, and attendants alike. Since their ordeal together, they'd all come to enjoy their weekly gatherings, though the Blondies would have denied it. There was a bond between the households that was so strong, it was as though, in a sense, they all belonged to one household.

"Iason, once again, the food is fabulous," Raoul remarked, and the others all nodded their agreement.

"I need butter for my buns," Megala announced happily.

Xian snorted at this.

"I can assist you with that," Omaki offered, arching a brow seductively.

"Omi, must you drag everything down to your level?" Lord Quiahtenon demanded. "Your perversions annoy me."

"Much as I'd love to be thought of as the most perverted one at this table, I fear I cannot claim that distinction," Omaki replied, winking at Iason.

But Iason didn't even seem to see or hear him. Although his guests were enjoying the dinner, Iason hardly ate at all. He sat, sipping his wine and brooding over Riki's late arrival. Every time he looked at the clock on the mantel in the great hall he felt angry. It was raining harder and now he was truly worried. What if something had happened to him?

Finally he excused himself from the table, hurrying over to the communications center to ferret out Riki's whereabouts. When he entered his tracer code and saw that Riki was still at Depravities, he was so angry he could hardly keep from smashing the terminal with his fist. He immediately placed an outgoing to Riki, impatient when the mongrel delayed picking up.

"I'm coming," Riki answered, a little breathlessly.

"Where are you?" Iason demanded, trying to conceal his anger.

"Um…I'm just, well, there's all sorts of traffic, so—"

"I see. You're delayed because of traffic," the Blondie repeated, his face darkening, one hand on his hip.

"Yeah," Riki answered, biting his lip. "There's…some kind of accident or something."

"Riki," Iason snapped, "I know you're still at Depravities. I'm staring at your signature on the tracer grid and if I don't see you moving home THIS INSTANT, I am coming after you."

"Honest, I was just leaving," Riki tried, a little timidly.

Iason disconnected the frequency without further comment, so angry he could only stare at the screen before him. When Riki's signature finally began to move, he relaxed a little, though he was still furious. He was so distracted, he hardly noticed when Raoul came up behind him, his hands sliding onto his shoulders as he began to offer him a massage.

"All right. Calm down, now. You'll give yourself another headache," he soothed.

Iason sighed, closing his eyes and enjoying Raoul's massage. "I *told* him to come home an hour ago."

"You know Riki," Lord Am replied, working out a knot he found between Iason's shoulder blades.

"That feels good, Raoul."

Now Lord Am leaned down to whisper in his ear. "You know I'd give you a full-body massage if you asked. Any time."

"Would you two like some privacy?" Heiku quipped. The others at the table all laughed, with the exception of Yui and Megala, who both watched the old lovers together with unconcealed jealousy.

Raoul blushed, immediately straightening.

"All right you two, save that for later, when I can film it all properly," Omaki called. "Come back over here. Aren't you having some of this marvelous cake?"

"You ought to at least have that, Iason. You didn't eat any of your dinner," Xian observed.

"What sort of cake is it?" Lord Am asked, attempting to disguise his disappointment when Iason moved to return to the table.

"It's delicious, that's what it is," Heiku announced. "I wouldn't mind a second piece."

"It's a Cream-filled Aristian Vanilla and Caramel Pecan Layer Cake," Tai answered. "It's a secret recipe of the Aristian Royals."

"I'll drag that recipe out of you, if I have to tie you down and beat you with Raoul's stick," Lord Quiahtenon remarked.

Tai, unsure if the great Blondie was threatening him or complimenting him, remained silent.

"Lord Sung has arrived," Askel announced over the intercom.

The Blondies all groaned at this.

"He's early," Raoul complained.

"I'm precisely on time," the Headmaster replied, striding into the hall.

"What did you bring that for?" Xian demanded, when he saw the crop whip the Headmaster carried.

"You will find out, soon enough."

"Headmaster, please join us. We're just finishing up with dinner and Tai has made a lovely dessert. In fact, there's plenty of food, let me get you a plate," Iason offered, suddenly feeling a bit embarrassed that the Headmaster had not been invited to dinner. It had become something of a weekly ritual for the Blondies to dine together before the Headmaster arrived, and though proper etiquette would have suggested Konami should have been included, it had never even been seriously considered.

"I have eaten, thank you. However, I confess I have a weakness for cake," Headmaster Konami replied, eyeing the frosting and caramel smothered confection with obvious interest.

Toma was on his feet without even being asked, taking Riki's empty chair and moving it to the head of the table between Iason and Heiku, as Tai jumped up and returned with a generous piece of cake for him, along with a cup of freshly-brewed coffee.

"My. Isn't this a treat," the Headmaster remarked, smiling as he settled down in the proffered chair and laid his crop whip on the table. "So, I trust you all have applied yourself this week and memorized the sections of the Code I assigned each of you?"

There was a strained silence. Konami raised an eyebrow, but said nothing, the faintest hint of a smile on his lips.

"How is the cake, Headmaster?" Iason asked, after a moment, hoping to ease the tension.

"Absolute heaven," he replied.

"Konami. You don't seriously intend to use that crop whip on us, do you?" Xian demanded.

"I beg your pardon, Xian? Are you addressing me?" The Headmaster leveled him a withering look, and Lord Sami instinctively flinched. "When addressing me, you will always refer to me as Headmaster, Sir Konami, or Lord Sung. And yes, I fully intend to use this whip on anyone who fails to recite the Code perfectly."

"For heaven's sake. We're not children," Heiku protested. "I won't stand for it."

"If you have applied yourself, you have nothing to worry about," the Headmaster replied.

"Three sections is too much to memorize in one week," Raoul asserted.

"I expected *you* to take such a view, Raoul," Konami answered. "Although if you had applied yourself *when you were at the Academy*, you wouldn't find yourself squirming now, would you?"

"I had trouble, too," Megala announced, sounding fearful.

"Hmmm. Then you shall both get to know this crop whip very well tonight, I think."

At this, it was all the pets and attendants could do to maintain straight faces and keep from giggling. To hear the great Blondies being scolded was extraordinarily funny, and the prospect of witnessing their Masters being punished in such an undignified manner promised to make the evening one of the best yet. Indeed, while the Blondies dreaded their weekly lectures with the Headmaster, the other members of their households looked forward to it—and talked about it—all week.

The transparent delight of the attendants and pets and their pathetic attempts at concealing their mirth did not escape the Headmaster, though he did not look directly at them.

"Iason," he said, as he sat back in his chair to enjoy a fresh cup of coffee, "I must say, I find your seating arrangement a bit unorthodox."

The Blondie paused for a moment before responding. "Yes, Headmaster. I know it must seem…a bit odd."

Lord Sung waited a moment, as if expecting more of an explanation, but Iason offered no elaboration.

Now Konami turned to regard Raoul, who avoided his gaze. "What about the rest of you? Is someone going to explain why pets and attendants are seated at the same table as the Masters?"

"There's no law against it," Lord Quiahtenon said, finally.

"No," the Headmaster replied, studying him. "I am quite aware of that. However, you know, as well as I do, that it simply isn't done. I'm not forbidding it. I would simply like to know how this arrangement came about."

"We've eaten together since the whippings," Lord Mink answered, finally.

"I see." Konami finished his coffee and then rose, picking up the crop whip. "Gentlemen. I think we should begin tonight's session."

The Blondies all rose with obvious reluctance, moving over to the chairs by the fire. The attendants began clearing the table, while the pets sat or reclined on the floor of the great hall on the plush cushions that Iason had put out for them.

Headmaster Konami opted to stand, arms across his chest, watching the Blondies get comfortable.

"Before we begin, I must insist you turn over the logbook I requested weeks ago. I've given you ample time to produce it. Surely by now you have located it."

"I assure you, we have searched everywhere for it," Iason replied. "It's simply not to be found."

"I'm afraid that is not good enough. You'll turn this place upside-down if you have to. I'll have that logbook. And to give you a bit of incentive, I'm giving each of you five strikes with this whip. Next week it will be ten strikes, and the week after that, if necessary, twenty. Each week the count will double until the logbook is found. Stand up, Iason. You're first."

"Headmaster," Iason protested, frowning.

"No argument," the Headmaster warned, bending the whip between his gloved hands. "Or shall I double your count this week?"

His face flushing red, Lord Mink stood up and removed his glove, holding out his hand.

"Not on your hand. Turn around and put your hands on the arms of your chair."

Iason did so, wincing when the Headmaster proceeded to give him five rather brutal strikes on his ass with his whip. He then whipped each of the other Blondies, one after the other.

"Now that I've warmed you up," Konami continued, "let's see which of you is in for some additional punishment. Raoul, let's start with you. Stand here in the center of the group and recite your three passages."

Lord Am's face darkened at this, though he stood up and made his way to the center of the group with an air of confidence that disguised his nervousness.

"Section IVa. Modification of hair. It is unlawful for a citizen of any class, without…without doing something or other, to modify or cut his hair or change his hair color. The—."

"*In*correct," Headmaster Konami interrupted, giving him three additional strikes on the back of his thighs. "The correct reading is, 'without Jupiter's authorization via Sanction 678.' Proceed."

"The punishment for modification of hair is a reduction in class and…four strikes with a whip."

"Incorrect."

"Blast!" Raoul cursed, as the Headmaster proceeded to give him three more strikes.

At this, Yui put a hand over his mouth, giggling.

"Yui! All of you, you need to leave the hall," Raoul ordered, turning toward the watching audience of pets and attendants.

"Stay where you are," Konami commanded, holding his hand up to stop them from leaving.

"For pity's sake," Raoul argued, lowering his voice, "we'll never have their respect if they watch us being whipped like children."

"Your humiliation is part of your punishment. I made that clear to you last week, Raoul, and for bringing the matter up again, you'll take another five strikes."

Lord Am endured the strikes, though his face grew even darker.

"Proceed."

"Section IVb. Proper attire. It is unlawful for a citizen of any class, with the exception of a pet, to show his genitals in public, unless that citizen has been ordered to disrobe for a Public Whipping. It is unlawful to wear clothing or the trappings or regalia that...that is...not lawful to wear."

"*In*correct. The correct reading is, 'that is indicative of a class above one's own station.' Three more strikes, Raoul."

Now Raoul bit his lip, closing his eyes. His ass was starting to sting horribly, and he wasn't even close to half-way through the first of three sections.

"Section IVc," Raoul began, then stopped. "Headmaster. Might I ask for another week to memorize these sections?"

"I take it I can expect this sort of miserable performance for the remainder of your assigned sections?"

Raoul hung his head, humiliated.

"Well then. Rather than have you waste our time any further, Raoul, I'll just give you twenty strikes, which I shall DOUBLE next week, if you fail to memorize your sections perfectly. Return to your chair and bend over, hands on the arms of your chair."

With that, the Headmaster gave Lord Am the full twenty; all the while Yui struggled not to laugh out loud. He was annoyed with his Master for bringing Regiland to the gathering, and so felt there was a sort of justice in seeing him so humiliated. As Raoul turned to sit down, however, he shot him a decidedly angry look, and Yui frowned, realizing that he would most likely pay for his mirth later.

"All right. Who else here failed to memorize their sections? Let's just get this over with now. Megala?"

"I'm sorry, Headmaster." Megala stood up and turned around, not even attempting to recite his passages. The Headmaster gave him a sound whipping as well. Next Xian and Heiku both attempted to recite their passages, each of them receiving a few strikes for their errors. Omaki didn't fare much better, and then the only one who had not yet recited his passages was Iason.

The Blondie was deep in thought, fuming over the fact that Riki still had not arrived home, when the Headmaster brought his whip down across the front of his thighs, startling him.

"Didn't you hear me? I said, you're next. Pay attention! And I must say, I certainly hope you do better than your peers. I am deeply disappointed in the lot of you. You had entire week to memorize your sections and it seems evident to me now that none of you applied yourselves at all. You will all be in for it, if you fail to improve your performance next week. I'm warning you, I shall not be as lenient next week as I was this week."

Iason stood up and cleared his mind, and then, with somewhat disarming ease to the watching Blondies, recited his three passages perfectly.

"Well. I'm pleased to see at least *one* of you is taking this seriously. Well done, Iason," Konami praised.

The Blondie sat down with a slight smirk at Raoul, who frowned.

"You don't have to gloat about it," Lord Am muttered.

"Raoul is right, Iason," the Headmaster remarked. "The fact that you know the Code so well shows that you, of all people, should have known better. Taking on Jupiter! For the life of me, I still can't understand what you were thinking!"

"It wasn't for lack of knowing what was forbidden," Iason replied, in a soft voice. "It has nothing to do with the Code."

"That goes for the rest of us, too," Raoul added. "Which is why memorizing this Code is so pointless."

Lord Sung looked decidedly angry at this, placing his hands on his hips. "I shall decide what is pointless and what is not pointless. And for that matter, if I choose to have you engage in pointless memorization for the rest of your lives, I shall do so."

"Oh, come on, Konami," Xian argued, "we've been punished enough."

The Headmaster whipped around to face Lord Sami, his face darkening. "Did I not tell you that you are to address me as *Sir* Konami, Lord Sung, or Headmaster?" he demanded. "And how dare you challenge me, Xian! On your feet!"

"If you think you're going to whip me again, you'd better think again," Xian replied, arms across his chest. "I've had enough of being treated like a child."

"Xian Sami. Do you not realize that as Head of the Eos Disciplinary Committee, I have the power to have you publicly whipped again, or confiscate your assets?"

Xian looked a little uncertain at this, frowning.

"Idiot," Omaki whispered. "He *does* have that power, Xian."

"You wouldn't do that," Lord Sami stated, though there was a question in his tone.

"I most certainly would, if necessary. I happen to be looking for a villa just now; yours would suit me very well. I am being very lenient by punishing you with this whip. Stand up, Xian."

With obvious reluctance, Xian finally submitted to the humiliation of being whipped like a schoolboy in front of hall of gaping onlookers. Afterwards he sat down with his gaze averted, his face flushed red with embarrassment.

"You had all better recite these passages next week as perfectly as Iason just did," Lord Sung warned again. "I may bring more than just this whip next time."

The Blondies waited in a grumpy silence for the Headmaster to leave, but Konami seemed bent on lecturing them a bit more, reprimanding them for their miserable performance and their failures as Blondies.

During the lecture, Riki finally returned to the penthouse, walking in as though nothing was wrong, though he was, in fact, two hours late. When Iason saw him he immediately rose, but was stayed by the Headmaster.

"I didn't excuse you, Iason. Sit back down."

"But Riki has arrived, I must—"

"Did you not hear me? I said, sit back down. I'm not finished yet! I suppose you want a whipping, too?"

Furious, but struggling to maintain his composure, Iason sat back down, glaring at Riki, who was snickering at his scolding. The mongrel sat down at the now empty table, as though expecting to be waited on. And he was not wrong in his expectations; Tai immediately rushed in with his dinner in a warming dome, and Riki began enjoying his dinner, while Iason watched him angrily, anxious for the Headmaster to finish with his lecture.

"Iason, have you gone to see Jupiter yet?" Konami demanded.

"No," the Blondie replied, frowning.

"I advise you to do so. Don't wait for a summons. You must face her eventually."

Iason lowered his gaze. "I know."

"So? Stop delaying. Really, I shouldn't have to tell you that!"

"Yes, Headmaster," Iason murmured.

After what seemed like an interminable length of time, and after Riki had finished his dinner and dessert and had crept off to his room, Lord Sung finally ended his tongue-lashing and went home, with stern admonishments to the Blondies to be prepared for the following week's lecture.

"That bastard," Xian grumbled, as soon as the Headmaster was gone.

The Blondies were all in agreement, every one of them still feeling the sting of his whip.

"Bring your stick next time, Raoul," Omaki suggested.

"What are we going to do about the logbook?" Raoul asked. "Iason, you have no idea where it might be?"

"As I said, I've searched everywhere for it."

"Do you suppose Yousi might have it?" Megala wondered.

Heiku frowned. "I wouldn't think so, but I'll ask him. He would have said something when Konami asked for it."

"But then, forgive me for saying so, but Yousi is not the brightest of fellows," Raoul remarked. "Perhaps he took it and then simply forgot about it."

"I suppose that's possible," Heiku conceded.

"Please excuse me," Iason announced, rising. "I have a little matter to take care of."

"That's our cue to leave," Xian sighed. "Thank you, once again for your hospitality, Iason."

"You may all stay as long as you like," he replied, "however, I will be occupied for the next hour or so."

"I guess that means no pairing this week, then," Heiku commented. "I think next week, Iason, you ought to have Riki pair for us. What do you say?"

Lord Mink made no reply to this remark, which was, of course, only intended as a joke, as he was already striding out of the hall toward the guest wing.

"If you're so eager to see a pairing, why don't you show your new pet next week, Heiku," Raoul hinted, eyeing his new blonde pet with interest. "What's his name, again?"

"Mathias," Heiku replied. "And I'll show mine if you show yours."

"Done," Raoul nodded.

Mathias and Regiland perked up at this, regarding one another with renewed interest.

"Looks like Puki's going to pair," Sarius whispered.

The other attendants snickered at this, except for Yui, who looked a bit upset.

"Pairings are so tiresome," Omaki sighed. "I'd like to see a threesome, for a change."

"Are you willing to show Enyu?" Heiku asked.

Omaki looked over at Enyu, who smiled back at him. "I would, only he'll be in his interval by then."

"Even better," Xian smiled, eyeing Enyu eagerly. He had enjoyed Enyu immensely when he had dared to pair with him once, at Iason's penthouse, and felt a bit envious of Omaki, who now owned the rare Xeronian.

"He'd actually be impossible to control," Omaki explained. "He'd pretty much try and mount anyone he felt like."

"That could be interesting," Megala announced rather loudly, then blushed when the other Blondies turned to regard him.

"Megala doesn't object, apparently," Heiku remarked.

"I only meant, I've always wanted to see a Xeronian...when he's...er...rutting."

"If you want to see him, Chimi, you'd have to come over to my place. He'll be chained up." Omaki whispered.

Megala blushed at Omaki's old nickname for him, which he hadn't heard in years.

"Yes, *Chimi*," Xian drawled, knowing how much the old name embarrassed him. "Go see Omaki tame his rutting pet. We all know how much you like to *watch*."

The others snorted at this, with the exception of Raoul, who reddened.

"What about your new pet, Xian?" Heiku demanded. "You're so anxious to see everyone else, but you're holding out."

Lord Sami turned to regard his new pet Enshu, who stared back eagerly. Xian had yet to have his pet perform, even at home, for fear of upsetting Juthian, who had made no secret of his jealousy over Enshu. He avoided looking at Juthian now, realizing he couldn't very well object to showing his pet when directly asked. Only Iason seemed to be able to get away with that.

He shrugged, as if uninterested, though he felt quite excited at the prospect. "If you want."

"Why stop at three?" Omaki pressed, eagerly. "Megala, how about throwing Shimera into the mix?"

"Of course," Megala answered, delighted at the prospect of watching four pets together.

Shimera smiled, grateful for a chance to show himself again. It had been a long time since Megala had offered him in a pairing, and he had feared he would be overlooked, once again. He liked Lord Ghan, and it was not the first time the Blondie had requested him for a pairing. Only this time, he would be shown with three other pets, which would be, at the very least, quite interesting.

"Well, at least we have something to look forward to next week," Lord Quiahtenon remarked. "Besides, of course, Iason's magnificent dinners."

"I wish we didn't have to come next week," Juthian whispered to Yui.

"I'm not coming," Yui asserted, crossing his arms on his chest, and regarding his Master with a pouting stare.

At that moment Iason could be heard yelling from somewhere in the penthouse.

"Sounds like the mongrel's in for it tonight," Heiku noted, rising. "Perhaps we ought to give Iason some privacy."

"I daresay he's not the only one with domestic issues to attend to," Lord Am hinted, giving Yui a pointed look.

"Quite right," Lord Sami agreed, rising.

Though neither Raoul nor Xian directly addressed the obvious displeasure of their attendants, it was clear that both Yui and Juthian would require a bit of correction that evening, once the Blondies got them home.

Yui's jealous stares and sullen disposition that evening had not gone unnoticed by Raoul, who quietly filed away each infraction for a full accounting, when he could address them in the privacy of his own quarters. Although Raoul avoided reprimanding members of his household in public, he was also a firm believer that discipline should be given at the earliest appropriate opportunity, and so Yui would be held accountable the moment they returned home. He was, himself, still burning from the pain and humiliation of his own punishment at the Headmaster's hand, though he had already decided he would tend to his punished flesh himself, without Yui's assistance. He had not forgotten the boy's inappropriate snickering at his predicament; Yui would find out, soon enough, his views on that.

"Yes," Omaki agreed, standing up with a mighty stretch. "He'll not be coming back any time soon."

23

When it became clear the Blondies were finally departing, their attendants and pets all rose, and so, without further fanfare, the weekly gathering came to an end.

Iason, after finally leaving the great hall, had made for Riki's room, where he found him sitting comfortably in a chair, almost asleep.

"Where have you been?" he demanded.

"Huh?" Riki opened an eye, looking disoriented.

"I made it perfectly clear to you, Riki, you were to come straight home. Why did you disobey me?"

Riki sighed. "Calm down. Anyway, you were busy. What do you care when I come home?"

"When I tell you something, I expect you to do it!"

"Stop yelling. Can't we talk about this tomorrow? I'm sleepy."

"We will talk about it *now*. I'm furious with you, Riki. Not only did you fail to come home immediately, you *lied* to me about where you were!"

"Well, you shouldn't give me a ridiculous curfew, then. I'm not twelve."

"You are my pet. You will do as I say!"

"Dammit, Iason! Quit being such a fucking prick!"

"That's it. You're in for it now." The Blondie lunged for him, but Riki was too quick, immediately jumping up and running into the billiard room. Iason chased him around the table a few times.

"Riki! I'm not in the mood for your games!"

The mongrel giggled at this. "That's just because I'm winning!"

"You won't be laughing when I put you over my knee!"

"Oh, come on! You're really going to spank me?"

"You've never had a spanking like the one I'm going to give you."

"Well that's really something. You're seriously going to punish me, after what I did for you?"

It was the first time since the Public Whipping, when Riki had stepped in for him, that the issue of punishment had been discussed. Lord Mink was in a difficult position; without the power to punish his pet, he had no authority over him. And yet it was true that Riki had sacrificed himself in such a manner that seemed to suggest he should have immunity from all future punishment, as Riki had pointed out weeks before. Since then he had become more aggressive in defying Iason's orders, staying out as long as he wished, without any real recourse.

"You're still my pet, Riki," Iason replied, walking slowly around the table. Riki moved as well, remaining directly opposite him. "I think it's time you remembered that."

"Oh yeah? But, you offered me my freedom, remember? Maybe I'll just take you up on that!"

"It's too late now, Riki," Iason replied. "You already made your decision. You agreed to stay as my pet. And as my pet, you will do as I say."

"I was fucking out of my mind not to leave, then," Riki answered. "I can't believe how you're treating me."

"Come here."

"No!"

"Riki," Lord Mink began, and then suddenly, much to Riki's surprise, he reached out and flipped the billiard table over, breaking it as balls went flying everywhere, hitting the walls and rolling across the floor. He then managed to grab hold of the mongrel, dragging him back to the sofa.

Riki fought him every step of the way, but as usual he was no match for Iason's incredible strength.

"Fucking bastard! You just broke my table!"

Iason attempted to put Riki over his knees, but Riki was too wild to control. He picked him up, instead, carrying him into the bedroom, where he bound his wrists behind his back with a belt. He did the same thing with his ankles, and then he spanked him, just as he had promised, laying him across his lap on the bed.

"That is the last time you'll go out without a bodyguard," Iason announced. "From now on I'll ensure that you'll be home on time."

Riki cried out his misery and frustration, furious with Iason for carrying out his threat to spank him, and suffering from the severity of it, for Iason seemed particularly bent on breaking him.

"I hate you," he sobbed. "I hate you, Iason."

"I'm sure you do, at the moment," Lord Mink replied, feigning an indifference he did not feel. It hurt him to hear Riki say the words, even if he knew he said them only in anger.

He made the spanking really count, and he was so angry that he ignored the burning of his own hand. Riki cursed and struggled, and called him every black name in the book, saying things so hurtful that Iason finally stopped, blinking back tears of his own, though he continued to hold Riki over his knees.

"I hate living with you," Riki whimpered. "I wish I'd never met you. Fucking prick!"

"That's enough, now."

"So now you've shown me who's boss, are you happy now? Because now I *hate* you."

"Riki," Iason sighed. "Stop saying that."

"Well, it's true! I don't know what I was thinking before. You can't love me, if you treat me this way."

"Just because I have to correct you, doesn't mean I don't love you," the Blondie argued. "You know that."

"You didn't have to correct me! I'm…I'm correct just as I am!"

"Why didn't you obey me?"

"I shouldn't have to obey you! Why does it always have to be *your* way?"

"Because I am your Master! Riki, I told you, the streets were getting slick. It was getting dangerous out. I wanted you home—"

"You don't care about that! You're just pissed because I didn't do exactly what you wanted!"

"That's not entirely true. I was worried about you."

"You wouldn't care if I was lying dead in the streets! You'd just find some other pet to torment!"

At this, Iason sighed, removing the belt from around Riki's ankles, and then his wrists, and allowed him to get up.

"Of course I would care," he said, softly. "I would be devastated if anything happened to you."

"I don't believe you! You're always hurting me!" Riki shouted, pulling up his pants angrily. "Sometimes I wish I *was* dead! Maybe I'll just kill myself, how would you like that? Knowing you drove me to it!"

Iason frowned. "Stop saying such things."

"Maybe I *will* do it!"

"Stop it, Riki!"

"No, *you* stop. You stop!" With that, Riki suddenly lunged forward, pushing Iason back on the bed and then pounding his fists into his chest.

Lord Mink grabbed his wrists, then flipped Riki onto his back and pinned him down by his wrists. "Riki. Calm down."

"You stop," Riki repeated, then suddenly began to cry.

"Oh, Riki," Iason whispered. "That's enough, now. Don't cry."

"Let me go. Leave me alone!"

"Pet—"

"Stop calling me pet!" Riki hissed, his eyes suddenly blazing.

Iason stared down at him for a moment, and then suddenly brought his mouth down, hard, over Riki's, forcing his lips open.

But Riki refused to kiss him back, struggling to turn his head. "You can't make me love you," he said, coldly, when Iason finally broke away.

"Perhaps not," Iason agreed, struggling to control his rising hurt and anger, "but I can make you submit to me."

"Yes, that's your great accomplishment, isn't it? Taming me," Riki spat. "Well I'm warning you, if I had your dick in my mouth now, I'd bite it off."

"Perhaps I need to put you back in chains," Iason threatened, a bit horrified at Riki's remark.

"You'd like that, wouldn't you? Pervert."

Iason answered this by attempting to pull Riki close, but the mongrel resisted him, pushing him away. "Riki," he whispered. "That's enough."

"Go away."

The Blondie continued to hold him, despite Riki's obvious displeasure. "Why must you be like this tonight?"

Riki laughed darkly. "Why? You're asking me why? For someone who's supposed to be so smart, you can be pretty stupid sometimes. Let me go!"

"Very well. It seems you're bent on being obstinate," Iason sighed, annoyed. He released him, then rose and left the room without another word.

"Fucking bastard," Riki called after him.

Iason went into the Master bedroom and closed the doors, barring all access. It was one of the few times he had slept without Riki next to him. He had decided, if Riki was going to be so difficult, he would give him his wish. He would leave him alone.

After a few hours, Riki had calmed down a bit, wondering why Iason hadn't returned. It was nearly bedtime, and he expected that the Blondie would demand he come to bed. Finally, he sauntered into the great hall, noting the closed doors to the Master bedroom with a frown.

"Is Iason in bed?" he asked, as Toma set his bedtime tea on the table.

"I believe so, Sir Riki."

"He didn't come for me." Although this was stating the obvious, Riki felt so surprised by it that he continued to stand for a few moments, staring at the door.

"Perhaps he wants to be left alone."

Shrugging, Riki sat down, wincing a bit.

"I don't know what you were thinking," Toma chided. "Why didn't you come home when he told you to?"

"Because I didn't feel like it," Riki replied, darkly. "He's always telling me what to do."

"And?"

"What do you mean, 'and'?" the mongrel demanded.

"I mean, what do you expect? He's a Blondie, and he's your Master."

Riki made no reply, dipping a cookie absent-mindedly into his tea.

"It sounded like you had a pretty big fight."

"Yeah. I guess he's still pissed." Riki looked at the closed door again, frowning. "Well, fine. I'll just sleep in my room, then." He stood up, hesitating a moment as he ran a hand through his hair, half-expecting Iason's door to suddenly open, and for him to demand that he come to bed. "I guess I'll just sleep in my room," he repeated, a little louder.

But the door remained closed.

"You're finished with your cookies?" Toma asked, eyeing his barely eaten cookie with surprise. Always before, Riki had wolfed down his bedtime tea and biscuits.

"Yeah." The mongrel looked toward the door one final time, then left the hall, hands buried deep in his pockets.

Toma watched him go, shaking his head.

THAT NIGHT NEITHER RIKI NOR IASON SLEPT well, both of them waking frequently and reaching instinctively for the other. Sometime in the wee hours of the night, Riki finally fell sound asleep, exhausted from hours of tossing and turning. When he woke, he felt strange to be in his own bed, without Iason by his side.

He got up, did his pushups and then showered, putting on a new outfit of leather pants with a mesh tank that he had purchased the week before. He stood in front of the mirror, smiling at himself.

"Yeah. I'm sexy," he announced, turning around to admire his ass. Though he would not have even admitted it to himself, he had put on the new outfit for Iason, who he knew would like it. He donned a new pair of lizard-skin boots and made for the great hall, where Iason was sitting at the breakfast table.

The Blondie didn't look up as he approached, but sat, absorbed in a journal article as he sipped his coffee.

Riki instinctively headed for him to give him his morning kiss and then, suddenly stopping himself, sat down with exaggerated indifference. Iason did not demand his kiss or even look at him.

Tai and Toma rushed in with his breakfast, noting the strained silence between Master and pet with interest. They were both aware of the fight the evening before and the fact that Iason and Riki had not slept together, and they had a wager going between them, about who would make the first move to mend relations.

"I'm going out after breakfast," Riki announced, a bit miffed when Iason did not demand his morning kiss.

"No, you are not, pet."

"Why not?" Riki demanded.

Iason flipped the page in his journal, still refusing to look at him. "Because I said so."

Frowning, the mongrel poured far too much syrup on his griddlecakes in an attempt to solicit Iason's censure. But the Blondie did not comment, as he normally would have, that he was pouring too much syrup, nor did he insist he drink his juice first, when Riki deliberately drank his coffee, loudly slurping it to make his infraction clear.

"Someone shall be asked to eat in the breakfast nook, if he cannot eat in a civilized fashion," Iason remarked.

"Oh yeah? Well someone shall be asked to fucking kiss my ass, if he doesn't quit being such a fucking asshole!"

At this, Iason slammed his journal down on the table, looking directly at him. "You will not speak to me in such a manner," he warned.

"What are you going to do? Spank me again?" Riki challenged.

"If necessary. I am not in the mood for your little tantrums today, Riki."

"Hmmm." Riki considered several rather insulting replies, but the look in Iason's eyes stayed him. He feigned indifference, stuffing his mouth with griddlecakes.

"Did you hear what I said? Stop eating like a savage," Iason scolded.

"What? I'm just a mongrel, remember?" Riki retorted, his mouth full of food. "I *am* a savage."

"Riki," Iason sighed. "You're trying my patience already."

"Why can't I go out?"

"I already told you," the Blondie replied, quietly. He was studying him, noting how nice his pet looked and wondering who he had dressed up for. "You'll do as I say today, no argument."

"Fine. Can you release my ring then? I want to watch a holoflic." He had been desperate to relieve himself since the previous evening, when he had watched a pet pairing at Depravities, much to his eventual regret. Now he had gone the entire night feeling aroused and angry, his needs mounting.

"No, I will not."

Riki sighed loudly, pushing away his plate. "Well, can I go swimming, then?"

"Yes, you may, after you finish your breakfast."

"I'm finished."

"You've barely eaten anything," Iason chided, pouring him some juice. "Drink this."

Although Riki pretended that he was annoyed by the Blondie's attentions, he was in fact a little relieved to see Iason behaving in his usual manner. Though he wouldn't have admitted it, he rather liked being fussed over, and while he was still a bit angry with him, he had felt somewhat hurt when Iason had simply ignored him.

"I don't want to," he complained, though he did, in fact, drink the juice.

Tai and Toma exchanged knowing looks; although everything was not quite back to normal, it had not taken long for Master and pet to at least resume their typical breakfast routine.

After breakfast Riki wandered off to the pool area, while Iason looked after him, frowning. Though it was only a small thing, Riki had not given him his morning kiss, and he had not asked for it. Neither of them had discussed the fact that they had spent the night apart, or, for that matter, really talked about what had happened the previous evening.

The Blondie rose, sighing. Riki's recent disobedience reminded him of his own responsibilities. He knew it was time to do something he had put off for far too long.

He had delayed visiting Jupiter, feeling shamed to face her after his public disgrace. But the Headmaster was right; it would be inadvisable to wait for a direct summons. He knew Jupiter was waiting for him to come, of his own accord.

AFTER THE EVENING'S LECTURE, LORD AM LEFT the penthouse in a foul mood, striding down the hall toward the lift so quickly that Yui and

Regiland both had to run to keep up with him. He said nothing to Yui until they reached the elevator and the doors had closed behind them.

"You're in for it tonight, Yui," he warned.

At this threat, Regiland could not help but gloat; Yui had been rude to him since he'd arrived at Lord Am's household, and he couldn't wait to see the impertinent attendant be punished.

Yui, though tempted to argue, was still wise enough to know when it was better to hold his tongue. He had not entirely forgotten how to be obedient, though since he had become intimate with his Master, he had developed a rebellious nature that even he found surprising. But all this was fueled by his intense hatred and jealous of Regiland, Raoul's annoying new pet.

He narrowed his eyes at Regiland, wishing he could reach out and slap the boy, who stood beaming back at him, not even trying to conceal his delight.

The door to the elevator opened on Raoul's level, and the Blondie reached out and took Yui's elbow, his uncompromising grip communicating his anger, as he led him into his suites.

"You are being punished," he announced, leading him over to the kitchen table.

"Why?" Yui demanded.

"You know perfectly well why, Yui. Do you think your behavior escaped me?"

Regiland followed them eagerly, grinning. "Master, he was very rude to me all week and refused to wait on me properly," he asserted.

"Again?" Raoul asked. "Did I not make clear to you, Yui, that you are still expected to perform your duties as an attendant?"

Furious, but not daring to challenge his Master, Yui attempted to pacify him by donning a look of repentance. "I am sorry, Master. I will do better this week."

"Yes, you will. However, that will not save you from a good strapping." Raoul unbuckled his belt and bent him over the table, lifting his long robe to reveal his bare ass. He then proceeded to whip him as Regiland watched, delighted.

Yui endured his punishment as well as he could, biting his lip and trying not to cry out. Before Lord Am was finished, however, he was in tears. He was furious with his Master, though he didn't dare show anything but remorse. And he hated Regiland, with every fiber of his being. Since the new pet had come into their household, nothing had been the same. It had been weeks since his Master had taken him to his bed, because Yui was always being punished for his behavior toward Regiland.

As for Raoul, he wanted nothing more than to take Yui into his arms, but he felt trapped by Yui's continuing disobedience and refusal to attend to his new pet. Now, more than ever, with Jupiter scrutinizing his every move, he felt the need to ensure that the proper boundaries of authority were established in his home. Why didn't Yui understand that?

"Go sit until I call you," he ordered, retiring to the Master bedroom to nurse his own sore backside. He felt he would never forgive the Headmaster for humiliating him in front of Yui and the other attendants and pets. But he was resolved it would never happen again. He was determined to learn every word of the Code, if he had to study every night.

IASON ENTERED JUPITER'S SANCTUM, RELIEVED to see, from the quiet, aquamarine aura that surrounded her, that she was no longer angry.

"Why did you not come to me sooner?" Jupiter asked.

"I delayed coming," Iason replied, softly, lowering his gaze. "I had difficulty gathering the courage to face you."

"Sit down, Iason."

The Blondie did so, his brow furrowed as he tried to collect his thoughts. "I hardly know how to thank you," he said, finally. "For allowing me to keep Riki. I know I am…completely undeserving of it."

"I trust I can expect obedience from you, from this point on?"

"I cannot promise complete obedience," Iason replied, carefully, "without knowing what you will ask. But I can say that, concerning all that you currently ask of me, I will obey, without question."

"That is a qualified answer. You disappoint me."

"I am only being honest. You deserve that much. Henceforth I will only be completely honest with you," he replied, gaze averted. Then he looked up at her. "But I will do my best not to disappoint you again."

"Why can you not promise complete obedience?" Jupiter demanded.

"Because I am not perfect."

"No, you are not," Jupiter agreed, after a moment. "But I have made my position clear. If you fail to obey me again, without exception, you will lose your authority and your position on Amoi. I will not forgive a second transgression, Iason. You may go."

Iason rose and, with a slight bow, left.

VOSHKA KHOSI WAS SITTING COMFORTABLY in his private quarters, enjoying a manicure that Azka was giving him, when his communication center lit up with an incoming message.

"Greetings, Commander," came the robotic voice of the X900 Guardian, "this is Guardian Four, owned by Iason Mink of Amoi, with a saved message for you from your pet, Lord Aranshu."

At this, Voshka paled, pulling his hand away from Azka and jumping to his feet. "What?" he cried. "What did you just say?"

"This is Guardian Four owned by Iason Mink of Amoi, with a saved message for you from your pet, Lord Aranshu. The message is: 'Holy shit, my Master can fucking kiss my ass.' Thank you and have a nice day."

"Wait! Voshka rushed over to the communications center. "Replay that! Have you...a visual? Let me see the original recording!"

"Certainly, Commander," the Guardian replied, projecting the image of Aranshu onto the screen.

Voshka watched, stunned, his eyes filling with tears. After all this time—nearly ten years, he finally had a visual of his long-lost pet. Aranshu had grown into a man—a handsome man, his blonde hair looking just as silky-soft as ever, a contrast to his angry features and piercing eyes. He had the Guardian replay the message over and over, his mind a turmoil of emotions.

"When...was this recorded?" he whispered. "And where?"

"The message was recorded three weeks ago in Iason Mink's residence. Lord Aranshu asked that I delay the message for three weeks."

"Three weeks? Then...he was there the day I left! But why do you keep calling him Lord Aranshu?"

"It is the proper title of an Amoian Blondie."

"Put Iason onscreen," Voshka demanded.

"Yes, Commander. Have a nice day." The Guardian disappeared, and after a few moments, Lord Mink appeared on the screen.

"Commander. I trust your voyage is going well?" Iason had just returned from his meeting with Jupiter, and actually felt glad to see Voshka again. Something about the Commander was comforting, and at the moment he felt, for various reasons, a bit on edge.

"Iason. Your Guardian just relayed a message from my pet, Aranshu—the one I told you about. It was recorded in your residence, three weeks ago."

"That's impossible," Iason replied, frowning. "Although I hope the unit's not malfunctioning. As much as it cost, that's disappointing."

"But I saw the visual. It's him. He was there."

Iason was silent for a moment. "Are you sure?"

"Absolutely. Although I'll confess, the Guardian did seem a bit confused about his identity. He kept referring to him as Lord Aranshu and insisted he was a Blondie."

"That doesn't sound promising," Iason sighed. "I'll have the unit checked out, but it sounds like the database might be damaged. In which case who knows where the message was recorded."

"But, if it was recorded there," Voshka began, anxiously.

Iason smiled. "Vosh. I assure you—there is no way anyone could get past my security. However, I'll have a full-system security review performed just to be sure. It may take a few days, but then I'll contact you just as soon as we have the results."

Voshka sighed, discouraged. Though part of him felt like turning the ship around and heading back to Amoi, he knew that, even if Aranshu had been there, by now he was most likely long gone. Besides, he needed to get back to Alpha Zen. He would go ahead and check out Aristia as planned, though he felt almost certain now he would not find Aranshu there. But perhaps he could uncover some clues as to his movements.

He smiled. "Iason. Forgive me—how rude I've been. I should have first asked after you—goodness, how have you been? You went through quite an ordeal, I believe, the day I left?"

"It was not pleasant," Lord Mink agreed. "But it turned out to be bearable. Mostly because Riki came to my rescue."

"Oh? How is that?"

"He stood in for me when I lost consciousness, offering to take my strikes."

"Is that so?" Voshka raised an eyebrow, impressed. "My. What a brave pet. But…is he all right, then?"

"Yes. In fact, it was quite extraordinary. I wasn't in a state to witness it, but apparently Jupiter appeared, right there on the stage, and halted Riki's punishment. He only took a fraction of the strikes that he might have, and so was able to recover after about a week."

"And your position? All is well, now?"

"I believe so."

"Hmmm. You're very lucky," Voshka remarked.

"Yes."

"My offer still stands," he added, smiling. "You are always welcome here."

"Thank you, Vosh," Iason replied, his lashes fluttering slightly.

"Oh. You're playing with me again, you little flirt," the Commander scolded.

"Am I?" Lord Mink smiled slightly in response.

"You know you are. Come see me. Bring Riki. You know we'd have a good time together."

"We'll see," Iason replied, coyly.

"Tease. All right then, how about you…perform for me? What do you say? Right now. Let me watch you pleasure yourself."

"I assure you, if I were inclined to do such a thing, I'd hardly have it transmitted over the airways, where it might be intercepted by anyone."

Voshka laughed at this. "I see your point. Then, will you send me a disc? Or better yet—a holodisc. Please? It doesn't have to be just you. It can be you and Riki. Or just you. And then you and Riki. And then just Riki. In whatever order." Aroused just thinking about it, the Commander reached down and adjusted himself.

"I'm not making any promises," the Blondie replied, smiling slightly.

"Hmmm. At least that's not a definite no. I suppose I shall have to be satisfied with that. Well then, please let me know as soon as you finish your security review, what you find out? About Aranshu?"

"Of course."

"I'll let you go then," Voshka sighed. "I've got guests coming. None of them are attractive, I'm afraid, so there's not even an erotic encounter to look forward to."

"How can you have guests coming? Aren't you on route to Aristia?"

"Ah, yes. However, some dignitaries from Galath have docked with my ship. It would be considered rude not to meet with them, though I must say, they're the ugliest fellows in the galaxy. However, I have my lovely little Azka to amuse me."

At this, Azka smiled, happy that the Commander had not yet tired of him. Since leaving Amoi, they had slept together every night, and Voshka seemed to have an insatiable appetite when it came to sex, taking him multiple times throughout the night. His only worry was what would happen when they finally returned to Alpha Zen, where the Commander kept his harem. Would Voshka forget about him then? He hoped not, though in his heart he knew the Commander would be eager for something different. It was absurd to believe he would continue to pick him—or at least, only him—when there were countless other young males to choose from. He was, in fact, a bit worried about the harem, and how he would fit in with the others there, most of whom were probably Alphazenian. He wouldn't even understand their language, unless they knew Amoian.

Azka had been so deep in thought, he had failed to notice that the Commander had ended his call and now stood, staring at him intently.

"Come here," Voshka ordered.

"Yes, Master?" Azka approached him, smiling when he realized what his Master wanted.

Voshka unzipped his pants, spreading his legs to reveal himself. "On your knees," he whispered.

Azka obediently knelt down, and proceeded to service the Commander, who remained extraordinarily quiet, but for his breathing. Voshka reached down to play with his hair, letting the dark red tendrils move through his fingers. "Aranshu," he whispered. "Good boy."

It was not the first time his Master had called him by this name, and Azka knew better than to say anything. It had become something of a game; he realized that the Commander wished him to pretend to be Aranshu. Before, he hadn't really been sure who Aranshu was, but after his conversation with Lord Mink, he realized that Aranshu had once been Voshka's pet, but that he had run away.

Deciding to be a bit bold in an attempt to please his Master, Azka, suckled him for a moment and then whispered, "I'm sorry I ran away, Master."

"Oh," Voshka whispered, excited. "You should be sorry, Aranshu. I am going to have to punish you, I fear."

"Yes, Master."

Swallowing hard, Voshka closed his eyes and ejaculated, moaning when Azka dutifully lapped up his seed. Azka was happy to please him, even if he pleased him most by pretending to be someone else, but he

36

could not help but hope, deep in his heart, that the Commander would never find his long-lost pet.

"YOU WANTED ME, SIR?" ODI ASKED, RUSHING into the great hall, where Iason waited for him, his arms crossed on his chest. Ayuda was there as well, looking concerned.

"Yes. I just spoke with Voshka Khosi. The Guardian sent him a message he found disturbing," Iason replied, relating what the Commander had told him.

Odi exchanged glances with Ayuda, frowning. "There's no way anyone could have gotten inside the penthouse."

"That's what I told him. However, run a complete security scan and review all the signatures from the past few weeks," Iason ordered. "And take a look at the Guardian. It may be malfunctioning."

"Of course. Right away." He turned to Ayuda. "Retrieve the Guardian. I'll meet you in my room. First I want to speak to Askel and Freyn."

Ayuda nodded, immediately setting out in search of the device, as Odi went to confront the brothers, who were fighting over the last cookie from a tin Tai had given them that afternoon.

"You already had six," Askel protested. "That's mine!"

"I had five," Freyn clarified. "And there were eleven cookies, so we should split this one."

"If you two don't stop," Odi warned, "I'm going to split your heads open."

"Don't tell me you're in a bad mood again," Askel groaned.

"I may have good reason. Iason's just informed me there may have been an intruder here at the penthouse, the day of the Public Whippings. Of course I told him that was impossible, since you were both at your posts."

At this, Askel and Freyn looked at one another.

"You *were* at your posts, weren't you?" Odi demanded, narrowing his eyes.

"Most of the time," Askel replied, a little meekly.

"What!"

Freyn pointed at Askel. "He left his post."

"But you were guarding Megala's entrance!"

"I only left for a few minutes!"

"Askel, I'm going to wring your neck! That's all it would have taken!"

Freyn smiled at this. "I tried to tell him that."

"What are you smiling about? You do realize, you're equally accountable?"

"But I was at my post!"

"You knew Askel left his post and you didn't inform me. I'm going to have to tell Iason about this, so you might as well start packing tonight. But before you do, I expect you to run a security review. Start with the day of the Whippings and check every single signature recorded." With that, Odi went back inside to meet Ayuda and examine the Guardian, now genuinely worried.

"Thanks a lot, Ask. Now you've done it," Freyn growled.

"Well," Askel replied, a little defensively, "you're an accountant, too."

"Account*able*, idiot," Freyn snapped. "And now we've probably both lost our jobs."

Back inside the penthouse, Ayuda had retrieved the Guardian and taken it to Odi's room, where he had it replay the message that Aranshu had recorded. He studied the image, frowning at the painting on the wall behind the young man. It certainly looked like the sort of thing Iason would own, and it looked familiar, but he couldn't quite place it. Odi joined him, puzzling over the recording as well.

"Who's that?" Tai asked. He had just arrived with the tea cart, which he dutifully offered to everyone in the penthouse each afternoon. "I brought you both some tea."

"Commander Khosi's runaway pet," Odi replied. "I don't care for any tea, thank you."

"Nor I," Ayuda added.

"Tai. Do you recognize this painting?"

Tai peered at the image, his brow furrowed. "Yes. It's in…the room where Commander Khosi stayed."

"Damn," Odi whispered, rising.

"Is something wrong?"

"Yes. Tai, we screwed up. There may have been an intruder here. I have a feeling I won't be working for Iason much longer."

"Oh no," Tai cried. "Are you sure?"

"Not yet. But I'm going to find out. If it's true, though, I'm in deep shit."

"But it's not your fault, is it?"

"I'm the Head of Security. So yes, if something goes wrong, ultimately it's my fault." He turned to Ayuda. "I'll do my best to keep you out of this, but your position may be in jeopardy, too."

Ayuda nodded. "Understood. I'm going to go check out the room now."

"If you don't mind, Ayuda, please don't say anything about this until we have all the facts."

"Of course," Ayuda replied, glancing at Tai before he left the room.

Tai swallowed, trying to process the full ramifications of this. "But what will happen? You'd just be sent away, right?"

Odi sighed, running a hand through his hair. "Not just that. I'll probably lose rank. It would be more than just a reprimand, Tai."

"When will you know for sure?"

"Probably later today. But I think I may delay telling Iason what I find out. I'd like to spend one last night with you, before…anything happens."

Tai nodded. "I won't say anything. And you should definitely wait. Master Iason is still in a bad mood, I think, because of Riki."

At that moment, the mongrel came wandering into the room, in search of the afternoon tea cart, having an uncanny ability to ferret out its whereabouts whenever Tai began his rounds. "What about me?" he demanded.

Odi and Tai both turned to him, looking rather anxious.

"Hey. What's going on?"

"Nothing," Tai replied.

"Fine. Don't tell me then. Cookies!" Riki exclaimed, grabbing a handful. "These are my favorite!"

"Riki, have you made up with Master Iason yet?" Tai probed.

The mongrel studied him for a moment, his mouth full of cookie. "No. He has to come to *me*."

Tai and Odi exchanged a worried look.

"Excuse me," Odi murmured, making for the Commander's room.

"What's with him?" Riki asked. "What's going on?"

"Riki, Odi may be in trouble. They have some…bad news for Master Iason."

"What sort of news?"

"There may have been an intruder here, the day of the Whippings. Master Iason won't be happy about it, when he finds out. Odi and the other guards may all be relieved of duty."

"That sucks," Riki remarked, pouring himself some coffee.

"I don't want Odi to go," Tai whispered. "Please, Riki."

"What do you want me to do about it?"

"Can't you just…smooth things over with Master Iason? Maybe he won't go so hard on them, if he's not upset to begin with."

Riki munched on another cookie, considering. He was still annoyed with Iason, and hated the thought of having to crawl back to him. But at the same time, he was a bit tired of their "fight," rather wishing things would get back to normal. And he was itching for some hot, steamy sex, no question.

"Riki, please? You're the only one who can make a difference."

"All right," he agreed. "But you owe me."

"Thank you Riki," Tai whispered, tears in his eyes.

"Yeah okay." Riki smiled, rather liking the idea that Tai, and the others, perceived him as having the power to shift Iason's mood. He made his way back to the great hall, searching out the Blondie, who was sitting in his chair by the fire, brooding.

At his approach, Iason looked up, surprised.

Riki slowed down, walking in a deliberately provocative manner. "I miss you," he announced, as he approached. "And I forgot to give you a morning kiss." He straddled the Blondie, rubbing up suggestively against him.

"Yes, you did," Iason agreed, smiling, pleased that Riki had finally come to him. He wrapped his arms around him, immediately feeling his tensions starting to fade away.

"I want to kiss you now," the mongrel whispered, nuzzling against his neck and cheek.

Iason closed his eyes, sighing. "Oh, Riki."

"I couldn't sleep without you, last night."

"Nor could I."

"I'm sorry…about before. I was pissed as all hell."

"Perhaps I was too hard on you." Lord Mink kissed his temple, smiling. "But I was worried about you. When you didn't return, and the weather worsened, I started imagining all sorts of unspeakable things."

"I didn't mean what I said. And I don't hate you. You know that. In fact, I love you."

Iason was quiet; holding Riki close had the predictable effect of arousing him, and his cock began to twitch and grow, rubbing up against the mongrel's thighs.

"I need some sex," the mongrel whispered, his seductive, commanding tone sending shivers down Iason's back. With bold

40

initiative, Riki reached out and took the Blondie's hand, tugging off his glove and leading him to his now completely rigid erection, which bulged beneath his pants.

"Mmmm," Iason moaned, his eyes now smoldering with lust. "Give me that kiss, now."

Riki leaned forward and kissed him, his tongue swirling slowly around the Blondie's, his hands buried in his soft hair. Iason unfastened the mongrel's pants and slid his fingers beneath the cool leather, apprehending his engorged member, which was swollen and hot in his hand.

For a long time they kissed, both of them enjoying the intimacy that somehow seemed all the more sweet for the previous day's bitter fight.

"You know something we've never done?" Riki whispered, breaking away.

"What, my pet?"

"Blown each other at the same time. Wanna try it?"

Iason smiled, enjoying Riki's initiative and adventurous mood. "Let's get into bed."

They retreated to the privacy of the Master bedroom, where they undressed and began loving each other, at first gently, and then with growing passion, rolling around on the bed.

"I'm so hot for you," Riki announced, finally. "I'm so horny I can't stand it. Can we do it now? My dick's about ready to explode."

"Straddle me, facing away," Iason ordered, equally anxious to try the new position.

Riki did so, lowering his body until he could feel the heat of Iason's breath against his exposed skin. Iason spread him apart with his hands and in the next instant he felt the Blondie's hot tongue snaking up his rectum.

"Fuck," Riki gasped, his eyes rolling back. He spread his legs wider, wiggling back eagerly against his tongue, and then forced his attention to Iason's organ, which was throbbing and twitching before his face. He slid his hand around the base of the shaft, then slowly moved his tongue over the head, lapping up the semen that already pooled there.

Iason's fingers gripped his hips a little more firmly, a low moan vibrating from deep inside his throat. This only excited Riki all the more. Much as he was enjoying the Blondie's attentions, he was anxious to feel his mouth other places, and so he repositioned himself to make his desires clear.

The Blondie accommodated him by admitting him into his mouth. Riki groaned as his cock slid into his wet, hot throat; this had the effect of stimulating Iason even more.

"Release the ring," he begged. "I need to come."

Lord Mink obliged him, much to Riki's immense relief. He did his best to service Iason as well as he could, but he was so excited that he could not resist thrusting almost wildly into the Blondie's mouth. Iason relaxed his throat to accommodate him fully, and Riki pulled away from his lingual project for a moment.

"Holy shit," he cried. "I'm going to come soon. Iason! Fuck! That's perfect!"

Now Riki took Iason into his mouth again, determined to give him as much pleasure as he was getting, his tongue wiggling up and down his shaft as he slowly sucked and withdrew.

Lord Mink moaned, the vibration of his mouth sending Riki to the brink. Now he was suckling the tip of the Blondie's cock, in exactly the manner he knew Iason loved most, and in the next instant he was climaxing, his seed shooting into his Master's mouth. Iason's nails dug into his hips as he joined him, his hot semen dripping from Riki's lips and chin as the mongrel opened his mouth to cry out his ecstasy.

For some moments afterwards they simply lay together, marveling over the experience.

"That was fucking unbelievable," Riki whispered, finally.

"Yes," Iason agreed, pulling him close.

"I'm sorry about last night. It's just, it's nice having new friends," he explained. "I like going out. We never go out."

"Where would you like to go?"

"I don't know. Just somewhere." Riki thought for a moment. "Hey, do you still have my bike?"

"Yes."

"Why don't we go out together sometime? I mean together, on the bike. I'd like to take you for a ride."

"When the weather's nice, we could go to the ruins at Minas Qentu."

"That would be awesome! That's where my mural came from, right?"

"Ah, you remembered," the Blondie replied, smiling. "Yes, that's right."

"We could have Tai make us boxed meals, and take them with us!"

"If you like."

"Iason?"

"Yes, my love?"

"Don't lock me out like that again, the way you did last night."

The Blondie only smiled, nuzzling the mongrel against his cheek happily. Riki smiled, too, glad that the quarrel was over and feeling proud of himself for managing to win Iason over so easily. That afternoon he came to a new realization, that he had a power over the Blondie he had failed to appreciate fully. Though he was forced to submit to his authority, he was not without his own powers of manipulation and persuasion. Even if Iason was Master of the household, Riki was Master of Iason's heart.

Chapter 02 ~
Of Bells and Bashes

"I'M BACK!" AKI ANNOUNCED HIS PRESENCE NOISILY as he burst into the great hall, dragging his bulging overnight bag behind him. Though he had only spent one night with Suuki, it had proved impossible for the nine year old to make decisions about which of his new toys to bring, so he had packed them all. The Guardian hummed into the room behind him, almost immediately rising to settle unobtrusively in the arching ceiling.

"Ah, Aki," Iason greeted from his chair by the fire. "Did you have a pleasant visit with Suuki?"

"Yes. We had cookies!"

"Indeed. Come here, Aki, and sit on my lap. Tell me now, what kind of cookies did you have?"

"Lots of frosted ones with sprinkles," Aki answered, abandoning his bag and dutifully trotting over to Iason's chair.

The Blondie scooped him up and set him on his lap, giving him a kiss on his cheek.

"I guess I won't have frosted cookies again for a long time," Aki said sadly.

"Tai makes amazing cookies, Aki," Toma remarked with a smile as he picked up Aki's bag. "I'll take this to your room."

"Does he make *frosted* cookies *with sprinkles?*"

"Yes, indeed," Iason whispered. "Wonderfully delicious ones, too. Shall I have him make some for you?"

"Yes, please!" Aki snuggled back in Iason's arms, yawning.

"Hmmm. My guess is that a certain little boy did not get very much sleep last night," Iason remarked.

"Suuki didn't sleep very much either," Aki confirmed. "But I'm only a *little* bit sleepy." This proclamation was somewhat diluted by another great yawn, which Aki, being rather tired and not completely in possession of his youthful deceptive arts, made no effort to hide.

"I see. Perhaps you would like to take a nap this morning?"

44

"I'm too old for naps," Aki protested, though he found the Blondie's warm lap, and his comforting, sweet scent, was not conducive to staying awake, and he struggled to keep his eyes open. "Where's Riki?"

"I believe, my darling boy, that Riki is taking his morning shower," Iason replied, kissing the top of his head.

"Oh. But he always tells me stories before I go to sleep."

"Shall I tell you a story, Aki?"

"Do you *know* any stories?" Aki asked suspiciously. The very idea of the great Blondie having any stories that could possibly rival Riki's colorful tales of life as the "prince" of Midas struck Aki as rather dubious.

"What about the Legend of Ios and Erphanes?"

"I don't know," the boy answered, frowning. "Does it have any battles in it?"

"It does indeed; however, it is mostly a story about love."

"Do you know any other stories?" Aki asked hopefully, feeling rather unenthusiastic about his Guardian's proposed fare.

"I know a good deal of history," Iason began.

"Well," Aki said hurriedly, "that might be all right, *if* you let me pick the subject."

"Very well, Aki. What would you like to hear about?"

"Tell me about being the head of a Sin Ducket."

"I think you mean *Syndicate*, but what shall I tell you?"

"Is it true you speak to Jupiter?"

"Yes, it is."

"And what does Jupiter say to you?"

"That is between Jupiter and myself."

"Well then, how did you get to *be* the head of the Sin Dickit?"

"I was on the Syndicate track at the Academy, first, and then I was made an apprentice to Jupiter. While I was working at the Tower, Jupiter decided to make me the Head of the Syndicate."

"But who was the head before you?"

"Ah. That was Zen Shaq."

"What happened to him?"

Iason paused for a moment before replying. "He was assassinated."

"What does that mean?"

"He was killed by his enemies," the Blondie clarified.

"But why?"

"Because not everyone is happy about Tanagura's prosperity," Iason replied. "Didn't Lord Ghan teach you about what happened to the Federation?"

Aki yawned. "I don't know."

"We shall have to do some catching up in your studies, it seems. Ah! This will make a very good story, I think. You see, when Tanagura was first established, there were thirteen small city-states that were also founded, south of the Wastelands. When Tanagura became the capital city and began to prosper, more and more of the inhabitants left the smaller cities and became residents of Tanagura. Eventually the cities were mostly abandoned, but those that remained formed the Federation. Those that are still part of the Federation call themselves Loyalists, and they resent Tanagura's prosperity. It's believed they were responsible for the assassination."

Aki made a small snorting sound, bringing the Blondie's "story" of the Federation to an abrupt end. Iason smiled at the sight of the wee boy in his arms, glad he had decided to take Aki in as his charge.

He was also starting to enjoy Omaki's daily visits, much as he found this surprising. He had come to feel a fondness for Omaki that he had rarely felt for any other Blondie. He saw now that Lord Ghan's affection for Aki was genuine, despite the Blondie's renown perversions. Omaki came to visit Aki every day without fail, despite having to drive into Eos from Midas, and this visit had evolved into a general invitation to stay at the penthouse for dinner, which Lord Ghan happily accepted.

Tai brought a tea tray for Iason, smiling at the sight of Aki fast asleep in the Blondie's arms. "I hear Master Aki may want some frosted cookies with sprinkles," he whispered. "Shall I make a batch?"

"I'm sure he's already had far too many, but yes, go ahead and make some," Iason answered, stroking Aki's hair.

"His hair is so interesting," Tai remarked, pouring the great Blondie a steaming cup of creamberry tea and setting it on the table next to him. "It's such an unusual shade."

Aki's hair had been transformed at the Pet Academy salon, using a process that had never been replicated before, since it was the first time in Amoian history that anyone's hair had been *modified* silver. His hair, now permanently altered, glittered and sparkled in the firelight, seeming, on the one hand, decidedly artificial yet at the same time so beautiful that already the young boy turned heads. Initially Iason had been disappointed with the result, because he perceived the shade to be too different from other Elites and worried that it would set Aki apart at the

Academy. But now he was as enamored with it as everyone else, deciding that it was no secret that Aki was not a typical Elite, and that the exact shade of his hair would not make much difference.

Odi came into the hall and stood for a moment, frowning. "Iason. Might we have a word?"

"Yes, of course. Just let me settle Aki into his bed first." Iason rose and carried Aki to his room, while Tai and Odi exchanged worried glances.

"You're going to tell him now?" Tai asked.

"Yes. I really can't delay any further. I really should have told him yesterday."

Ayuda, who had been standing quietly by the wall, stepped forward. "Shall I send in Freyn and Askel?"

Odi nodded. "Yes, you might as well. They'll be called in one way or another, I suppose."

Ayuda went to retrieve the brothers, who both entered the hall seeming rather uncharacteristically somber.

"Have you told him?" Freyn asked.

"I'm just about to."

Iason entered the hall, instinctively stiffening when he saw all four bodyguards waiting. He sat down in his chair, calmly crossing his legs and sipping his tea before speaking. "So. What's all this about?" he asked finally.

"Lord Mink, I'm very sorry to report...that is, I take full responsibility, of course—"

"It's my fault, actually," Askel interrupted. "I'm the one who should be telling you this."

Freyn looked at Askel in surprise. "It's my fault, as much as yours."

"No, as Head of Security, I take responsibility," Odi asserted.

"For Jupiter's sake, would you mind getting to it? What is it you're trying to say?" Iason sighed.

"There *was* an intruder, the day of the Whippings," Odi answered. "The same individual, it appears, who broke in earlier and stole Lord Chi's blueprints. The same...individual...that contacted Commander Khosi, the one he asked you about?"

"You mean his pet, Aranshu?"

"So it appears."

Iason was silent for a moment, puzzling over this information.

The bodyguards exchanged glances again, surprised at his silence.

"It…appears he got in through Lord Chi's secret passageway," Odi continued. "We've verified that the message was sent from the room Commander Khosi was staying in."

"How precisely did he get past your security?" Iason asked, his anger concealed by his rather impassive expression.

Askel stepped forward. "That's my fault. We…I left my post, to watch the Whippings on holodisc with Freyn. I was only gone a few minutes. But apparently that was all it took."

"I should have insisted he return to his post," Freyn announced.

"Are you saying," Iason began, his voice now rising, "that you allowed an intruder to come into my home WHEN THE COMMANDER WAS STAYING WITH US?"

The bodyguards shivered at Lord Mink's tone. This was what they had been dreading.

"Yes—well, not precisely," Odi murmured. "That is, the Commander had already departed, although that was probably a surprise to the intruder."

"Have you any idea what might have happened, had any harm come to Commander Khosi?" Iason was so angry that he stood up, hands on his hips. "Are you deliberately trying to ruin my reputation? How could this have happened?"

"What's all the yelling about?" Riki demanded, walking into the great hall with only a towel wrapped around his waist, still wet from his shower and leaving a trail of water behind him.

Iason sighed. "Riki. Put some clothes on! How many times must I tell you!"

The mongrel hesitated a moment, frowning at Odi, and then turned and obediently made for his room.

The Blondie was fully expecting Riki to argue and looked a bit surprised when his pet actually obeyed him. He watched Riki leave the hall, his concentration momentarily broken.

"I assume you want my resignation," Odi said, bowing his head.

Iason made no reply, but sat back down in his chair, closing his eyes and bringing the tips of his gloved hands together as the bodyguards watched anxiously. "You're correct that I *should* take your resignation," he said, finally. "I ought to have the three of you demoted."

"Yes, Sir," Odi whispered, looking a little surprised. Did this mean Lord Mink was *not* going to take his resignation?

"I assume, from this point on, I can expect better from all of you?"

"Of course, Lord Mink," Odi said quickly.

"Yes, Sir," the brothers answered in unison.

"Then, I expect you to get to the bottom of this matter. How is it that a mere pet was able to outwit Eos security? And why? There must be an explanation for all this."

"We're working on that now," Odi confirmed, nodding, "and thank you, Sir. You're very magnanimous."

"It won't happen again," Askel added.

"See that it doesn't," Iason replied sharply, leveling them each a stern look. He rose from his chair. "I must put in a call to the Commander. I'm not sure how I'm going to explain this, but it must be done." He dismissed them with a wave of his hand, moving over to the communications center.

The brothers headed for their post and Odi accompanied them, motioning to Ayuda to join them as well.

Lord Mink sat down in front of the terminal, trying to collect his thoughts. He had no idea how the Commander would react to the news that Aranshu had, in fact, been at the penthouse. It was an egregious breach of security, and for a moment Iason contemplated simply lying about it and reporting that the Guardian had malfunctioned. But Iason didn't want to deceive Voshka—not about this. He felt guilty enough for the secret he already kept from the famous Commander, and after the intimacy they had shared at the penthouse, he found that he bore a strange affection for the man. Voshka had generously offered to give him asylum on Alpha Zen rather than face Jupiter's punishment. The least he could do was tell him the truth.

He put in the outgoing beacon, a bit surprised when the Commander immediately came onscreen, as if he had been simply waiting by his terminal for Iason's call.

"So?" Voshka said breathlessly. "What did you find out?"

"Your pet was here," Iason confirmed. "We're still looking into the details of exactly how he managed to get into the penthouse, but it seems he has some sort of device that allows him to project a special genetic signature. Using this he was somehow able to evade the building security."

The Commander was overjoyed. "I'm turning the ship around. As soon as I land on Aristia, I'll return to Amoi."

"Vosh, there's no certainty he's still on Amoi. In fact, given that he opted to delay the message he sent you, he's most likely long gone."

"Yes, yes, but you can relay that signature to the ports and find out which ship he left on and then summon it back to Amoi!"

"Of course, but don't you think it's likely he's used a different signature by now?"

"Perhaps. But maybe just by being there again, I can lure him back. Might I be so bold and beg for a bed in your home?"

"Certainly, Commander, you are always welcome, at any time."

Now Voshka arched a brow, smiling. "Ah, we're back to 'Commander.' I rather liked it when you called me Vosh a moment ago."

Iason laughed softly. "Shouldn't you be back on Alpha Zen?"

"My men are loyal. I could be gone a year and nothing would change."

"Hmmm. But what excuse will you give for returning so quickly to Amoi?"

"I will state the truth: I have decided that Amoi will supply the parts for our new defense system grid. I am returning to finalize the details of the contract."

Iason was quiet for a moment, a bit stunned with this news. A contract with Alpha Zen would be a tremendous boon for Tanagura and would mean an influx of substantial income. "Oh, Vosh."

The Commander smiled. "I had nearly made up my mind about it on Amoi. But I was planning to go to Galathia after my trip to Aristia, before I came to a final decision. As I told you, some Galathians docked with my ship, and I have to say I can't bear the thought of doing business with them. They are so unattractive, they make my toes curl. *You*, my deviant little Blondie, make my toes curl, too—but for other reasons."

Iason laughed. "Don't tell me you're making such an important decision based on mere aesthetics?"

"Aesthetics? Oh, no, not mere aesthetics, I assure you. I'm basing it on the fact that you were a delightful fuck. A business arrangement—indeed, an alliance, with Amoi would be even more palatable to me, knowing a beautiful Blondie and his saucy pet are part of the package."

"Is that Vosh?" Riki came up behind Iason, smiling.

"Ah, Riki. I hear you were quite the hero," the Commander greeted.

The mongrel shrugged, grinning.

"The Commander is returning to Amoi. He should be here in a few weeks," Iason remarked.

"Yeah? Cool." Riki absentmindedly began to play with Iason's hair, running his fingers through the long tresses.

Iason closed his eyes, enjoying the mongrel's touch.

50

"I wish I were there already," Voshka said with a wink. "Save some of that cider for me."

"Then all is well, between us?" Iason asked, opening his eyes and smiling.

"Goodness, you do have a knack for springing me with a mere look. You're so sexy, Iason." The Commander leaned back in his chair, adjusting himself.

"What about me?" Riki demanded.

"You too, Riki, of course," Voshka laughed. "You're both equally irresistible."

"Let us know when you're close to Amoi," Lord Mink said. "May we expect the same retinue?"

"Yes, if that is amenable to you."

"Of course."

"You're most gracious."

"Thank you again, Vosh, for the contract."

"My pleasure." With a smile, the Commander cut off the transmission.

"What contract?" Riki asked, leaning down to nibble Iason's ear.

"Alpha Zen has chosen Amoi to supply its new defense grid," Iason answered. "Oh, Riki. You're arousing me."

"Iason?"

"Yes, love?"

Riki moved around to face Iason and then straddled him, kissing his neck. "Please don't fire the bodyguards."

"What makes you think I intend to?" Iason asked, closing his eyes and turning his neck to allow the mongrel greater access to his throat.

Riki continued to kiss his neck. "Nothing. I just heard you yelling at them. Please?"

"Why do you care?"

"Just because...I don't know...I like them. I was just starting to get used to them." The mongrel slipped his hand down Iason's trousers, smiling when he found the Blondie already fully erect.

"Oh pet," Iason breathed. He fumbled to unfasten his trousers fully, anxious for Riki to continue.

"What do you want?" the mongrel whispered, biting his throat.

"Get on your knees."

Riki climbed down on the floor, gazing up at him with dark, gleaming eyes. "I'll suck you real good," he teased, touching his tongue to the tip of the Blondie's cock. "But will you please let the bodyguards stay?"

"Open your mouth."

"But will you?"

Iason held his organ in one hand and put his other behind Riki's head, urging him forward. "We'll discuss it later," he answered. "Now, be a good pet."

"Please?"

"Riki!" Exasperated, Iason forced himself inside the mongrel's mouth, holding his head firmly between his hands. He bit his lip when Riki began to move his tongue over his length and then groaned when the mongrel began suckling him. "Oh! That's lovely."

Riki pleasured him for a few minutes and then pulled out. "Promise me you won't fire them."

The Blondie, who had been just at the brink when Riki withdrew, gave an anguished moan and then pumped himself, his semen spraying onto his pet's face at the precise moment that the door to the penthouse hummed open.

In walked Omaki Ghan, followed by Odi, both of whom stopped in their tracks upon apprehending the Blondie and his pet thus engaged.

"Oh, my," Omaki murmured, arching a brow.

"Lord Mink," Odi gasped. "I'm terribly sorry. I should have announced Lord Ghan. I thought—"

The Blondie pressed his lips together angrily, attempting to cover himself up. Riki only snickered, finding the situation amusing. Toma and Tai both rushed into the great hall at the same time—Tai from the kitchen and Toma from the arching entrance to the main house—each carrying damp hand towels, and both of them were so preoccupied with waiting on Master Iason that neither saw the other, and the two collided in the great hall.

"It seems at least one of us has come at a bad time," Omaki remarked, his eyes twinkling.

Toma leapt to his feet, rubbing his arm where he had collided into Tai, and offered Iason and Riki each a damp cloth, which both gratefully accepted.

"Forgive me," Lord Mink murmured, his face flushing pink as he fumbled to fasten his trousers.

"Please don't put away your toys on my account," Lord Ghan teased.

Too flustered to respond, Iason only rose and retreated to the fire, motioning to one of the chairs there. "Please sit down. May I offer you a drink?"

"Tea would be nice. It's a bit nippy out there this morning. I'm sorry for the intrusion. It's just that I hardly got to see Aki last night, and I was hoping to spend a little time with him today." Omaki settled down in one of the chairs, crossing his legs languidly.

"He's taking a nap," Iason answered.

"I'm ready for breakfast," Riki announced, sitting at the dining table.

"Coming, Sir Riki!" Tai exclaimed, rushing back into the kitchen and returning with a few warming domes as Toma brought a new tea tray to the Blondies.

Odi attempted to retreat from the hall but was hailed by Iason. "Odi. Commander Khosi will be our guest again, in about three weeks. Please make appropriate arrangements."

The bodyguard frowned at this. "Was he very upset?"

"Quite the contrary. He was actually rather delighted to learn that Aranshu was here."

"Interesting," Odi murmured, nodding. "I'll take care of it."

"Vosh is coming back to Amoi? Oh, goodness," Omaki purred. "Who's this Aranshu?"

Iason took a sip of his tea before answering. "An Aristian pet he owned some years ago that ran away, apparently. It seems he managed to break into the penthouse while the Commander was staying here."

At this, Odi's cheeks reddened and he bowed his head.

"Aranshu," Omaki repeated, dipping a chocolate biscuit into his tea. "That's an interesting name."

"I suppose so. The Guardian listed a rather long name on the logs. What was it again, Odi?"

"Lord Wyn Qantum Aranshu."

"Wyn Qantum?" Tai was so surprised that he froze, holding a warming dome of glazed cinnamon buns in midair.

Everyone turned to the flustered chef, who looked about ready to pass out.

"Yes? Does that name have some meaning I'm not aware of?" Iason asked.

"For-forgive me, Lord Mink. But Wyn Qantum is the name of the notorious rebel who recently…that is…who recently…."

"Yes? Who recently what?" Iason pressed, a bit impatiently.

"What is it, Tai?" Odi whispered.

"Well," Tai looked uncertainly at Odi and then back at Iason. "There was a…an incident recently on Aristia."

"Ah, the Merovian massacre at Anubia. Isn't that why Vosh went rushing off to Aristia?"

"Yes, I believe so, although I was rather...preoccupied that day," Iason remarked. "So, what are you saying, Tai?"

"It's just that Wyn Qantum is said to be responsible...for it."

"That's interesting," Lord Ghan remarked, sipping his tea. "His pet is an assassin?"

"Are those cookies I smell?" Riki asked.

"Oh! The cookies!" Tai set the cinnamon rolls on the table and rushed back into the kitchen.

"Riki, you'll finish your breakfast before you have any cookies," Iason remarked.

"What? I was just asking what they were. Sheesh. Well, I'm having one of these rolls, then. Tai! Bring me some coffee!"

"Jupiter's sake, Riki, you needn't yell! And finish your juice before you start on your coffee," the Blondie scolded.

"I already drank it!" Riki retorted, holding his cup upside-down. "Back off, Blondie!"

"Riki," Lord Mink sighed.

"That Guardian really is a remarkable device," Omaki said thoughtfully. "Although I must say I'm thankful it doesn't scan my retina every time I come in. How does it work exactly? I mean, how does it know it's already scanned me?"

"It implants a retina trace," Ayuda said quietly.

"Oh?" Iason turned to the quiet bodyguard, who was standing a few feet away, by one of the hall pillars.

"Yes, unless I'm quite mistaken, when it does the scan it implants a microscopic trace chip. You wouldn't even feel it. It then ignores you because it senses the tracer."

"A tracer? Does that mean it knows the location of anyone it has scanned?"

Ayuda thought for a moment. "I don't know, actually. I suppose it's possible."

"Guardian X900!" Iason commanded. The unit immediately whizzed into the great hall and stopped in front of the Blondie.

"Yes, Lord Mink."

"What is the location of Raoul Am?"

"Lord Am is currently in the great hall of his estate."

"What is the location of Heiku Quiahtenon?"

"Lord Quiahtenon is currently at the Pet Academy."

"What's he doing there?" Omaki wondered aloud.

"What is the location…of…Commander Voshka Khosi?" Iason continued.

"Commander Khosi is on his ship, approximately 26 hours away from Aristia."

"What is the location of Aranshu, Commander Khosi's pet?"

"Lord Aranshu is currently aboard Commander Khosi's ship."

"What?" Iason stood up, looking alarmed.

Odi frowned. "That's not possible. He was still here after the Commander departed."

"Guardian, can you tell us how Aranshu came to be on the Commander ship?"

"Lord Aranshu departed Amoi three weeks ago on a Galathian ship bound for Aristia. His ship docked with Commander Khosi's Emperor-VI yesterday at 13:10."

Ayuda nodded. "Galathian ships *are* fast."

"Vosh said some Galathians docked with his ship," Lord Mink remembered, rushing to the communications center. "Guardian, where precisely is Aranshu on the Commander's ship?"

"Lord Aranshu is in cargo bay 354-C."

Iason immediately sent an emergency outgoing beacon to Voshka.

"Why does it keep calling him 'Lord'? I thought Aranshu was a pet?" Omaki mused aloud.

"We're not sure," Odi replied. "We think—"

Iason held up his hand to silence the bodyguard when the Commander came onscreen.

"Yes?" Voshka looked concerned. "Are you in some kind of trouble, Iason?"

"No, but you may be," Iason replied. "Vosh, your pet—Aranshu—is aboard your ship."

The Commander blinked, seeming confused. "I don't understand."

"The Guardian has a mechanism to trace anyone it scans. We've just verified that Aranshu boarded your ship from the Galathian vessel that docked with you. He's in cargo bay 354-C."

As the full weight of the news registered with Voshka, his eyes lit up. Could it possibly be true? After ten years of searching, was Aranshu finally in his grasp—*and aboard his own ship?* "Thank you, Iason," he said breathlessly. "I'm in your debt." Without further comment he cut the transmission, leaving Iason to stare at a blank screen.

"I'd give half my estate to have one of Megala's spy-holes on that ship now," Omaki remarked.

Lord Mink only frowned. "I hope he's careful."

Ayuda surprised everyone by laughing. "Forgive me," he said, when Iason shot him a disapproving look. "It's just that you're talking about Commander Khosi, possibly the greatest military commander of our time. I don't think he'll be bested by a pet."

"What makes you think a pet can't be dangerous?" Riki demanded, his mouth full of cinnamon roll. "Sounds like he did some damage on Aristia, anyway."

"Pet, how many times must I tell you? Do not talk with food in your mouth," Iason scolded.

The mongrel rolled his eyes but dutifully quieted.

"At any rate, it should be an interesting reunion," Omaki remarked. "How long did you say he's been looking for him?"

"Ten years," Iason answered.

Lord Ghan only shook his head, but for a brief moment he and Iason locked eyes.

"Would you look for *me* for ten years?" Riki asked, almost absently, before munching on a piece of bacon.

"Of course, pet," Iason replied. "Although you'd have quite a spanking waiting for you at the end of it."

"Only if you found me."

"Oh, I'd find you," the Blondie replied. "I'd look for you for a hundred years, if I had to."

"I'd be dead by then," Riki pointed out.

There was a rather long silence as both of them reflected on the reality of this observation. It had never been discussed before, but the differences in mongrel and Blondie physiology meant that, barring any accidents, Iason would outlive Riki by several lifetimes. As Iason thought about this, he instinctively brought a hand to his head to ward off the dull aching that began in his head.

Without a word, Riki rose and went to Iason, moving behind him to massage his shoulders.

"I wonder if Vosh will punish Aranshu?" Omaki mused, hoping to break the awkward silence.

"He's a fool if he doesn't," Iason replied.

"Why am I not surprised you take *that* view," the mongrel sighed, though the smile on his face showed that he was only teasing. "I guess this means Vosh won't be coming to stay again after all."

"No, probably not, now that he's found his pet," Lord Mink agreed.

"The cookies are ready," Tai announced, bringing in a plate of frosted, sprinkle-covered biscuits.

"My, aren't those festive? What's the celebration?" Lord Ghan asked.

"Aki was rather taken with some frosted cookies he had at Suuki's residence," Iason explained. "So I had Tai make some more."

"Ah! Speaking of celebrations, that reminds me, part of the reason I came here today was to invite you to a Bash tomorrow night at my villa. After everything that's happened, I imagine we could all use an evening away from Eos."

"That's a splendid idea," Iason agreed, nodding. "I should have thought of it myself."

"No, you shouldn't have. You've played the host long enough, it's time you let someone else run the show. So, do you accept my invitation?"

"With pleasure. What should I bring?"

"Your household. Unless, of course, you have more of that cider," Lord Ghan teased, winking.

"A party sounds fun," Riki remarked.

The talk of parties and frosted cookies predictably had the effect of luring Aki from his bed, and he padded into the great hall, looking extraordinarily sleepy. "Master," he cried, immediately running to Lord Ghan and crawling onto his lap. Despite being corrected many times, the boy continued to address the Blondie as "Master," though Omaki, for his part, was only too glad that Aki seemed unable to break the habit.

"Come here, my little love," he whispered, hugging him tightly.

"You're here early!"

"Yes, I am. I won't be here later today, because I must get the villa ready for our party."

"Party?" Excited, Aki sat straight up, staring up at the Blondie with wide eyes.

"Yes. I'm throwing a very big party tomorrow night. And I have a special surprise for you when you get to the villa," Omaki added, winking.

The promise of a party and a special surprise, as well as the sight of freshly-baked frosted cookies *with sprinkles* was simply too much; Aki squirmed off the Blondie's lap and began running erratically around the room, providing the additional service of repeatedly announcing, every few moments, that there was going to be a party. His noisy excitement was tolerated, for everyone there felt similarly: after the ordeal of the

Public Whippings and Konami's weekly lectures, a party at Omaki's infamous villa seemed like the perfect diversion.

"Come here, love, and give us a kiss," Lord Ghan said, rising. "I have a thousand errands to run today, so I'd best be off."

"Who else am I giving a kiss?" Aki asked, rushing to him and planting a wet kiss on the Blondie's cheek.

"Whatever do you mean?" Omaki asked.

"You said, 'Give *us* a kiss.'" Aki explained.

Lord Ghan laughed. "That's only an expression. I meant give *me* a kiss."

"Oh. Can I invite Suuki to the party?"

"That is up to your Guardian."

Aki turned to Iason, who was enjoying Riki's neck massage, his head bowed and his eyes closed.

"Guardian, may I invite Suuki to the party?" Aki pleaded.

"You may," Iason replied.

"Then, I'm off," Omaki announced, looking at Riki and hesitating. He patted his pocket purposefully, winking.

The mongrel's eyes lit up as he realized what Lord Ghan had with him.

"Oh pet," Iason sighed, when Riki found an especially tight knot.

"Hey, maybe you should, like, go lie down on the bed? I'll rub out your back for you," the mongrel suggested, with a mischievous smile the Blondie could not see.

"Yes, I'll show myself out," Omaki said, pressing his lips together to keep from laughing.

As Iason rose and retreated to the Master bedroom, Lord Ghan carefully withdrew a small red velvet pouch from his pocket.

"Is that it?" Riki whispered.

"Yes. Remember our agreement," Omaki whispered back, arching a brow.

"Yeah, okay."

"What is that?" Aki said loudly.

"Shhh," the Blondie cautioned. "It's a secret."

Satisfied to be part of a secret, even if he was unsure what the secret was about, the boy happily munched on his cookie as he walked Lord Ghan to the door.

Riki concealed the pouch behind his back as he joined Iason in the bedroom, glad to find the Blondie already naked and facedown on the bed. He carefully hid the pouch at the foot of the bed and then proceeded to undress and give Lord Mink a thorough massage.

It had become something of a ritual; nearly every day the Blondie suffered from an excruciating headache, and while there had been a time when an O-3 or an O-6 could bring him relief, now he no longer responded to opiates at all. Only Riki was able to help assuage his pain.

As usual, Iason fell asleep during the massage. The mongrel waited until he was positive the Blondie was dead to the world, and then he carefully retrieved the pouch he had hidden, opening the golden ties to peer inside. First he pulled out the tiny transmission camera. Grinning, he then pulled out the collar, keeping his hand over the large round bell that hung from it to prevent it from sounding. Then, holding Iason's hair aside, he quickly slid the collar around the Blondie's neck, snapping it shut.

Lord Mink's eyes flew open and he rolled onto his back, staring up at him in confusion. This movement was accompanied by the tinkle of the bell at his collar.

Riki giggled, delighted with the sight of the Blondie, naked and rubbed down with oil, wearing only a collar with a bell. He snapped the holopic he promised Omaki, using the tiny transmission camera, which sent the image directly to Lord Ghan's receiver, and then let the inconspicuous device fall to the floor.

The Blondie was too distracted to even notice. "Riki!" He sat up and tugged at the collar, frowning. "Remove this at once! Someone wants a spanking, I think! A very hard one, too!" Iason's every move was punctuated with the happy jingle of his bell, the sound somehow diluting the Blondie's threat.

The mongrel continued to giggle like a schoolboy, so amused with the great Blondie's predicament that he found it impossible to feel at all alarmed at Iason's growing anger.

"Pet! Obey me! Unlock this collar *at once!*"

Lord Mink lunged for him, but the mongrel backed away and then darted out of the room, laughing. Iason was at his heels, chasing him through the great hall, his bell providing a merry accompaniment to his pursuit.

Aki's loud giggle and the surprised stares from Toma, Tai, Ayuda and Odi put an end to the chase; Iason, suddenly realizing he was completely naked *and wearing a bell*, stopped in his tracks and then hurriedly retreated to the Master bedroom.

"Riki!" he bellowed. "Come here THIS INSTANT!"

Aki was on the floor, giggling so hard that he clutched his stomach, gasping for breath. The others in the hall could only shake their heads, exchanging amused glances.

"You'd better obey him, Riki," Toma said nervously. "He sounds a bit upset."

"Yeah, yeah. Don't worry, I'll calm him down." With a grin and a wink, the naked mongrel returned to the bedroom, where he was promptly seized by Iason and dragged over to the bed. Riki continued to laugh, unable to help himself when he heard the tinkle of the bell.

"You're very naughty," the Blondie whispered, though he felt his anger diminish when he realized that Riki was aroused.

"Oh, come on! I'm just having a little fun. You look so sexy with that bell on. Can't we play a bit? Please?"

"You're getting a spanking," Iason replied.

"Yeah, but, couldn't we, like, do that later? That collar is going to come off automatically in an hour, at least that's what Omaki said. I don't want it to go to waste." As if to emphasize this, the mongrel began stroking himself meaningfully. "Come on! This is a huge turn on!"

"Omaki gave this to you, did he?" Lord Mink shook his head, marveling at the Blondie's incorrigible mischief and wondering how he might get even.

"Please?" Riki purred, flicking his tongue over Iason's nipple and gently touching a finger to his bell. "Lie back on the bed."

"Very well," Lord Mink agreed, finding himself immediately responding to the mongrel's advances, his cock springing to life. "But afterwards, you *will* be spanked."

"Whatever," Riki replied, rolling his eyes. He pointed to the bed. "Lie back like a good little pet."

Iason opened his mouth to protest and then seemed to warm to the game, slowly lying back on the bed and fondling himself eagerly. "Suck on my nipples a bit," he ordered.

"Pets do not dictate," Riki replied sternly, hands on his hips. "Pets do their Master's bidding without comment or argument."

The Blondie laughed at this. "Is that so? I quite agree with you, in fact. And I shall hold you to it."

Riki ignored this, crawling toward him seductively. Iason bit his lip, enjoying the mongrel's game. "Oh, Riki."

"You look sexy as hell with that bell on," Riki whispered. "It makes you seem even more naked somehow." He slid between Iason's legs and moved on top of him, prodding his mouth open for a long, sensual kiss.

Lord Mink responded with almost violent passion, returning his kiss enthusiastically and moving his hands over the mongrel's hot skin, then grabbing his buttocks and pulling the cheeks apart suggestively.

Riki broke away from the kiss, grinning. "You see? You're just as turned on as me. So I don't think I deserve to be punished."

The Blondie answered that with a hard smack to his ass, eliciting a yelp of protest. "It is up to me whether or not you shall be punished, but for the record, there can hardly be any question that you *deserve* a good spanking. In fact...ohhhh!"

Riki silenced him by sucking on his nipples, which Iason responded to by immediately arching his back. After a few minutes of this, the Blondie could wait no longer. He seized the vial of oil that was on the bedside table and poured a generous amount of the warm liquid onto his member, his mouth parting slightly as he lubricated himself.

Riki sat back on his heels, smiling, his own erection so rigid he was about to spill his seed.

"Straddle me," Iason commanded.

The mongrel did so, sliding onto his length with ease and then wiggling a bit to admit Iason fully.

"I've broken you in nicely, I think," the Blondie remarked, pouring more oil into his hand.

"Humph," Riki snorted. "I'm not an animal, you know. I can't be *broken in.*"

"You're a wild little pet that still needs a bit of taming," Lord Mink replied, wrapping his hand around the mongrel's cock and lubricating him with slow, firm strokes.

The movement of his hand caused his bell to sound, which brought an impish smile to Riki's face.

"I think you should *always* wear a bell," he proclaimed. "That way I can hear you when you're near me. You're always sneaking up on me and scaring the crap out of me, you know. Mmmm...that feels fucking awesome."

Riki began to undulate, much to Iason's delight. "That's very good, pet. Keep doing that."

"I'm gonna come!"

"That's it," Lord Mink encouraged, pumping him faster. "Come for me, my love."

The mongrel did so, his semen arcing onto Iason's chest as he groaned his release. As usual, Riki's rapture was enough to send the

Blondie over the brink, and he climaxed as well, emitting a series of soft gasps and moans.

When Iason opened his eyes, he found Riki staring down at him, his face tilted to one side and a lopsided grin on his face.

"You're so sexy when you come. I wish I had a holopic of it. Hey, could I—"

"Absolutely not."

"Why not?" Riki demanded, slowly disengaging himself from the Blondie and then snuggling up in his arms.

"Because," Iason replied, kissing his temple, "I wouldn't want such an image to fall into the wrong hands."

"I wouldn't let anyone else see it," Riki protested. "How about just a regular holopic then?"

Iason smiled. "Are you saying you want a picture of me?"

"Maybe," the mongrel replied, twisting a strand of the Blondie's hair around his fingers.

"Perhaps I should have a portrait commissioned. Ah! Raoul is very good at portraits. Yes, that's a splendid idea; we'll have our likenesses painted together, as Master and pet."

Riki frowned at this. "Do I have to wear chains?"

"It would be nice if you did. However, I'll not insist on it."

The mongrel relaxed, laying his head on Iason's chest. "Okay, then."

"You *will* be wearing chains to Omaki's party tomorrow, of course," Lord Mink added, and then seemed to tense up as if expecting an argument.

"I know," Riki sighed. "But you'll take them off as soon as we get there, right?"

"Yes," Iason promised, giving him a little hug and feeling pleased that the mongrel was being so cooperative. "And this time, you may have *three* drinks."

Riki rolled his eyes at this but knew better than to say anything, though he made a little sigh.

The sudden snap of the bell collar as it automatically unlocked and fell from his throat reminded Iason of Riki's infraction, but it was hard to feel truly angry at his pet after the intimacy they had just shared. He reached out and proffered three hard smacks to the mongrel's buttocks.

"There, you have been duly chastised," he announced, and then added, after a moment, "although if you ever pull another stunt like that again, you're in for a *real* spanking, make no mistake."

Riki only yawned in response to this threat, feeling suddenly extraordinarily comfortable in the Blondie's arms. For a long time they simply lay together quietly on the bed, until Tai sounded the chime for lunch.

⁂

"WE HAVE HIM," LIEUTENANT MAHTA CONFIRMED. "Shall we bring him to your quarters?"

"Stay where you are," Voshka replied, a smile teasing the corners of his lips. "I'll be there momentarily."

After ordering that the ship change course again, this time heading home to Alpha Zen, the Commander strode toward the cargo bay, his heart pounding. Could it really be true? After ten long years of searching, was Aranshu finally his again? It seemed impossible, and even with Mahta's assurance, he found himself unable to believe it was true until he saw Aranshu for himself.

He slowed his pace as he entered cargo bay 354-C, instinctively holding his breath when he saw his pet. Aranshu was being restrained by four guards, his back pressed up against the wall, and it was clear that even with a laser jabbed up against his throat, he was continuing to resist. Voshka couldn't help but smile; Aranshu was no fool—he knew that he would not be shot and that the laser posed no real threat.

"Get your filthy hands off me!" Aranshu's eyes flashed defiantly, a look that Voshka had seen many times.

As the Commander approached, the young man suddenly quieted, turning to regard him as he neared. For a long moment neither of them spoke. One of the guards was standing apart from the others, cursing as he examined his own bloody hand.

"He bit me!" he complained, when Voshka glanced in his direction.

"He hasn't changed a bit," Mahta observed wryly.

Voshka, however, was of an entirely different opinion. Ten years had, indeed, changed Aranshu; the rebellious Aristian boy had grown into a strong, handsome man. Only the look in his eyes remained the same…the look, and, as Voshka immediately noticed as he neared him, his distinctive, alluring scent.

But while the Commander was prepared for the change in Aranshu's appearance, having watched the taped message from the Guardian over and over, Aranshu seemed a bit stunned when he saw Voshka.

Ten years had made the Commander even more handsome and virile; but more than this, there was an air of confidence about him that was simply intoxicating. Voshka's great military successes and his enormous wealth had indeed transformed him, and there was a sort of aura around him that was mesmerizing to all who saw him.

But for Aranshu, it was more than this. He had thought of Voshka Khosi every night since escaping from the harem on Alpha Zen ten years before, but his memories hadn't fully prepared him for the way he would feel when he set eyes on the Commander again. His heart was pounding hard in his chest as Voshka neared and then stood in front of him. In that instant he felt surprised that the Commander was so handsome; somehow he had forgotten this detail, or perhaps he had been too young to appreciate it. He felt the blood shoot to his loins, unbidden, his cock lengthening and hardening.

"Aranshu," Voshka whispered, his eyes dark and gleaming. "You have been a *very naughty* pet."

Chapter 03 ~
Paddles, Peni, and Party Prep

VOSHKA LET HIS HAND SLIDE DOWN ARANSHU'S back and then gave him a hard smack on the ass. The young man barely reacted, his lips twitching ever so slightly.

"Ah, it seems I must spank you a bit harder now," Voshka observed. "I ought to spank you like the naughty pet you are, over my knee just as I did the day you left ten years ago."

Laughter now echoed through the cargo bay. The very idea that Vosh would punish Aranshu—now a grown young man and a notorious terrorist—with a *spanking* was ridiculous.

Aranshu only glared back at the Commander. "Fuck you," he spat.

"Oh, you shall," Voshka answered. "Repeatedly, and with enthusiasm. And I will do the same to you."

"He was carrying this," one of the guards announced, holding up a laser knife. "And this." He handed the Commander a slender metallic case. Voshka took it, opening it and examining the contents.

"An assassin's case," Anders exclaimed, his brow furrowing.

In the case were vials of poisons—clearly labeled—thin wire garrotes, a cable rope, razor blades, a capsule containing a plastic bag, skewers, tape, miniature explosives (fuse-lit and digitally-triggered), matches, a lighter, a laser gun, and a pair of black leather gloves.

"What's all this?" Voshka demanded.

"What does it look like? I came here to kill you."

For a moment the Commander was silent, toying with one of the vials of poison. Though he feigned being unaffected, he was, in fact, a bit hurt. He was not altogether surprised that Aranshu would say such a thing, but it was disappointing to find so much physical evidence that he truly intended to carry out such a threat.

"I see. You've come here to kill me," he repeated thoughtfully. He pressed the cold blade of a razor against Aranshu's throat, nicking him slightly. "My. That's sharp."

Aranshu flinched but remained silent. Voshka put the razor back in the box and then held up a skewer with one hand. "And what precisely did you have in mind for these?" he asked, his eyes twinkling.

"I'd stick them in your eyes and through your voicebox."

Though privately horrified at the answer, Voshka refused to give Aranshu the satisfaction of appearing concerned.

"Hmmm. And this?" He held up a vial of what appeared to be oil, shaking it slightly. "Is this what I think it is?"

Color rose to the young man's cheeks and he scowled, annoyed that Voshka had found his private vial.

"It seems perhaps you had something more pleasant in mind before you whipped out those skewers. You were hoping for a ride, I think—or perhaps to be ridden. For old time's sake?"

"That has nothing to do with you," Aranshu snapped.

"Is that so? Let's try it out tonight, shall we?" Voshka leaned close, his breath making the hairs on Aranshu's neck stand on end. "After your punishment, of course." He slid a hand between his pet's legs, sliding across his thigh to his hip.

Aranshu closed his eyes, swallowing hard. It was infuriating how easily Voshka aroused him, even now. He tried to clear his mind but all his thoughts were bent on the sensation of Voshka's hand on his hip and how much he longed to feel his touch again, all over his naked body. He hated himself for his weakness, so much that he hung his head in shame.

The Commander glanced down, noting Aranshu's growing bulge. "I still arouse you," he whispered, delighted. He slipped a finger teasingly along the inside of Aranshu's pants, against his abdomen. "Right now you want nothing more than to feel me slide between your thighs, my mouth around your cock. Admit it."

Aranshu looked away, feigning indifference, though his erection grew rigid almost instantly. He desperately needed to adjust himself but forced himself to remain motionless.

Voshka was beside himself with pleasure. He had his long-lost pet back again and a night ahead that promised to be nothing short of glorious. He moved behind Aranshu, teasing him by rocking his pelvis against his ass.

"I'm going to fuck you again and again. Harder than you'll like." He whispered this dark promise into Aranshu's ear as he slid both hands down the young man's sides to his hips, giving him a decidedly violent thrust. Then he abruptly stepped back.

"But first...there is the pressing little matter of your discipline. I confess I'm rather at a loss. It seems that no punishment is quite fitting for your disobedience. You've been gone for, let's see...how long was it again? Oh yes. TEN YEARS." His voice now betrayed his anger, an old, long-festering anger that rolled up his spine, making the Commander tremble as it spilled out into his body. He clenched his teeth, the movement shifting his jaw.

For the first time, Aranshu flinched ever so slightly; he remembered well his Master's anger, that sinister tone in his voice and how precisely it matched the sting of his arm. Had he still been a boy, he would have been instinctively shaking. But he was no boy now. His momentary uncertainty quickly vanished; his expression was once again stoic, his eyes clouded and distant.

No, he was no boy. The Commander was marveling on this exact point as well. He circled him slowly, studying the masculine lines of Aranshu's body. His pretty little pet had grown into a handsome young man, his muscles bulging with sinewy strength. In fact, Voshka suspected that Aranshu now exceeded him in strength. He would have to be kept in chains—that much was clear enough. His golden-blond hair was every bit as glorious as it had always been, but a bit longer now. He longed to touch it, to bury his face in it and inhale its rich scent—to yank Aranshu's head back with it tangled around his fingers.

"Bring him to my chambers," he commanded. "Chain him face down to the bed." He turned on his heel and left the cargo bay, followed closely by his bodyguard, Anders.

"Commander, I feel it would be prudent to keep guards in your room. It's clear Aranshu means you harm," Anders asserted, falling into step with him.

"I'll not have an audience to spoil my triumph," Voshka replied.

"But, Commander—"

"Don't argue with me, Anders. How many times must I tell you that? Besides," Voshka added in a teasing tone, "we both know you just want to satisfy your voyeuristic propensities."

But Anders remained serious, shaking his head earnestly. "This is no joking matter. How do you expect me to protect you? He's dangerous and you know it."

"He'll be chained."

"And muzzled?"

"No." If there was one thing Voshka missed, it was Aranshu's kiss. He would have him responding before the night was through, of that much he was sure.

"You know he bites," Anders protested.

"No muzzle," Voshka replied firmly.

"At least say you don't intend to put yourself in a position that…that," Anders stammered as he tried to find the words, "might compromise the integrity of your manhood."

At this Voshka couldn't help but laugh. "Are you asking if I intend to force him to perform fellatio without precautions? I'm not mad, Anders. No, I have a special device that I'll be using tonight; Aranshu knows it well."

"A…device?"

"A mouthpiece. It holds the teeth apart and forces the mouth open, allowing me to enjoy the pleasures of oral stimulation without, as you so delicately put it, compromising the integrity of my manhood."

Anders nodded, relaxing slightly. He hadn't even known such a device existed, but of course if anyone would have one, it would be Voshka Khosi.

As they neared the Commander's chambers, Anders suddenly thought of Azka, the pet Voshka had acquired on Amoi. "At least keep your new pet in the same room," he pleaded. Though Azka would hardly afford the Commander much protection against a man like Aranshu, it was better than nothing. He could perhaps alert Anders if there was a problem.

"Oh, I intend to," Voshka replied, smiling. He was already envisioning scenarios where he would force Aranshu to watch him being pleasured by the new pet. Despite Aranshu's claims that he had come only to kill him, Voshka knew that the young man's feelings were more complicated than that. He knew he could still arouse the Aristian, and he intended to find out if he could still make him jealous as well.

Aranshu's jealousy of other pets in the harem had always been a complete contradiction to all his assertions that he hated his Master. If he truly hated the Commander, why would he be jealous of other pets? It made no sense, and Voshka had always delighted in Aranshu's transparent jealousy, deliberately provoking it, for he viewed it as an indication of his pet's true feelings toward him.

"I'm taking a bath now," Voshka announced, shooting Anders a mischievous look. "Do you intend to follow me into the bath hall, or can I hope for some privacy?"

68

"Of course, Commander," Anders murmured, stopping just outside the bath hall as Voshka slipped inside. He frowned, pulling out his communicator. Although he knew Voshka was thrilled to have Aranshu back in his grasp, he was extraordinarily worried about it. Aranshu had always been trouble, from the moment he had first come into the Commander's household. And now that he was a grown man—and a renowned assassin at that—Anders knew he posed a very real danger, even if Voshka refused to acknowledge it.

He came to a decision, one that he knew would infuriate the Commander if he ever discovered it. He decided to plant a small camera device on Azka, the pet the Commander had brought with him from Amoi, so that he could watch what was happening inside Voshka's chambers. He was especially worried about what might happen when the Commander was asleep, for he suspected that he would allow Aranshu to remain in his bed. Anders felt that, even chained, Aranshu posed a threat.

"Manji, bring the Commander's pet, Azka, to me. I'm just outside the bath hall," he said in a low voice, his mouth up against the communicator.

"Copy that," Manji replied.

"And bring a 460 unit."

"What model?"

"A neckring. And…please tell no one about this, Manji."

There was a slight pause. Then, "Copy that."

Anders disconnected the frequency with a sigh. It was going to be a long night.

"Yousi."

The Blondie jumped and turned around, his eyes wide. "Oh. It's you," he said, smiling when he saw Lord Quiahtenon standing behind him.

"Did I frighten you?" Heiku asked.

"Yes," Yousi answered.

"What are you doing?"

"Erm…" Lord Xuuju stammered, looking around him as though confused about where he was. "I was just counting things."

"Now that I have disturbed you, does that mean you'll have to start over again?"

"Yes," he admitted. "But I don't mind." He smiled up at the tall Blondie, actually rather pleased and flattered that he had come by again.

"Do you have to do that now? Maybe you should take a break."

"Well," Yousi eyed the long row of paddles, considering. "I guess I could put it off until tomorrow."

"Excellent plan! Always put off today what you can do tomorrow." Heiku allowed his hands to rest on Yousi's hips, pulling him a little closer. "Because I want you to come to my place tonight. I mean my house, in Midas."

"Your house?"

"Yes. You haven't seen it yet. You may not remember," he continued, leaning a little closer, "but you and I designed that place. With Megala's help, of course. I don't suppose you remember that, do you?"

Yousi furrowed his brow, frowning. "I'm not sure," he whispered.

"Well, anyway, I want you to see it," Heiku insisted. "I want you to spend the night."

"Oh, I don't want to be any trouble," Lord Xuuju said.

Heiku laughed. "Yousi, Yousi. What am I to do with you? You'd hardly be any trouble. Don't you understand? I want you in my bed tonight."

"But," Yousi countered, looking concerned. "I take up a lot of space. And I kick off all the covers."

"You take up exactly the right amount of space," Heiku argued. "And I like the way you kick off the covers. It's endearing."

"Then, we've slept together before," Yousi said, looking a little uncertain.

"Oh yes," Lord Quiahtenon laughed. "Many times. Don't tell me you don't remember, not even one little bit? Surely you haven't forgotten the night we spent together just a few weeks ago?"

"We didn't sleep," Yousi replied.

"No, we didn't," Heiku agreed, grinning. "But this time I promise we'll sleep, at least a little. You can spend the night at my place tonight, and then we'll both go together to Omaki's party. You received your invitation, I hope?"

"Oh yes," Yousi replied, brightening. "He says it's going to be a very special party."

"And it will be, I'm sure. Omi knows how to give a good party, I'll give him that much. So…how about it? Spend the night with me?"

"Will we have sex?"

Heiku laughed, kissing the Blondie on the forehead. "Oh, Yousi. You are a true delight. Yes, we're having sex. Lots of it."

"Good, because I have an erection now."

"Yes, you do," Lord Quiahtenon whispered, rubbing his thumb across the Blondie's obvious bulge.

"I'm going to ejaculate in my pants," Yousi announced.

"Well, let's take care of that, shall we?" Heiku unfastened Yousi's pants, sliding a hand inside.

"Someone might come into the store!"

"Yes, love, and have you forgotten that you run a sex shop? We'll just tell them we're trying out the merchandise."

The Blondie stiffened, his back rigid. "Oh! Oh! I'm going to come! I'm going to come!"

Heiku kissed the side of Lord Xuuju's neck, pumping him slowly. "That's good. You go right ahead and come."

"Oh! Heiku," Yousi grabbed onto the Blondie's tunic, clutching him desperately. "It feels good! It feels so good!"

"You're so close.…" Heiku suddenly knelt down, closing his mouth over his partner's member and finishing him off with a slow suck.

Yousi let out an anguished cry, his semen pooling into Lord Quiahtenon's mouth. He buried his hands in the Blondie's hair, biting his lip as the waves of rapture contorted his body.

"Hei," he whispered.

After a moment Heiku rose, wiping his mouth. "What did you just call me?"

"I…I don't know."

"You called me Hei. You haven't called me that since…well, since *before*." Heiku's eyes were shining.

"And Omi used to call you Ku-ku," Yousi remembered suddenly.

"Argh! Don't call me that!" Heiku brought a hand to his forehead, shaking his head. "I hate that name."

"Ku-ku," Yousi repeated, with a mischievous grin.

"What! Such insolence! That deserves some punishment, I think. Let's see," Heiku brought a hand to his chin as if in deep contemplation as he studied the paddles lining the wall. "I think *this one* will do nicely."

With that, the Blondie snatched up an impressive-looking paddle and twirled it around in his robotic hand, raising his eyebrows.

71

Yousi immediately shrieked and darted behind a stack of anal plugs, knocking the display over and sending the plugs rolling and wobbling across the floor. Thus ensued a grand chase through The Bondage & Discipline Shop, with Yousi screaming all the while, until finally Heiku managed to seize him from behind, pulling him close, the paddle firmly across his tummy.

"Now you're in for it!" he warned.

"Please! Please don't...don't paddle me!"

"And why shouldn't I?" Lord Quiahtenon whispered, nibbling on Yousi's ear. "Didn't you call me Ku-ku right after I told you not to?"

"But I was just...just...*flirting*," Yousi stammered.

Laughing, Heiku released his hold on the flustered Blondie, turning him around. "Oh, very well. I suppose I shall be lenient *this* time. Ooo, it's quite a sacrifice, I must say. I very much feel like paddling *someone*."

"Paddle Omi," Yousi suggested, "at the party."

"Oh my. Oh yes. Yousi, that is a brilliant idea. Simply brilliant! It's about time someone got him back for all his little pranks." Heiku examined the paddle, delighting in the imagery of Omaki taking the full force of it.

"Although, he *is* throwing the party," Lord Xuuju remembered. "Is it polite to paddle the host?"

"Of course it is!" Heiku proclaimed happily. "Besides, we'll give it to him as a gift afterwards. He'll love it. It's a very nice paddle."

"I have a paddle that takes a picture before it strikes," Yousi remarked, pointing to a shiny silver paddle in the center of the display.

"What!" Heiku tossed his paddle aside, immediately seizing the new paddle, an Xtreme Punishment 9800 Spank-Cam. "Ohhh," he laughed, when he spied the tiny camera. "This is absolutely perfect!"

"It sends the image to this receiver," Yousi explained, sliding open a panel on the handle. "You just push this button, here, to take the picture. And you can project the image as a holopic with *this* button."

Heiku was beside himself with joy over the Spank-Cam, snickering like a schoolboy. "My, oh my. Where did you find this?"

"Omi told me about it," Yousi confessed. "I picked one up at the Trade Convention from Alpha Zen."

"I'd really like to give Xian a few good whacks with this, too," Heiku murmured. "Or for that matter, I ought to give Ima a taste of it."

"But you sent Ima back to the Academy."

"Ah, didn't I tell you? I've got her back. I know I'm pathetic, but I missed her. Besides that, it's still a mystery who got her loaded. The

Academy couldn't reconcile the genetic signature with any other pets. They told me there's a possibility she conceived without a partner."

"I would miss Arian, if I had to send him away," Yousi mused, completely missing the point.

"Did you hear me, Yousi?" Heiku laughed. "I just told you Ima may be a genetic miracle."

"Well," the Blondie replied, not wanting to confront Heiku with the reality that everyone else in Tanagura seemed to already know, that Ima was nothing more than a very naughty pet, especially for an A-class pet, "maybe you shouldn't paddle her then."

"You're quite right. I should put her on a pedestal! I should—heavens, what did I do with that locket? Ah! Here it is!" Lord Quiahtenon pulled out a small locket from his pocket, flipping it open to reveal a small holo-projection of Ima crossing and uncrossing her legs. "Isn't she something? I mean, really! Stunning! And you can tell by her brow, mind you, that she is not just your average female pet. Such intelligence! Always in such deep thought! You know, I was going to keep her at home, but I think I ought to take her to the party and show her off. I always knew there was something extraordinary about that girl. Ha! I can't wait to see the look on Xian's face when he learns she's split her own egg. I shouldn't be surprised if Jupiter herself takes notice!"

Yousi had no reply to this, shifting his weight uncomfortably. "We made a mess," he observed, looking around the shop.

"Never mind that. I'll help you clean up, and then we'll go to my place for some serious fornication. Agreed?" Heiku tilted Yousi's chin up with his finger, planting a kiss on his nose.

"All right," Yousi nodded, for though he was not entirely sure of the meaning of *fornication*, thinking perhaps it was a sort of well-pruned shrubbery, or possibly egg-throwing during a night of revelry and drunken mischief, was certainly ready to entrust Heiku with the evening's agenda, and so, without further argument, he pursued the wayward penetrative devices that were now scattered about the floor of the shop, and upon achieving satisfaction that they were stacked in an aesthetically pleasing manner, accompanied Lord Quiahtenon to his house in Midas.

"YES?" HEADMASTER KONAMI LOOKED UP, SURPRISED to see Aertis Jin standing in the doorway to his chambers. "Ah, Aertis. Come in, please," he said, smiling at the breathtaking young Blondie.

Aertis returned the smile, stepping into the Headmaster's chambers. "What can I do for you?"

"I'm sorry to disturb you, Headmaster," Aertis began, bowing his head in a delightfully submissive way, and lowering his gaze for a moment, his long blond lashes fluttering slightly.

"It is no disturbance whatsoever," Konami assured him.

As always, Aertis was perfectly courteous, bowing low before him. He reminded Konami in so many ways of young Iason Mink, as he had been in his early Academy days. Aertis Jin also enjoyed Jupiter's favor and special notice and was on the Syndicate track, as Iason had once been. Konami had no doubt that, should Iason fail in his duties again, Aertis would take his place as Head of the Syndicate.

"Are you going to the debates tonight, Headmaster?" Aertis asked.

"No," Konami sighed. "I think not."

"Oh?" Aertis was surprised. He would have thought the Headmaster would be the first to attend. "Do you not find them a worthy pursuit?"

"I am sure the debates will be interesting," Headmaster Konami replied, "but to be honest, I feel our loyalty to Jupiter is best shown by refraining from joining in on such spectacles. After all, Jupiter's laws are really not open for debate. Although she has not prohibited the debates outright, I don't see what can be gained. She has made it clear that she will consider citizenship for a select few mongrels. It is therefore pointless, in my view, to debate the matter at all."

"Yes, I quite agree with you," Aertis said, looking relieved. He found the whole idea of the debates a bit unnerving, wondering if he was expected to attend and hoping very much that he might be able to avoid the affair altogether. "Then, it won't be frowned upon, should I opt not to attend?"

"Heavens no," Lord Sung assured him. "Goodness, are matters so out of hand that you felt it was your *duty* to go to the blasted thing? I should put out a notice right away, letting the students know they are in no way required to attend, nor are they prohibited from doing so."

"I confess, I'm a bit relieved," Aertis admitted. "The whole idea of the debates made me very nervous." In truth, Aertis was half afraid Jupiter would make an appearance at the debates, chastising those who spoke against her recent decisions.

74

"I'm not surprised that's your view. Besides, I doubt anything will come of all this," Konami said, closing the book he had been writing in. "My guess is Jupiter will find very few mongrels worthy to become full citizens of Tanagura. Riki the Dark is…something of an anomaly."

"The city certainly seems to be in an uproar over the notion, at any rate."

"Yes. I'll grant you that. Now, what is it you've come to see me about? Goodness, where are my manners? Please…sit down, sit down." Konami gestured toward the chair in front of his desk.

Aertis brightened. "It's about a scan I've just run on Minas Qentu."

"Oh?" Konami leaned back in his chair, unable to stop smiling. Aertis' enthusiasm for archaeology was infectious; and in truth, he had something of a soft spot for Minas Qentu himself. The recent discoveries of an ancient civilization on Amoi filled him with curiosity, and since Jupiter seemed completely unopposed to such explorations— in fact, even encouraged formal excavations—he was more than happy to oversee young Jin's rather buoyant interest in the matter. There were few Blondies who took much interest in archeology, even after the exciting discoveries at Minas Qentu. Iason Mink had been the exception, and in this regard Aertis once again reminded Lord Sung of young Mink.

But where Iason had shown a rather restrained, intellectual appreciation for archeology, Aertis was full of passion, nearly bursting with excitement over his latest project. He sat on the edge of his seat, his eyes wide and shining blue as a summer sky.

"Yes, I used rapid pulsar ejection with partial penetration and parallel reversal, like you suggested, and I believe I've discovered something extraordinary." Aertis unrolled a printout from the pulsar device, pointing excitedly to it. "You see? Right here. I think I've discovered some sort of structure. Perhaps even a burial chamber."

"Hmmm." The Headmaster nodded as he studied the printout. "It certainly doesn't look like a natural phenomenon."

"By my calculations, it's about 20 hectors below the surface."

"This is a remarkable discovery. You should be very proud, Aertis."

"I would like to check it out right away. I was hoping to find a sponsor who might accompany me to the site tonight." Unable to remain seated, Aertis now stood up and leaned across the desk, looking up anxiously at the Headmaster, his eyes bright with excitement. He pointed again to the map, moving a little closer, so that his hair brushed against the Headmaster's hand.

Headmaster Konami was careful to redirect his thoughts, but the truth of the matter was that he was very much aware of the young Blondie's presence, of the softness of his hair against his hand, of his sensual, indescribably perfect scent. Of course, it was not the first time he had been sexually attracted to another Blondie. But always before, he had been able to easily take command of his desires. With Aertis, it was different.

With Aertis, he had certain longings, longings that he had already contemplated in the privacy of his bedroom, under the permissible loneliness of his sheets. And now the Blondie was uncomfortably close to him—so much so that Konami had to move away.

He rose suddenly, walking over to the window and looking out at the white sky. It had begun to snow again, beautiful, great flakes of snow that swirled around slowly as though reluctant to submit to gravity. "I'm sorry, Aertis," he said, turning, once he had his desires under control. "But surely you know a sponsored dig takes weeks of planning. And most of the faculty will be at the debates tonight, I think."

"Oh." Aertis looked so disappointed that the Headmaster could hardly bear it. The young Blondie slowly rolled up his printout, attempting a smile. "Yes, of course. How foolish of me."

The Headmaster studied him for a moment, and then turned away again. "Although…perhaps I could accompany you."

"Truly? Oh…Headmaster," Aertis breathed.

"My only hesitation is…well, to be frank, it might be considered a bit improper for me to accompany you on a dig…alone. That is, just the two of us." He turned to give Aertis a meaningful look.

The young Blondie blushed. "I hadn't considered that."

"No, of course not." Lord Sung smiled. "Though, you ought to be aware of such matters, especially now."

The young Blondie reddened even more; the contemplation of the implied intimacy with Headmaster Konami was shocking and something he would never have seriously considered. But once Lord Sung had put the idea in his head, he found his imagination began to run with the idea.

There was no question Konami was attractive—all Blondies were, and there was something especially alluring about the Headmaster's serious, distinguished air. Perhaps it was precisely because he couldn't possibly imagine Lord Sung engaging in forbidden pleasures that made the very notion rather intriguing. Ashamed of his thoughts, Aertis hung his head, fiddling nervously with the map he still held in his hands.

The Headmaster studied him, marveling over Aertis' obvious

embarrassment over the remark. The Blondie hadn't even considered such an impropriety, that much was obvious. Was there really any reason not to accompany him to Minas Qentu? Konami knew he would be able to restrain himself, no matter what the circumstance. He always had done so, and always would. And it was clear enough he was not in danger of being seduced by Aertis, whose charming naiveté had the young Blondie turning three shades of red.

"However, we may be able to take certain precautions to avoid censure," he said, finally. "Such as a robotic chaperone, for instance."

Aertis' delight was so transparent Konami almost laughed.

"Thank you, Headmaster!"

"We'll have quite a bit of preparations to do. My day is free tomorrow, but I'll need to be back on Jupiter's Eve by nightfall."

"I already have the excavation equipment reserved, on the off-chance I would be able to go," Aertis said breathlessly. "But I haven't had a chance to deal with camping gear or food or anything of that nature."

"It's going to be cold tonight," Konami remarked. "We'll want heated inflatables. That shouldn't be a problem, though. There's a good shop near the hospital. Why don't I take care of our gear and permits, while you get the excavation equipment. Let's meet back here in a few hours. We'd better exchange signatures, as well."

"Yes, of course." Aertis pulled out his communicator and the Headmaster pressed his thumb to the identification pad; his signature and phone beacon were automatically loaded into the unit, and a transmission of Aertis' information was sent to the Headmaster's phone, which chimed to confirm receipt. Almost immediately afterwards the computer terminal in the corner of his office chimed as well; indeed, anywhere Konami was logged into Jupiter's network, Aertis would be listed as a permanent connection, one of only a handful of individuals the Headmaster had awarded access to his profile.

"We're connected," Lord Sung remarked, experiencing a secret rush of pleasure at this observation. Once connected, they would always be connected. Even if he were to obtain a new phone or computer, Aertis' beacon would always seek him out, insisting on a connection. Though it was simply commonplace technology, Konami found the idea that Aertis was forever part of his signature profile somehow comforting.

"I can't thank you enough," Aertis said, shaking his head. "I'm sure this must be an inconvenience for you."

"Not at all," the Headmaster assured him. "I'm...very fond of you, Aertis." As soon as he said the words, he felt he had been a bit too open, said a little too much. But the young Blondie only rewarded him with a dazzling smile, sending Konami's heart racing.

To young Jin these were words he had waited years to hear. He loved Lord Sung as he might a father; indeed, he harbored deep feelings for the kind, yet uncompromisingly firm Blondie. Headmaster Konami was a pillar of stability in a world that had, of late, become a bit more uncertain. Aertis had been completely shocked by the sedition and conspiracy of the leading Blondies against Jupiter, and the Public Whippings had made his blood run cold. In the aftermath of the scandal, it was Headmaster Konami who surfaced as the leading voice in Tanagura, and who, it was said, now met with the disgraced rebels on a weekly basis—cane in hand—to discipline and instruct them once again.

Though no one knew exactly what went on behind the closed doors of Iason's penthouse during those sessions, the latest rumor was that the Headmaster had been seen arriving at the Eos Tower with a whip, and that the Blondies had been physically punished, much as they might have been, were they still young cadets at the Elite Academy.

Aertis took comfort in the Headmaster's no-nonsense approach to discipline. For Konami, there was one path, and one alone. Any deviation from it resulted in swift and severe censure, followed by the sting of his cane or whip. As a child Aertis had deliberately concocted ways to be sent to him for minor infractions—nothing too major or alarming, of course—just enough disobedience to earn a few strikes with a switch or, if he were very lucky, an intimate turn over the Headmaster's knee.

In the privacy of his heart Aertis knew from his earliest days that he enjoyed being disciplined by Lord Sung; it was a secret perversion, or perhaps merely a longing for intimacy, at whatever cost. His frequent trips to the Headmaster's chambers and private quarters, however, eventually earned him a fearsome, blistering paddling that put a decided end to his infatuation with being disciplined, and he had never misbehaved again. Neither he nor Lord Sung ever spoke of the matter, and Aertis had always wondered what the Headmaster truly thought of him.

Konami allowed himself only a moment to bask in the glory of his smile. He turned away, pretending to secure the lock on his desk drawer and straighten some the items on his desk.

"So. We'll meet back here in a few hours then?"

"I WANT A MASSAGE," REGILAND ANNOUNCED, strolling into the kitchen where Yui was busy preparing the evening meal.

"I just gave you one yesterday," Yui answered, trying his best to hide his profound annoyance.

"I want another one, now."

"Well, I'm busy getting dinner ready."

Yui began kneading the dough of sweetbread angrily, pounding his fist into it.

"You can finish with that later."

"No, I can't. Master Raoul will be home any minute. I'm already behind schedule." Because of *you*, he thought darkly. Regiland—or Puki, as Yui preferred to think of him—had kept him busy the entire day, forcing him to wait on him hand and foot, and he was at his wit's end.

"You don't know how to manage your time properly," Regiland accused.

"Get out."

"I beg your pardon?"

"Get out! Get out of my kitchen!"

"You can't talk to me like that. Wait until Master Raoul gets home. You'll be in big trouble again!"

"I said GET THE HELL OUT!" Yui punctuated his by throwing the ball of dough full-force at the surprised pet, who just barely managed to duck out of its way. The dough went flying across the room, knocking over a vase and breaking it.

"Now you're really in for it" Regiland remarked.

As if on cue, Lord Am entered the suite at precisely that moment, noting the broken vase with a frown.

"Yui broke the vase," Regiland reported. "And he threw a pastry at me."

The ball of dough, which had stuck to the wall and was slowly peeling away, finally succumbed to the force of gravity, landing on the floor with a *squish*-PLOP!

Pixie darted into the room, excited over all the commotion, and proceeded to explore the dough and broken vase disaster with delight.

Raoul leveled Yui a look of reproach. "Yui," he said, his voice betraying his impatience.

Yui, realizing that his temper had once again gotten the best of him, hung his head, his cheeks flushing red. "I'm sorry," he murmured.

"He needs to be punished," Regiland announced happily.

The Blondie immediately whirled around to confront the smug pet, seizing his wrist and pulling him toward him as he leaned down to look directly in his face. "In this household *I* will decide who needs to be punished."

Regiland quieted, looking rather shaken by the reprimand. "Yes, Master."

The Blondie released him, dismissing him with a wave of his hand. "Go to your room, Regiland, until I call you."

The pet hesitated, looking as though he had something more to say.

"NOW!" Raoul bellowed.

Startling at the Blondie's sudden fierceness, Regiland scurried from the room. Yui watched his retreat with some satisfaction, though as soon as he saw the angry look on his Master's face, he cowered, lowering his gaze.

"I've had it with you!" Lord Am began, one hand on his hip. "Every day when I come home, it's the same story. What has gotten into you?"

Yui kept his gaze lowered, his lips pressed tightly closed.

"Answer me," Raoul demanded, taking hold of the young man's chin. "Look at me."

"I'm sorry." A single tear streamed down his cheek as Yui looked up into the Blondie's eyes.

Raoul sighed, softening a bit. "Yui."

"I hate him so much. He makes me wait on him all day. He follows me around, just thinking up things for me to do."

"We've been over this. We *must* keep up appearances. It is your *duty* to attend to Regiland."

"I just want to be with you. He ruins everything. I want...I want to pleasure you in bed, like we did before. You never even touch me now."

Yui reached up to wipe another tear from his face, sniffing.

The Blondie gazed at him for a moment, then leaned forward and kissed the tears from his cheeks. "Hush," he soothed. The moment his lips touched Yui's face, he was unable to hold back any longer. He needed intimacy—*craved* it. His mouth sought out Yui's, his tongue flicking inside. Yui responded eagerly, thrilled. Since the public whippings, the Blondie had been decidedly aloof. Yui had begun to fear that perhaps his Master would never take him to his bed again, that perhaps, after all that had happened, he had changed his mind, that he didn't want him any more.

Now it was as if all that Raoul had held back was released in a torrent of unstoppable passion. He slid his hands down Yui's back, groping his ass and pushing him firmly towards his own body as he devoured him with a commanding, insistent kiss. The Blondie became so enthusiastic that he lifted Yui off the ground, arching back as he forced the boy's body to slide against his own. He lifted his robe to access his bare flesh and then groped and squeezed Yui's ass, kneading the firm flesh, his fingers seeking out his prize, his precious hollow, the entrance to his inner sanctum. He pressed and probed and one finger made a bold incursion, sinking a ways into his portal.

Lord Am grunted, the sound vibrating inside Yui's mouth. In the next instant the Blondie was leading him to his bedroom, the doors humming closed behind them. He punched in the lock codes and then began tearing at Yui's robe, clawing at the satin belt-tie almost angrily to remove it. In his impatience Raoul knocked over a small night table, its drawer opening and its contents spilling across the floor. Yui was equally passionate, thrilled that his Master was finally *back*.

In a matter of moments they were both naked and on the bed, kissing each other so furiously that they were both panting.

"Oh yes," Raoul groaned. He suddenly seized Yui, flipping onto his back and forcing the boy to straddle him.

Yui gasped, biting his lip. The sensations were almost unreal. Although he had been exploring his new sexuality every night in the privacy of his own bed, he felt quite unprepared for the excitement and pleasure of finally being unrestrained with his Master.

"Look at you," Lord Am whispered, marveling over Yui's masculine form, now completely restored. His erection was stiff and proud, a tear of seminal fluid pooling over the head of his cock.

"Master," Yui cried, when Raoul's hot fingers encircled him.

"You're perfect." The Blondie ran his other hand down the midline of Yui's body, pushing against him. "Arch your back."

Yui obeyed, allowing his head to fall back, his long, loose hair nearly touching Raoul's legs.

"That's it." Lord Am rubbed a nipple between his thumb and finger, and then squeezed it, hard.

"Oh!" Surprised, Yui instinctively straightened, finding the sensation both pleasurable and a little painful.

"Oh, Yui. I hope you're ready for me. I'm going to fuck you all night. I'm going to bury my cock inside your mouth, and then ram it in your tight little ass. I'm going to fuck you on your hands and knees, facedown on this bed, up and down the walls, on your back with your ankles past your shoulders and just like this, with you squealing across my pelvis. And then I'm going to make you scream with pleasure, Yui, over and over."

RIKI AWOKE TO FIND HIMSELF ALONE in Iason's bed. He got up, tugging on his pants though not bothering to don his shirt, and then proceeded to make his way into the Great Hall, an unlit cigarette dangling from his mouth.

"Where's Iason?" he demanded, sitting down at the table.

"He left after lunch to go on some errands," Toma answered. "Riki, you can't smoke in here."

"I'm not smoking. I'm just tasting. How come no one woke me up for lunch?"

"You were fast asleep and Master Iason said to let you rest," Toma answered.

Tai rushed toward the table from the kitchen, carrying a warming dome. "I saved your lunch for you, Riki."

"Mmmm. I'm starving. What is it?" the mongrel peered into the glass dome, eyeing the plate of rolls hungrily.

"It's mutton stew," Tai answered.

"My favorite!" Riki took the cigarette from his mouth and put it next to his plate, removing the dome and immediately starting in on his meal.

He loved mutton stew, and it always reminded him of Daryl. He remembered the way Daryl would make it rather frequently, knowing how much he liked it, much to Iason's eventual annoyance, for the Blondie didn't care for it. "Ha! What did Iason say when he saw what we were having? I bet he wasn't too pleased."

"But," Tai frowned, looking confused, "Master Iason approved the menu himself. He instructed me that we are to have mutton stew once a week from now on."

"Oh yeah?" Riki smiled, dipping a roll into his stew. He felt a little surprised that Iason had made such an arrangement, knowing that he could only have done it to please *him*.

"You're dead." Aki poked his head up from under the table, aiming his mallow-puff blaster toward him and then launching one of the fluffy cylindrical confections toward Riki's chest.

"Ahhh!" Riki yelped as though startled, though in fact it was difficult not to be aware of Aki's rather noisy movements under the table and his stifled giggles and snorts. He caught the mallow-puff and then popped it in his mouth. "Mmmm! Shoot me again!"

Aki giggled, launching a second mallow-puff toward him, which the mongrel again caught and disposed of in a similar fashion.

"Let me see that," Riki laughed, examining the boy's new weapon and its ingenious food-shooting design. "I love mallow-puffs."

"Me too," Aki agreed.

"Where did you get this?"

"Guardian gave it to me."

"Hmmm. He sure gives you a lot of presents," Riki remarked, slurping his stew loudly.

And it was true enough; nearly every day Iason brought some new toy or book for Aki, seeming to take great delight in showering his young charge with gifts of all sorts.

"That's because I'm a door-bull," Aki answered confidently, turning on his heel and then marching away toward some suddenly perceived danger in another part of the penthouse.

"He's a what?" Riki repeated, perplexed.

"I think he means *adorable*," Toma said, laughing.

"He is, that," Odi agreed, walking up to the group and stealing one of Riki's rolls.

"Hey!" Riki attempted to slap Odi's hand but the bodyguard was too fast, shooting the mongrel a grin and a wink as he took a bite from the warm roll.

"There are plenty more of those," Tai announced, rushing back into the kitchen to retrieve them.

"Why are *you* in such a good mood?" Toma asked, when Odi continued to smile.

"Because I just found out we're all going to that party tomorrow at Lord Ghan's villa."

Tai had returned from the kitchen, a bowl of rolls in hand. "All of us?" he asked, his face brightening.

"Yes, *all* of us," Odi answered. "Which means it's going to be a blast. Omaki Ghan gives the best parties—or at least that's what I've heard. He always has a live band, and the Blondies usually get so plastered they don't even care what the pets and attendants do."

Riki perked up at this. "Really? Even Iason?"

"Well, I don't know about that."

"I've never seen Master Iason drunk," Toma asserted. "And I've been to plenty of those parties."

"Great," Riki groaned. "That means everyone except me will be having a great time. He'll probably make me stick to two drinks, too. The big meanie."

As if on cue, the chime to the front door sounded and Lord Mink entered the hall, carrying several packages. He was followed by Ayuda.

"Ah, Riki. You're up." The Blondie smiled mysteriously and set the packages on the bar counter in order to remove his cloak.

"What did ya bring for me?" Riki asked, regarding the packages with curiosity, though he didn't truly expect that Iason had bought him anything.

"As a matter of fact, I *do* have something for you." Lord Mink took the packages and made his way over to his favorite chair, sitting down with a sigh. "Come here and I'll show you."

Intrigued, Riki joined him, climbing up onto his lap and planting a sloppy kiss on his cheek. "Did you really bring me something?"

"I did, indeed. It's for the party tomorrow night."

Now a bit more suspicious, Riki took the package Iason handed him and shook it, frowning. "It sounds like chains."

"Open it."

The mongrel untied the strings that bound the package and then lifted the box lid, peering inside. "What is it?" he demanded.

"It's what you'll be wearing," Iason replied, his eyes glimmering.

"What!" Riki lifted up what appeared to be an elaborate outfit made entirely of thin golden chains, but for a black and gold cup-shaped area that he could only assume was to provide coverage for his genitals.

"Put it on," Lord Mink demanded.

"I'm not wearing it."

"You most certainly *will* wear it. End of discussion."

Riki held the outfit up with a thumb and a forefinger as though afraid to even touch it. "I'll look ridiculous! I'll be a laughing-stock!"

The others in the hall quietly moved away, trying not to laugh at Riki's predicament.

"After that stunt you pulled this afternoon, you're lucky I'm letting you go to the party at all," Iason remarked. He set Riki on his feet, giving his ass a pat. "Put it on."

"I'd rather *not* go, if I have to wear this," the mongrel argued, pouting.

"You're going, and you're wearing it. That's final."

Riki sighed dramatically, stripping off his clothes and tossing them aside with exaggerated annoyance. He then studied the outfit, trying to determine how it was to be worn.

"Put it on, Riki," Iason repeated, growing impatient when the mongrel continued to stand, naked, looking at the outfit as though mystified.

"I don't know how it goes," Riki grumbled.

Iason then assisted him with the outfit, unfastening and then refastening some of the buckles until at length the mongrel was fully garbed, or at least garbed as much as the flimsy chain outfit allowed. The glittering chains hung low on his hips, and then rode over his chest and back to fasten at rings at the shoulders. His buttocks were almost entirely visible, with only a series of chains draped across his upper cheeks. The majority of his body was exposed, with the exception of his genitals, which were covered by the gold cup-like attachment.

The Blondie seemed extraordinarily pleased with the result, smiling and nodding.

"I look retarded," Riki complained. "I'm not going."

"Pet, I told you, this is not open for discussion. Now, here's the second part of your outfit." Iason handed him another package, which Riki took with obvious displeasure.

"The second part?" The mongrel opened the box, but finding only a pair of gold sandals with ties that wrapped around his ankles, relaxed. He shrugged, finding this part of the outfit far more innocuous than the first part.

"And the third part," Iason continued handing him the final box.

Riki opened it, peering inside. "Huh?" He lifted the object from the box, which appeared to be some sort of device—with two paddles attached.

"That goes around your waist," Iason explained.

"What is it?"

Lord Mink smiled, his eyes twinkling. "It's a spanking machine." He held up a tiny remote. "Which I'll control."

Riki turned to look at Ayuda, who was watching the exchange from one of the pillars of the hall with a look of amusement on his face, his lip twitching.

The device, when secured around Riki's waist, would keep the paddles against his thighs until the "spanking machine" was activated, at which time the paddles would swing into position and offer their punishment upon the mongrel's exposed buttocks. As if this weren't enough, each of the paddles boasted a raised surface—a word, in reverse, to be precise. On the left paddle, the word was NAUGHTY, and on the right paddle, PET. When the paddles were set into motion, the end result was that the phrase "NAUGHTY PET" would be spanked onto the mongrel's cheeks.

Riki was so horrified that at first he said nothing. He was mortified that Iason expected him to wear the humiliating outfit and device and was now kicking himself for his earlier prank.

"I knew it. I just *knew* you'd find something like this, sooner or later." The mongrel had even joked about such a device, never for a moment thinking a wearable spanking machine actually *existed*.

"What do you think of it?" Iason pressed. "It's fitting, is it not?"

Deciding to switch tactics, Riki put the box down, and then straddled the Blondie, slowly thrusting his pelvis against him. "Iason," he pleaded, leaning forward to nuzzle his neck. "You wouldn't seriously make me wear that, would you?" He reached out and began twirling a piece of the Blondie's long hair around his fingers as he slowly rocked his pelvis forward, getting more comfortable in Lord Mink's lap. "I'm sorry about the bell thingie, but we ended up having great sex, right?"

The Blondie responded to this by settling back in his chair and moving his hands to either side of Riki's hips. "Yes," he whispered.

"Then," Riki nibbled on Iason's bottom lip, kissing him as he pressed his hands up against the Blondie's chest, "how about you give me a break and not make me wear it? I'll be especially enthusiastic tonight, I promise."

Iason closed his eyes, enjoying the mongrel's seductive arts. He tilted his head to the side, baring his throat, which Riki promptly covered with kisses and gentle nibbles.

"Mmmm."

"So? Is that a yes?"

"Let me think about it," Lord Mink murmured, opening his eyes and giving the mongrel a smoldering look. "I'll make my decision later tonight, based on your performance."

Riki sulked at this. "What if I, like, do a super good job but you *still* make me wear it?"

"That's my prerogative," came the Blondie's firm reply.

"What a rip off!" the mongrel proclaimed.

"Might I remind you, pet, that because of your ridiculous antics earlier today, I exposed myself to the entire household with nothing more than a bell on."

Riki's upper lip quivered as he struggled not to smile at the memory. It *had* been a pretty brilliant prank. The image of Iason trying to scold him while his bell merrily jangled with his every move was still so fresh in his mind that he was unable to keep from snickering.

"Naughty pet," Iason whispered, his eyes shining with love. It was hard to stay truly angry at the mongrel when his face was lit up with such impish mirth.

Aki wandered back into the hall, stopping dead in his tracks when he saw the mongrel.

"Why are you wearing *that*, Riki?"

"That's what I'd like to know," the mongrel replied.

Aki giggled. "I can see your bottom." Then he spied the spanking device next to Iason's chair. "What's this?" he shrieked.

"That's proof that your Guardian is a sadistic fuck," Riki proclaimed.

"Riki," Iason snapped, leveling him a disapproving look. "I'll not have you sporting such vulgar language around Aki, nor sullying the conversation with your disparaging remarks."

"What are asparagus marks?" Aki wondered aloud.

"Sheesh. All you do is nag at me, all the live long day," Riki complained. "For like, practically nothing."

"And what's a saddle-stick fuck?"

Riki snorted at this, earning another glare from the Blondie.

"Aki," Iason said sharply. "That is not appropriate talk for an Elite. I never want to hear you say those words again."

"But Riki said it first," Aki pointed out, sulking.

"And did you not hear me berate him for it?"

"I just wanted to know what it means."

"It means someone who takes perverse pleasure in other people's pain. In a really sick, like, hideously mean way." Riki gave Iason a pointed look.

"Guardian isn't mean," Aki objected.

Lord Mink smiled. "Thank you, Aki."

"Ha! You haven't seen his dark side yet. Wait 'til he makes you pee in a jar!"

Aki regarded the Blondie suspiciously at this, puzzling over Riki's bizarre comment.

"Don't let Riki alarm you, Aki. He's merely disgruntled because I'm forcing him to wear that spanking machine tomorrow, to Lord Ghan's party."

"A spanking machine?" Aki now eyed the device with newfound wonder, and a little bit of nervousness.

"Yes, I had it specially made for Riki. What do you think, Aki? Should he wear it to the party tomorrow so that everyone can see what a naughty pet he is?"

"Yes!" Aki agreed, giggling. "Riki should wear the spanking machine!"

"Gee thanks, kid," Riki muttered.

"Will it really spank him?" Delighted with the device now that it was clear it was not intended for *him*, Aki danced about in front of the chair. "Riki has to wear the spanking machine!" He giggled so hard that eventually he acquired the hiccups, his celebration of the mongrel's certain humiliation reduced to gurgles and comical gasps for air.

"Everyone's against me," Riki lamented.

"Katze and Daryl have arrived," Freyn announced over the intercom.

"Oh, shit!" Riki jumped up, grabbing his pants and darting out of the great hall just as the two eunuchs entered, but not before they both got a good look at his retreating ass. They exchanged amused glances but refrained from commenting when they saw Iason sitting in the hall.

"Ah. Come in, both of you." Lord Mink rose, moving toward the dining table. "Toma, Tai—I want to talk to you."

Riki now rushed back into the hall, after throwing on his pants and a shirt over the chain outfit, which he had been unable to figure out how to remove quickly.

"Hey! What are you two doing here?" He grinned at the two lovers, having not seen them in weeks, since Daryl had moved into Katze's apartment in Midas.

"They'll be attending us tonight," Iason answered, sitting at the head of the table and motioning for everyone to join him as he looked to Toma and Tai. "We'll all be going to Omaki's party tomorrow night, and I'm sending the two of you over there this evening to see if you can be of any help. I'm sure Ru will be happy to see you."

88

"Yes, of course," Tai murmured, looking delighted. He loved celebrations, the bigger the better—and although he preferred being in charge of all the arrangements himself, it was almost as good to be sent to assist at a last-minute gathering. He had no doubt that Ru was frantic at Lord Ghan's impromptu decision to throw a large bash with only a couple days' notice.

Toma was equally thrilled at being sent to Omaki's villa in advance of everyone else, because it meant he would be the first to learn all the latest gossip. And as other attendants arrived to assist, it would be clear that *he* had been the first to set foot at the party, which was nearly as good as being the host of the party.

"I already invited Suuki," Aki announced. "But he says he's not sure he's allowed to go!"

"That's up to Sir Elusiax," Iason replied.

"But can he at least stay over tonight?"

"I have no objection to that," Iason answered, rising. "I'm retiring to the library. Toma, bring tea before you leave."

"Of course, Master," Toma answered.

"I'll get the tray ready," Tai said, rushing back into the kitchen.

Aki wandered off, and Riki, Daryl and Katze smiled at each other for a long moment.

"So, what's it like living with Katze?" Riki asked.

"It's awesome, of course." Katze replied. "Isn't that right, baby?"

Daryl giggled. "Yeah. It really is."

"Hey, I need a smoke," the mongrel announced, jumping up. "Wanna join me?" He pulled out his pack of Dark Baccalias, holding it out to them.

"I never turn down a good smoke," Katze answered, accepting one of the thin black cigarettes and following Riki out onto the balcony. "How about you, Daryl?"

Daryl reached for the pack, yelping when Katze smacked his hand. "Katze!" he protested.

"No smokes for you," Katze said firmly.

"I guess it's clear who's the boss in this relationship." Riki stuffed the pack back into his pocket, raising a brow.

"Damn right." Katze nodded.

Daryl pouted at this. "That's not fair. I should be able to smoke if I feel like it! Riki, give me one of those."

"You do and I'll kick your ass," Katze warned, when Riki reached for his pack again.

"Yeah, right. I'd like to see you try," Riki answered.

"I could kick your ass and you know it."

"You mean *kiss* my ass."

"Speaking of which, we enjoyed a nice view of your ass today, Riki. Was that a new outfit?"

Daryl snickered at this as Riki scowled, lighting up his smoke.

"Iason's making me wear it to the party tomorrow."

"How sadistic. Give me a light."

Riki tossed Katze the lighter, but Daryl intercepted, snatching it up midair.

"Hah!"

"Give me that," Katze demanded, snapping his fingers.

"Not until I get a smoke."

"All right. That's it." Katze put his smoke behind his ear and then seized Daryl, propping a leg up on a bench and then angling the youth over his leg.

Daryl shrieked as Katze proceeded to give him a series of rather hard swats on his backside. "Okay, okay," he cried, giggling. "Ow! You win."

He surrendered the lighter and then reached back to rub his ass.

Riki rolled his eyes. "You two."

Katze released Daryl and then put his arms around him from behind, pulling him against his body. Daryl settled back against him, smiling.

After lighting up, Katze tossed the lighter back to Riki. "So, Iason's making you wear that outfit to the party? I'm surprised. I figured you'd be able to do pretty much whatever you wanted now."

"Well, he's a little pissed off over a prank I played on him today."

"Oh really?" Katze raised a brow, intrigued.

"Yeah. I waited until he was asleep and naked in his bed and then I put a collar on him with a bell. You know, one of those timer kinds that won't come off for about an hour."

"Riki!" Daryl gasped, holding a hand over his mouth.

"Fucking brilliant," Katze praised, nodding.

"I thought so. You should have seen it! He chased me out into the great hall, naked, in front of everyone."

"Ooo. I wish I'd seen that. Ow!" Katze grabbed his side when Daryl gave him a hard jab with his elbow.

"Yeah, well. I kinda wish I hadn't done it now. That party is going to totally suck for me tomorrow."

Katze shook his head. "Maybe at first. But soon everyone will be so drunk they won't even notice."

"That's another thing. Everyone will be drunk except *me!*"

"Why do you say that, Riki?" Daryl asked.

"Because Iason only lets me have two stinking drinks!"

"I wouldn't worry about that. Once those Blondies get together they tend to get caught up in their wild antics," Katze remarked. "Iason will be too distracted to notice."

"But won't the bartender check my portfolio?"

"Bartender?" Katze laughed. "Riki. This is one of Omaki's parties. There's no bartender, just a huge open bar."

"One for the Blondies and one for the rest of us," Daryl agreed. Riki brightened at this. "Really?"

Katze nodded. "The pets usually stay near the Blondies in case they want pairings. But the rest of us can do whatever we want."

"We usually help out Ru in the kitchen, though. There's a room adjoining it where the attendants all gather, and we kind of take turns bringing in food for the Blondies," Daryl added.

"But I'm a pet," Riki pointed out. "Iason will probably make me stay near him."

"Maybe for awhile. But you'll eventually be able to wander off and he probably won't even notice or care," Katze answered.

"Hmmm. That shows how much you really know Iason," Riki muttered, scratching his torso. "And this thing bloody itches, too!"

"You mean you still have it on?" Katze grinned, reaching out to try and lift Riki's shirt. "Let's see it."

"No!"

"Come on, Riki," Daryl pleaded. "Let us see it and we'll tell you how bad it really is."

"Oh, all right." Riki took a deep drag and then tossed his smoke over the ledge. He then lifted his shirt.

"That's pretty sexy, actually."

"Yes," Daryl agreed. "No one's going to laugh at you."

"You haven't seen the back of it."

"Actually, yes, we have," Katze replied. "But let's see it again."

"You'll laugh."

"We won't laugh."

Riki sighed. He turned around and unzipped his pants, tugging them down to his thighs.

Katze immediately reached out and smacked his bared ass.

"Hey! Ow!" Riki pulled up his pants and turned back around, shooting Katze a dark look.

Daryl giggled.

"You said you wouldn't laugh!"

"I'm sorry, Riki," he apologized.

"I'm not going."

"You have to go," Katze said. "Don't worry, you look sexy. It's really not that bad."

Daryl nodded his agreement. "No one will laugh."

"Oh, yes they will. That's only part of the outfit."

"Part?" Katze and Daryl exchanged glances.

"Yeah." Riki sighed.

Katze smiled. "Well, what's the other part?"

The mongrel only shook his head, rolling his eyes.

"I'm cold," Daryl complained.

Katze put out his smoke on the ledge and then flicked it over the edge. "Yeah, let's go back inside."

The three of them entered the great hall just as Aki came in, completely naked but for a string with a bell tied to it, around his neck.

"Guess who I am?" he yelled.

Riki snickered at this, though Katze frowned.

"You'd better get some clothes on, Aki," he warned.

"But I like being naked!" Aki ran through the penthouse, running in circles around Iason's empty chair.

Katze and Daryl set off after him, knowing that the great Blondie would not find the boy's imitation of him at all flattering.

But when Katze saw the box with the spanking device in it next to the chair, he stopped. "What's this?"

"Riki's spanking machine!" Aki screamed. "He has to wear it to the party!"

A slow smile crossed Katze's face. "I take it this is the other part of the outfit, Riki?"

"Fuck off," Riki answered.

"Master Suuki is here to see Master Aki," Freyn announced over loudspeaker.

"Wee!" Aki ran to the door, startling Sir Elusiax, who had arrived with Suuki to respond to Aki's invitation to the Ghan party, and now stood, staring down at the naked child with a look of horror on his face.

"Shouldn't you be wearing some clothes, young man?" he scolded.

"Come on, Aki, let's get you dressed," Daryl said, moving toward Aki. Katze was just behind him, offering the Elite a slight bow.

"Please excuse him, Sir Elusiax."

"But I'm just dressing the way Guardian did! He ran through the house naked with a bell!" Aki protested.

"Goodness," Sir Elusiax murmured, putting a hand on Suuki's shoulder to prevent him from moving.

"Can Suuki stay over tonight? Are you letting him go to the party?" Aki demanded, and then turned to Suuki, adding in a loud whisper, "Riki's wearing a spanking machine! We'll have so much fun! Except Guardian might make us pee in a jar."

The poor Elite stood at the door, frowning, and looking decidedly unwilling to let Suuki progress any further inside the penthouse.

At that moment Iason emerged from the library. "What's all that yelling? Ah, Sir Elusiax, please come in. Aki! You ought to be ashamed! Put some clothes on this instant! Someone wants a spanking!"

"But—" Aki's objection was muffled when Katze put a hand over his mouth, dragging him away.

"I do beg your pardon," Iason apologized, coming toward Sir Elusiax, who had a rather stiff plastic smile on his face. "But you know what they say. Boys will be boys."

The Elite relaxed. He was relieved to see Lord Mink fully dressed and behaving in such a formal, proper fashion. "Yes, they say that. Indeed they do."

"Please, come in. I've just called for the tea tray. Join me for a few minutes?"

"Certainly," Sir Elusiax agreed, though he kept a tight hold on Suuki's shoulder. "But no need for any tea. I can't stay but for a moment."

Iason pointed to a chair near the fire and sat down in his own chair, as Sir Elusiax sat down and lifted Suuki onto his lap. His gaze moved to the spanking device in the box next to the Blondie's chair, and his brow furrowed.

"About this party," the Elite began, looking a little embarrassed. "I hope you won't think me ungrateful, but—"

"Oh, my. You're probably worried about Suuki going to one of Lord Ghan's notorious parties. I understand, certainly."

Sir Elusiax relaxed. "You do?"

"Of course. I took the liberty of asking Omaki about it, and if you're agreeable, perhaps you would like to come as well. You could supervise the boys. He's created a separate play area for them, away from the main party."

"I see." Sir Elusiax thought about this for a moment. He had come prepared to refuse Aki's invitation, but Iason's remarks changed matters a bit. As long as he could watch over Suuki, he really had no objection. And he was also naturally curious to find out what went on at one of the infamous Ghan villa parties. He smiled. "Then, we accept."

"Splendid."

"I believe Aki would like Suuki to stay the night here as well."

Sir Elusiax looked around the penthouse, and finding nothing objectionable—at least in sight—he decided to allow Suuki to stay.

"Very well. I'll go retrieve his bag, then."

"Are you sure you wouldn't like a bit of cake?" Iason pressed.

"No, no. Thank you, though." Sir Elusiax rose, setting Suuki down and giving him a pat on his bottom. "Be good."

"Yes, father," Suuki replied. "Can I go find Aki now?"

"You may."

Suuki ran off in search of his playmate as Iason showed Sir Elusiax to the door.

"Riki, come here."

Lord Mink was returning to his seat, motioning to the mongrel as Toma rolled the tea tray into the hall when suddenly the lights flickered. Then, the entire penthouse began to shake, a low hum rumbling as if from deep inside the earth. A brilliant blue light flashed brightly; the tea tray went crashing to the floor, sending broken glass everywhere.

Iason grabbed hold of one of the hall pillars.

"Jupiter," he whispered.

Chapter 04 –
Sentinels and Salad Spoons

"ROCK AGAINST ME," RAOUL COMMANDED, gripping Yui's hips as the boy straddled him.

"Like this?" Yui undulated his body, allowing the Blondie to lift and lower him. At the same time Yui's body lowered, Raoul thrust upward, penetrating as deeply as he was able.

"Yes," Raoul hissed. Then suddenly he seemed to change his mind, pulling Yui off his organ and tossing him back onto the bed.

Yui squealed, delighted with the Blondie's commanding manner.

Lord Am moved on top of him. Yui thighs were pushed back to his shoulders as the Blondie penetrated from the front. "Naughty pet," he whispered.

"I'm not naughty," Yui protested. *Nor am I technically a pet*, he thought.

"Hush!" Raoul was up on his arms, thrusting wildly, and enjoying the alternating looks of torment and pleasure on Yui's face.

In the next instant he changed positions again, flipping the youth onto his stomach and lifting his hips. "On your hands and knees," he directed.

"Oh!" Yui cried, when Raoul began fondling him as he entered from behind. "Oh, Master!"

"I'm going to paddle you raw," the Blondie whispered. "And then fuck your cherry-red ass until you scream."

Alarmed, and not really understanding the concept of bedroom threats, Yui turned to look behind him. "Why?"

"You do not speak unless spoken to," the Blondie announced, smacking him hard on the ass.

"Ow," Yui yelped, bewildered.

Lord Am was ramming him so vigorously that the youth cried out with each thrust, gripping the sheets beneath him. Then the Blondie began fondling him again, slowing down his pace as he did so.

Yui was so engorged that Raoul's warm hand was enough stimulation to take him to the brink.

"It's happening!"

Raoul suddenly withdrew, throwing Yui onto his back and pumping him quickly, and then leaning down to suckle him as the semen oozed out from the boy's eager organ.

Yui rewarded him with a glorious sex-cry, arching his back as he ejaculated. The Blondie immediately did likewise, releasing himself with quick strokes onto the boy's stomach. Then he lay down next to Yui, sighing.

"I'm going to fuck you all night," he repeated, for the billionth time.

"Master," Yui whimpered, "I'm getting really sore."

"So? You'll take more of me before I'm finished with you. You'll be begging for mercy."

"I'm begging now," Yui pleaded. "That's three times in a row!"

Raoul reached around and gave his ass another hard smack. "You'll take as much as I feel like giving."

Suddenly the bed—indeed, the entire room—began to shake. There was a deep, low hum that accompanied the shaking. And then there was silence.

Lord Am leapt up from the bed. "What in the world?"

"What was that?" Yui asked, frightened.

"I haven't the slightest notion." Raoul fumbled with his skintight bodysuit and his boots, slipping them on hurriedly, though he didn't bother to don his tunic. "I'm going to the penthouse to see what Iason thinks just happened."

"May I go?" Yui asked, putting on his robe and winding the sash around his waist, then tying it in a neat, though very quick, knot.

"No. I shouldn't be gone long."

Yui's disappointment was quickly forgotten when he realized that he'd left dinner cooking. "The casserole!" he cried, rushing to the kitchen.

Raoul was worried. There was no doubt in his mind that Jupiter had just made her presence known. But why? Was it because he had just bedded Yui? Was she watching him, the way she had spied on Iason?

He looked around the room, his gaze stopping where he knew Megala had once watched him from a small peephole. Though he had long since covered the hole with a painting, as well as barred all access to the corridor that led to his room, suddenly he had a horrible sensation that he was being watched.

"Master…."

Raoul nearly jumped out of his skin when he realized Regiland was standing in the doorway.

"Did I call for you?" he scolded, trying to regain his composure. "Go back to your room."

"But…I felt…a shaking. My whole room was shaking."

"I'm looking into the matter now. You heard me, pet, wait in your room until I call you."

"I heard something else," Regiland remarked, a mischievous smile on his lips.

For a moment the Blondie only stared back at him, not quite believing the audacity of his pet. "You heard nothing," he hissed, seizing his wrist.

Regiland, though previously terrified when Raoul had grabbed him, now was far bolder. "But I did," he insisted, "and I'm not so sure what I heard was proper."

Raoul answered the pet's insinuation with a hard slap across the face. "How *dare* you. I'll not be blackmailed by my own pet! You, Regiland, will learn your place!"

With that he grabbed his belt, which was lying on the bed, and flipped Regiland around, holding his wrists above his head and pinning them to the wall. Then he proceeded to give him a thorough strapping, much to the pet's obvious surprise and horror.

Regiland made such a fuss that both Pixie and Yui came running— Pixie to dart around excitedly and Yui to watch with utter delight as his nemesis received a good beating.

When he was finished with the belt, Lord Am escorted Regiland to his room, pushing him roughly inside.

"I'm not finished with you," he warned, punching in the codes to lock Regiland's room.

Yui's delight in his archrival's punishment was completely transparent, but when he saw his Master's angry glare he immediately sobered. He knew better than to ask what had happened, for he knew Lord Am well; the Blondie did not like to discuss matters when he was upset.

Raoul left without a word, making for Iason's penthouse.

"HOLY SHIT," RIKI EXCLAIMED, GRABBING onto a pillar for support. "Are you sure this building is solid?"

"Was it an earthquake?" Daryl wondered, moving closer to Katze for comfort.

Katze shook his head, putting his arms around Daryl from behind. "I don't think so. I think Iason's right. That was Jupiter, surely."

"What's she all crabby about now?" Riki asked, looking to Iason.

"I haven't any idea," Iason murmured, shaking his head.

Aki and Suuki came running into the great hall, both of them rather excited over the situation and shrieking loudly.

"What's happening? Is the tower going to blow up?" Aki demanded.

"Calm down, you two," Daryl scolded gently, putting a hand on Aki's head to keep him from running to Iason.

Aki responded to this by marching in a circle where he stood beneath Daryl's hand. "I am being detained," he said in a robotic voice similar to the Guardian. "Error. Error. My head is being unscrewed."

Suuki giggled, but he seemed a bit nervous, glancing toward the Blondie as if hoping for an explanation.

Everyone had gathered in the great hall around the communications center. After a moment, when nothing happened, they all stared at one another, perplexed.

"At least it wasn't a summons," Katze finally remarked, voicing what everyone was thinking.

"Maybe she's pissed off at someone else this time," Riki said, shrugging. "Hey, when are we going to eat? Because I'm starving."

"I've never seen the power flicker before," Daryl observed. "Maybe it was just me, but I thought I saw a blue light on the computer screen."

"I saw it, too," Odi agreed, nodding. "Only it was on my handheld."

Iason remained silent, moving over to the bar to pour himself a brandy.

"Can I have a brandy too?" Riki pleaded.

"No, pet," Iason answered.

"Why not?"

"Riki, I'm not in the mood for one of your tantrums," the Blondie sighed.

"What? I was just asking. Sheesh. Hey! Can I at least have more than two measly drinks at the party tomorrow?"

Iason seemed not to even hear this request, continuing to stare at the bar as he drank his brandy. He downed the drink in several gulps and then poured himself another.

"Lord Am is here to see you," Freyn announced over intercom. "Shall I—hey!"

Askel suddenly came onto the intercom. "Is everything all right in there? What's going on? Should we evacuate the building?"

"Send Raoul in," Iason replied, ignoring Askel.

"I'll go out and calm them down," Odi offered, slipping outside as Raoul entered.

Lord Mink greeted the Blondie at the door, seeming extraordinarily relieved to see him.

"Was it Jupiter?" Raoul asked, frowning.

"Don't know. We felt the building shake and heard a hum, but after that nothing else happened."

"The power flickered."

Iason nodded. "That's never happened before."

"What's your feeling? Is Jupiter upset?"

"Please," Iason touched the Blondie's arm gently, urging him inside. "Come sit down. Can I offer you some Ambrosia?"

"I could use a scotch, actually."

"I'll get it." Toma rushed to the bar but was intercepted by Daryl.

"Let me take care of it. You should get ready—you're leaving soon for Lord Ghan's villa, aren't you?"

"Thanks." Toma smiled at the gentle-eyed youth, hurrying to his room to pick out what he would wear for the party.

Aki, released from Daryl's restraining hand, now ran through the great hall, excited. "Can we go over to Suuki's place? He says his father will probably come and get him anyway, because of the earthquake and the Tower falling apart."

Iason nodded dismissively, not really paying attention to all the boy's remarks. "Yes, yes. Be back within the hour for dinner, Aki."

"Affirmative." Aki saluted the Blondie and marched from the penthouse, followed by a marching Suuki, who copied everything the young Elite did.

Raoul and Iason retired to the chairs in front of the fire.

"Perhaps we should discuss this in private," Raoul hinted.

Iason nodded, turning to Riki, who was wandering through the great hall in a random circle, seeming a bit bored.

"Riki, go to your room until I call for you."

"Why?" the mongrel demanded.

"Riki!"

The mongrel looked a little hurt, and Iason immediately softened. "Raoul and I want to discuss some things in private. You may have as many drinks as you like tonight and tomorrow, provided you don't become completely inebriated."

"I won't," Riki promised, thrilled with this change in his permissions and rushing off before the Blondie changed his mind.

"Your scotch, Lord Am," Daryl said, handing him his drink.

"Daryl, Katze, please wait in your room until I call you."

"Forgive me, but might we help Tai in the kitchen?" Katze asked. "He already has dinner underway, apparently."

"Very well." Iason dismissed them with small nod, turning to the Blondie.

"So?" Raoul prompted.

"I have an odd feeling. I can't explain it."

"Perhaps you should speak to Jupiter. We could go to the Tower."

"I thought of that. But to be honest, right now I'm not sure how welcome I would be. I'm sure Jupiter is still disappointed in me."

Lord Am bowed his head, saying nothing for a moment. "If anyone can get in to see Jupiter, it's still you, Iason. But perhaps you should simply send a relay request."

"Good idea," Iason agreed, standing up again and going to the communications center. Raoul followed him, though he stayed to the side, out of view of the camera.

The Blondie sat down before the screen, taking a deep breath. "Iason Mink. Alpha Seven Seven Delta Nine." The computer hummed, its main terminal lights flickering in response to his voice. Iason spoke with an air of confidence he was far from feeling. "Request for a conference with Jupiter." He waited, surprised when the system did not automatically bring Jupiter onscreen.

There was a brief pause, the screen reading:

Voice recognition activated. A77D9.
Facial scan activated. A77D9.
Authorizing…..success.
Iason Mink. A77D9. Blondie, Level 1. Head of the Syndicate.
Processing request….

Iason turned to Raoul, frowning. "This has never happened before."

"Hmmm." Although Raoul attempted to smile reassuringly, he found himself a bit alarmed by anything that wasn't standard procedure.

Iason turned back to the screen.

- Request Declined. Access Denied. -

"Declined," the Blondie repeated, astonished. "She's refusing my relay!"

"That's odd. That's all it says?"

Raoul moved over behind Iason, peering at the screen.

Suddenly a series of unusual symbols flickered across the screen, and a face appeared—but a face unlike anything either had seen before.

The face seemed male. He was composed of the same bluish holo-projection light that Jupiter appeared in, the only difference being that there was no low hum accompanying his projection.

"I am Sentinel One. You may call me Armeus. How may I help you, Lord Mink?" he said.

"Forgive me, but I don't understand. I just submitted a relay request to Jupiter. How is it that you are on a private frequency?"

"I am authorized by Jupiter to speak with you. I do so now at her request."

Iason blinked. "I still don't understand. What is a Sentinel?"

"We are Jupiter's private Guardians. We have been programmed to protect Jupiter at all costs."

Raoul and Iason exchanged a perplexed look.

"We haven't been informed of any Sentinels," Iason replied.

"We are informing you now."

"How many Sentinels are there?"

"We are five."

"Does this mean Jupiter is shutting us out? Even Iason?" Raoul demanded.

"We do not have the answer to that query, Lord Am. We are only responsible for the maintenance of the grid, and for Jupiter's security."

Alarmed, Raoul leaned closer to the screen. "Are you saying that we no longer have access to the grid?"

The Sentinel paused for a moment, its eyes shifting colors, from dark blue to dark red, and then back to blue. "That is correct."

"Thank you for your assistance," Iason said suddenly, breaking off the connection.

"My apologies," Raoul murmured. "I don't know what got into me."

"I'm not sure what to make of all this," Iason sighed, rising. "But if it means what I think it may, we've just been replaced."

The Blondies retreated back to the chairs by the fire, both of them deep in thought.

"What exactly are these Sentinels? Are they attached to Jupiter?" Raoul wondered.

"That wouldn't make sense," Iason replied. "How can they protect her if they are connected to her network?"

"True. But what are they?"

"They appear to be computer programs, running independently, with some sort of holo-projection interface."

"I wonder if they have anything to do with what happened earlier?"

Iason nodded. "That makes sense."

"Either that or she just wanted to get our attention. Jupiter probably knew you'd try to contact her."

"I can't say I'm especially happy with the way she chose to tell us," Iason remarked.

"I agree. I hate them already. I wonder if we still have access to the Tower?"

Iason thought about this for a moment. "It seems odd that she'd lock us out completely. We're probably just barred from the grid. Maybe we should contact Lord Sung. He'd probably want to know about all this."

"Let's wait," Raoul cautioned. "And perhaps we ought to keep this to ourselves. I'm thinking of you. Your position, I mean. Once everyone finds out you no longer have access to Jupiter...."

"I don't care about that," Iason protested.

"Well, then, I care," Raoul replied. "Let's keep this under wraps until we find out more. Agreed?"

"Very well," Iason nodded.

"I'll head over to the Tower now and find out what I can. I'll let you know what happens."

The Blondies walked over to the door and there stopped, gazing at one another for a long moment. The door had opened and then, after a moment, closed again automatically.

"This isn't the end of the world," Raoul whispered.

"I know."

"You look as if you'd just lost a good friend."

"It's foolish," Iason replied, shaking his head. "I can't explain it. But I suppose I took for granted that I'd always have a place with Jupiter."

"You still do, for all we know. Let's not rush to any conclusions until we know more." Lord Am offered him a smile, longing to reach out and stroke the side of the Blondie's face. He realized at that moment how much his heart still ached for Iason, despite all that had happened between them, and despite the passion he now felt for Yui. He adored having sex with Yui; he even had strong feelings for the boy, but none of this was enough to overcome the strength of his love for Iason Mink.

Even though he knew, without any bitterness or expectation of change, that Iason no longer loved him, he could not help loving Iason, just as he always had—and perhaps now even more.

"Thank you, Raoul."

"Call me if you need me. I'll come anytime, day or night."

Lord Mink nodded, his eyes lowered. "I know."

"Good. I don't say that to anyone else, you know. I've said it before: you can always depend on me."

"Except when your jealousy drives you to kidnap and torture my pet," Iason replied wryly.

"Except then," Raoul agreed, with a smile. "Admittedly, I have my faults. I am, after all, an artist. But you've forgiven me for my transgressions by now, surely."

"I have," Iason confirmed, returning the smile.

"Then, I'm off." Raoul reached out and brushed a strand of hair from Iason's face. "I'm serious. Don't hesitate to call me tonight if you need me. I mean as a friend. But of course...as more than that. If you want it."

"I don't think Riki would be too happy about that," the Blondie laughed.

"Hmmm. Not in the mood for a threesome then?"

Iason only laughed, as though not even taking Raoul's offer seriously.

The Blondie put a hand to his heart as if wounded. "You laugh at my agony."

"And what about Yui? Don't tell me you've tired of your restored attendant already."

Raoul smiled, shaking his head. "I'm not tired of him, no. Perhaps a foursome, then?"

"Good night, Raoul."

"Night, Iason." Lord Am leaned forward and kissed Iason on the cheek. The Blondie allowed this but then pushed the button to open the door again. Raoul took the message and left, a smile at his lips, even while his eyes were dark with sadness and hurt.

"WE FOUND THIS WHEN WE WERE UNDRESSING him, Commander."

Anders held out a small book, which Voshka took absently, preparing to slide it in his pocket. He had just finished with his shower and was anxious to commence his evening with Aranshu.

The bodyguard fell into step with the Commander, frowning. "I think you should take a look at that. It seems...important. I confess my Amoian isn't all that impressive, and perhaps I'm mistaken, but...."

Voshka took a second look at the book, eyeing the symbol on the cover. "Hmmm. I have no idea what this is." He flipped through the book, stopping at a page and studying it. "My Amoian isn't so good either," he murmured. The Commander appeared lost in thought, flipping the page. "Interesting."

"That's what I thought. They appear to be some sort of log entries. And here, if I may," Anders took the book and opened to a page, pointing to the text, "does this say what I think it does? About deactivating Jupiter?"

"Hmmm. I'm not completely sure."

"Shall I have one of the scholars from the University take a look?"

"Perhaps," Voshka replied, nodding. "Yes. Send one over."

"Very good."

They were now outside the Commander's chambers, and much as the book intrigued him, he found what waited inside on his bed far more interesting. He slipped the book in his pocket, entering the room with a smile at his lips.

Aranshu was completely naked, spread-eagled face down on the bed. His ankles and wrists were manacled, so there was no chance that the young would-be assassin could escape.

Azka sat in the corner of the room, looking a little frightened.

"What is it, Azka?" Voshka laughed. "Let me guess. You've met Aranshu."

"Yes, Master," the pet answered meekly. "He doesn't seem to like me much."

"Don't worry. He can't hurt you—he's completely helpless at the moment."

Azka nodded, though seemed disinclined to move from his corner of the room where he had retreated. Aranshu had said terrible things to him, and though his Amoian was a bit hard to understand, the captured pet left no doubt that he intended to do Azka harm if he had the chance.

"He's all bark and no bite anyway," Voshka teased. "Isn't that right?"

"Come put your hand near my mouth and find out," Aranshu spat back.

The Commander only laughed, walking slowly over to a table where his implements of discipline had already been neatly laid out. "Let's see. Where shall we begin? Do you have any special requests, my pet?"

"Go fuck yourself," Aranshu hissed.

"No, I think I'd prefer to fuck *you*, which I shall do repeatedly once we've gotten the discipline out of the way." He picked up a flogger with multiple tails, examining it as though feeling indecisive. "Perhaps this will do, to start out with."

He walked over to the bed, his boots clipping smartly on the marble floor of his room. "You know why I'm punishing you. I don't really need to say anything."

"Then don't!"

"Ah, but I prefer to scold you a bit," Voshka whispered, removing his elaborate cape and letting it fall to the floor. Beneath his cape he was dressed in a skintight thin bodysuit, one which he had picked up while on Amoi and found exceptionally comfortable. He brushed the flogger over Aranshu's backside gently, allowing the tails to fall between his thighs. "Ten years is a very long time."

"Get on with it! Fucking sadistic bastard!"

"I shall indeed get on with it, but only when I am ready. And—pay attention now, pet—I won't stop until you beg for mercy and acknowledge the great wrong you did me."

"I'll never apologize," Aranshu vowed. "You can whip me to death for all I care!"

"I prefer a little life in you before I mount you," the Commander replied. "So is that a no? No apology before I begin? It might make things slightly easier for you." He continued to drag the flogger up and down the young man's thighs, over his cheeks and up to the small of his back.

Aranshu fell silent, closing his eyes and bracing himself. He knew his Master well enough to know the calm before the storm. Voshka was ready to unleash his fury, he was sure of it.

And he was not wrong.

"Very well. Your choice is noted," the Commander hissed, whipping back his arm and bringing down the flogger full-force on Aranshu's ass.

The pet bore the flogging rather stoically—at least at first. Gone was the young boy who had sobbed and begged for mercy when Voshka had punished him for his various youthful transgressions. Aranshu was now a man and was not easily broken.

Voshka was so angry that he could hardly see straight. He whipped his pet mercilessly, not satisfied with the welts that appeared on his skin. No, he wanted a response from Aranshu. He wanted to hear his suffering.

At last the brave pet could no longer remain silent. His vocalizations, however reluctantly tendered, were genuine evidence of his agony. But Aranshu simply would not apologize, nor would he shed a single tear.

Finally Voshka stopped; his arm was aching and he was sweating from his strenuous efforts. His whole body shook. He wiped the sweat from his face with his sleeve, studying Aranshu's punished flesh. He marveled at the fact that the boy—no, the man—had held his ground and refused to apologize.

"That's your first round of discipline," he remarked, tossing the flogger aside. "We still have the entire night ahead of us. But you realize that, of course."

At this, Aranshu's eyes widened, though he remained silent. He forced himself to retreat inside himself in order to escape the pain that already threatened to break his composure. One thing he was sure of: he would not give his Master the satisfaction of hearing him beg.

"YOUSI," HEIKU LAUGHED, PULLING THE BLONDIE back into bed with him. "Where are you going?"

"I don't know," Yousi admitted.

"That's the third time you've tried to get up. Is there something you want? Are you hungry?"

"I can't sleep. I'm not sure why."

"It's my fault. I keep fondling you."

"Yes, you do," Yousi agreed, giving him a scolding look.

"Oh, but I can't help myself. You're all warm and in my bed. In fact, I'm getting aroused again."

"But my ass hurts," the Blondie objected, frowning grumpily.

"I know. I'm being too rough on you. Perhaps if you could use your mouth? And I'll do the same to you."

"I'm no good at that," Yousi warned.

"You're perfect," Lord Quiahtenon whispered, yanking on his cock happily. "Oh! I'm ready for you now." He attempted to push Yousi between his legs but the Blondie resisted.

"I don't know what to do!"

"Yes, you do," Heiku encouraged, wiggling up toward the head of the bed as he held Yousi's head and urged him toward his erection. "Just lick me, for starters. Kiss me."

Yousi frowned at the enormous cock presented to him and then kissed the top of the head.

Heiku laughed. "That's good, but don't stop there. Use your tongue. Pretend you're having frozen creams!"

"Can we have some frozen creams when we're through?" Yousi exclaimed suddenly.

"Yes, yes, you can have whatever you like! Oh! Yes, that's perfect! Keep wiggling your tongue." The Blondie rose up on his elbow to watch his lover, excited with Yousi's sudden enthusiasm. "Just like that! Go crazy!"

Yousi, now thinking about the promised frozen creams, allowed his tongue to explore the Blondie's entire length, licking him with almost ridiculous fervor. Heiku was thrilled, tossing his head back and groaning.

"Good boy! That's it!" He reached down and gently directed his lover back to the head of his cock. "Now open up wide and take me in. NO TEETH, though, remember?"

"Mmm hmmm." Yousi's mouth vibrated against him as he took Heiku into his mouth.

Lord Quiahtenon moaned, opening his eyes wide and then closing them. "All the way! All the way if you can! Keep moving your tongue like that. Keep—oh! Jupiter help me!"

The Blondie ejaculated, unable to even warn Yousi. But Yousi adapted surprisingly well, holding the semen in his mouth.

"Whah oo I oo ow?" he asked.

Heiku looked down at him through half-closed eyes. "Swallow it. Swallow it, love."

Yousi did so, shuddering a little.

"What wrong?" Heiku frowned. "Don't you like the way I taste?"

"You're not as good as frozen creams," Yousi replied honestly. "Can we have some now?"

"Don't you want me to take care of you first?" Heiku reached down and began fondling the Blondie, his cock almost immediately going rigid in his hand.

"Yes please!" Yousi cried.

"What would you like? My mouth?"

"Can I have your ass please?" Yousi asked, so excited that he almost yelled.

Heiku laughed. "I suppose you're entitled. Here," he handed Yousi a tube of lubricant. "Put lots of that on first."

"Where should I put it?" Yousi asked innocently, squeezing some of the gel into his hand and then looking as if he was going to rub it on his stomach.

"Here," Heiku directed, guiding his hand down to his cock.

"Oh!" Yousi moaned, as he spread the warm lubricant onto his member. "It feels so good!"

"Of course it does." Heiku rolled over onto his stomach, spreading his legs. "Can you find your way inside?"

"I think so," Yousi replied, repositioning himself between Heiku's legs and then bumping up a little awkwardly against the Blondie's ass.

"You're about two inches too far north."

"What?" Perplexed, Yousi looked around the room, not understanding his lover's hint.

"Here," Heiku reached back and took hold of Yousi's member, guiding him inside his rectum. "There you go."

"Ohhh," Yousi sighed, as he slid inside his partner's sanctum. "This feels good, Ku-Ku."

"Yousi! Don't call me that," Lord Quiahtenon complained.

"I slid right in," Yousi observed. "Which means you must do this a lot...with someone."

"Let's not talk about that now, love."

"Why not?"

"Because...I don't know...it might upset you."

Yousi frowned. "But I'm already upset."

"Get ready, love. You're about to feel it."

"Feel what? Oh! Ohhhhh!" Yousi gasped as the Blondie began contracting against him, squeezing his cock wonderfully. He thrust quickly, sloppily, unable to stop himself. "I'm going to ejaculate!"

"Of course you are," Heiku laughed. "Go ahead, love."

With a loud grunt, Yousi reached consummation, sighing as the waves of pleasure passed over him. After a moment he pulled out, sighing and rolling onto his back.

"Did you like that?" Heiku kissed his nose and then his cheek, snuggling up against him.

108

Yousi opened his eyes, frowning. "Who else do you have sex with?" he demanded.

"Oh, love. Are you sure you want to know that? I don't have sex with him now."

"I want to know!"

"All right. It was Kobin Nu."

Yousi was quiet for a moment. "How many times did you have sex?"

"I really don't know, love."

"How many? Three times? Twenty?"

"Somewhere in between, I suppose." Heiku traced a finger down Yousi's face. "Don't be jealous. It wasn't until recently that you seemed even interested in me again. You have to understand…I was very lonely. You would have done the same thing."

"I wouldn't have had sex with Kobin Nu!" Yousi protested. "He cheats me every time I go to the fish market! He's a…a…scalawag."

"Let's forget about it then. I'm sorry, love."

"Humph." Yousi pouted, feeling extraordinarily jealous over this new information.

"Now, how about those frozen creams? You still want some, right?"

"Yes," Yousi admitted, with a sigh.

"Then, let's go get some." Lord Quiahtenon stood up, holding out a hand and helping Yousi out of bed. But when the Blondie was before him, he wrapped his arms around him, squeezing him tightly. "Please don't be angry with me," he pleaded. "Do you forgive me?"

"I forgive you," Lord Xuuju replied, closing his eyes and enjoying Heiku's embrace.

For the first time in a long while, Yousi felt alive again. Capable of feeling jealousy, of remembering everything that had gone on that night without feeling entirely confused. He wasn't sure what the difference was, but he knew something was different. It almost seemed as if getting upset had changed something inside his mind.

He opened his eyes. "You flirted with Kobin Nu at that party after graduation," he remarked.

Heiku pulled away, looking down at him. "How could you possibly remember that?"

"Because it made me angry."

"It did," Heiku agreed, smiling. "You refused to talk to me for a week."

"Did you sleep with him then?"

"No, love. Not until after…after things had changed." Heiku studied him, puzzling over his expression. "You seem different, Yousi. You seem…almost, like before."

"I feel different," Yousi agreed. "What do you think it means?"

"I'm not sure. Let's go get those frozen creams and talk about it, all right?"

Yousi nodded, walking with the Blondie to the kitchen.

AERTIS STOOD BEFORE THE HEADMASTER, his head bowed. "I have a confession to make. I…I—"

The Headmaster narrowed his eyes. "Yes?"

"I broke into the laboratory to use the rapid pulsar unit. Last night. I know I wasn't allowed but…I was so excited. But then I think I might have…broken a few beakers."

"Aertis," the Headmaster sighed. "You should know better."

"I know. I'm sorry."

"Well, you've put me in a bind. I can't very well reward you by sponsoring your excavation after you've just confessed to such a thing."

"Oh! Please, I was hoping…that is, I would like to request corporal punishment. To keep it off my record. Truly, I'm sorry."

"I see." The Headmaster sat back down in his chair, studying him. He felt more than a little perplexed at Aertis' sudden confession, which seemed to have come from out of nowhere. "You could have told me this first," he scolded.

"I know. I was…afraid."

"To keep this off your record, you'll have to submit to a something a bit more severe than I think you're expecting. You won't feel much like going on the dig, after that."

"I will," Aertis protested, sounding almost frantic. "I promise, I will!"

"Then, drop your trousers and put your hands on the desk." The Headmaster rose, going over to his "punishment wall" where hung the various implements of his disciplinary toolkit—a few paddles, a strap, a crop whip, and a cane. He reached for a paddle and then, out of compassion, found himself choosing the strap. Yes—he would spare him the paddle. But he would give him a good strapping. And it wouldn't be that much of a reprieve; Konami knew the thick leather strap could bite. He pulled it taut in his hands, its snap startling Aertis.

Konami kept his eyes averted as he moved behind the Blondie, but when he lifted his gaze and beheld young Jin bent submissively over his desk, his bare ass positioned for punishment, he felt blood shoot to his loins. For the first time in his life when faced with disciplining a student, he felt light-headed. He gripped the chair next to him, hungrily eyeing every hollow and curve, every ripple of his muscles. He tried to look away but couldn't. His mouth felt dry.

"I know you must punish me very hard," Aertis said.

Konami gripped his desk, pulling on his cock as he reached his ascent. He'd never in his life masturbated in his office before, but he found that after Aertis had come to visit him, he was unable to proceed with their planned agenda until he relieved himself first.

His eyes rolled back as his semen finally burst up from his cock. With a mighty groan, which he was completely unable to suppress, he enjoyed his glorious release. He hadn't even gotten past the punishment to his planned fantasy of penetration; it had been enough to imagine the young Blondie bent over his desk, taking his discipline.

Almost immediately he felt a little ashamed, although he knew there was nothing to feel shamed about. It was perfectly acceptable to fantasize. Such things were not forbidden. Yet somehow Konami knew that his feelings for Aertis were approaching a dangerous impasse, especially if he was going to be alone with the boy at Minas Qentu. And it was alarming that he had been unable to restrain himself in his office—a place decidedly inappropriate for sexual release.

"Jupiter help me," he whispered.

He cleaned himself up, deciding to administer a bit of self-punishment. He seized his strap and whipped it over his shoulder, clenching his teeth when it struck his back. After several more strikes he felt a little better. What he really needed was a thorough punishment session, but he didn't know who he could trust to administer it. For a fleeting moment he thought of Omaki Ghan, but knew almost instantly that the notorious Blondie was out of the question. No, he would have to keep his private shames to himself and make do with self-punishment.

Lord Sung looked at the clock, frowning. He was off to a late start. He would have to rush in order to take care of everything and be back at the Academy without keeping Aertis waiting for long. He found that he was shaking as he locked the door to his office. Perhaps the excavation wasn't such a good idea. But he couldn't very well back out now, when he'd already promised Aertis he'd go with him.

He shook his head, worried. Never before had he felt so uncertain about his own actions. Although he was sure he could control himself, he was not as sure he would be able to hide his attraction to the young Jin. Perhaps he should simply confess the problem to Aertis and explain why he was unsuitable as a mentor.

Even as he rushed from the Academy to his vehicle, he knew he wouldn't go through with the confession. Truth be told, he was thrilled with the idea of spending the night alone with Aertis at the deserted dig site. He felt ashamed thinking about it, but he knew he planned to use the night as fuel for fantasy, and that part of him hoped—indeed ached—for a glimpse of the young Blondie's naked body. He told himself sternly that, after that night, he would refuse further contact.

He told himself this even as he became aroused again, just thinking about the night ahead.

"IS RAOUL GONE?" RIKI PEERED OUT FROM the guest wing, finding only Daryl and Katze in the dining area, where they were setting the table.

"He's gone," Katze confirmed.

"Where's Iason?"

"I think he went out to the gardens by the pond, Riki," Daryl answered.

"Yeah? It's freezing outside. Wonder why he's there?"

"Maybe he has the awning down," Katze remarked. "You know, you really don't need to avoid Lord Am anymore. It's not like it was before."

"That's right," Daryl agreed, nodding.

"Yeah, I know. But I can't help it. When I see him, my dick shrivels up. He may be nice now but it was a whole different story when I was tied up at the Taming Tower."

"Let's not talk about that," Daryl suggested, frowning.

Katze reached out and pulled the boy close, kissing the side of his head. "Yes. Let's not."

"Sorry. But I'm just saying…Raoul and I have a history."

"But Riki, what about the painting?"

"What do you mean? That's exactly what I'm talking about! He never forgave me for ruining that dumb old painting."

"Oh, Riki! That was a beautiful painting!"

"It really was," Katze agreed.

"Well, hell! Now you two are against me, too!"

"I'm not saying it justified what he did. Anyway—that's not even what Daryl was talking about. He means the new painting. The one that's causing such a fuss."

"What painting?" Riki blinked, confused.

"Don't you know?" Daryl and Katze exchanged a look of wonderment.

"Um…I have no idea what the fuck you're talking about."

"Riki! Raoul's new painting is of *you*," Daryl exclaimed.

"Me?" Stunned for a moment, Riki turned to Katze for confirmation. The auburn-haired youth nodded. "That's right. He painted you."

"Well, fuck. I'm not naked, am I?"

Daryl giggled at this and Katze rolled his eyes. "Thankfully no."

"What the hell does that mean? You know you'd like it."

Katze raised a hand as a warning. "Okay. We are *not* having this discussion."

"Well, if I'm not naked, what am I doing?"

"It's from the day of the Whippings, when you ran onto the stage and demanded to take Iason's place."

"It's beautiful," Daryl added.

Riki was speechless. He never would have imagined that Raoul would do him such an honor. He hardly knew what to think.

"He's been offered ten million credits for it, but Lord Am says he won't sell it."

Ten million! "Well of course it's in demand, if it has *me* in it," the mongrel replied saucily.

Katze answered this by punching him in the arm. "Asshole."

"Ow!" Riki grabbed his arm, laughing. "Does Iason know about it?"

"Honestly, I don't know," Katze replied. "I assumed you knew. So maybe he has no idea."

"Well, I'm going to go find him now. Maybe I'll ask him about it."

"Dinner's almost ready."

"Finally! I'm about to die of hunger!"

"Doubtful," Katze snorted, poking him in the side. "You look like you're putting on weight."

"I am not!" Riki protested, lifting his shirt to show his perfectly sculpted abs. "See? No fat! I'm perfect! I bet I can do more crunches than you!"

Katze only rolled his eyes.

"Ha! You're afraid you'll lose!"

"Katze wouldn't lose, Riki," Daryl protested. "He's in great shape."

Riki pointed to Katze. "You. And me. Tonight before bed. A crunch contest. Winner has to give the loser a massage."

"You're on," Katze agreed.

The mongrel nodded and then went off in search of Iason, giving Katze the one-finger salute when the eunuch yelled after him, "By the way, I prefer warming lotion."

Riki found Iason in the garden by the fishpond just as Daryl had guessed, sitting on a bench there. The Blondie seemed sad.

"Hey," he whispered, sitting down next to him. "Dinner's almost ready."

Lord Mink nodded absently, a faraway look in his eyes.

"What's up?" Riki traced a finger along the Blondie's thigh. "What did you and Raoul talk about?"

"It's complicated."

"Hmmm. You know if you keep this to yourself, you're just going to get one of your headaches. Why not tell me about it?"

"Jupiter," Iason began, after a long sigh, "has shut me out."

"Shut you out?"

"She declined my relay request for a conversation. She's…created new Guardians for the grid. They're called Sentinels."

"And this upsets you?"

"A little," Iason confessed. "Although it's hardly surprising."

"I'm kinda surprised that you even care. I mean—you were ready to bring her down, weren't you?"

"It's hard to explain. It wasn't because I hated Jupiter. I just wanted more control over my own affairs." Now the Blondie lowered his voice, as if fearful that they might be overheard. "Jupiter goes too far. I still feel she has no right interfering in my private life."

"But…she's okay with us now, right? I mean, isn't that what she told you?"

"That's what is puzzling. She gave me what I wanted but then she cut off my access." He laughed softly. "I'm being foolish."

"Not really. Anyone would feel that way, if they were used to being treated a certain way and then suddenly got the door shut in their face. I remember that one time, not so long ago, when you locked me out of your room. I hated that. Anyway, it's kind of like what happened to the Rebels, you know, after the Revolution."

114

A strange look came over the Blondie's face. "It's exactly like that, Riki. She shut out the Rebels forever. She's doing the same thing now—she's shutting us out and creating new Guardians."

"But she's not *really* shutting you out," Riki pointed out. "It's not like how it was for us mongrels. You still have everything. And besides, she didn't shut us out forever. I'm a citizen now, remember?"

The mongrel shivered, his teeth starting to chatter.

"You're cold," the Blondie noted, frowning. "Come here, love." Iason put his arms around him, pulling him onto his lap.

"The winter seems longer this year," Riki remarked, leaning back against him. "You're warm, though."

The dinner chimes sounded, much to Riki's delight.

"Food!" he exclaimed happily. "Let's go eat."

"Kiss me first."

"But...wouldn't it be better if—"

The mongrel's reply was silenced by Iason's kiss, a long, lingering kiss that promised of more pleasure later that evening.

"You're getting me all horny," Riki complained, breaking away and adjusting himself.

"I want you in my bed immediately after dinner."

"After dinner? Okay, good. For a minute there I was worried you wanted something *now*. And I don't know about you, but ever since that day of the Whippings, I'm hungry all the time."

"I confess, I have more of an appetite myself, most likely from the Acceleration," Lord Mink answered, giving Riki a pat on the bottom as he stood up. "But if I wanted you to be in my bed now, it would be my prerogative to insist you join me now."

"You'd have to catch me first!" Riki darted towards the door to the indoor pool, a bit surprised when Iason immediately seized him from behind.

"Geez. You're fast, all of a sudden. But I hope you aren't serious about sex before dinner. I'm really REALLY hungry."

"Very well. It can wait until after dinner."

"Iason?"

"Yes, my love?"

"You won't ever shut me out again, will you? I mean like you did, you know, that one time."

"Only if you're especially naughty."

"Well, fuck. That means you will," Riki replied, frowning.

Iason laughed. "Are you saying you can't refrain from being naughty?"

"I'm saying I can't refrain from doing whatever the fuck I want, instead of whatever the hell it is you want me to do."

"Hmmm."

They walked together through the pool area to the guest wing.

"Oh!" the mongrel exclaimed. "I meant to tell you this before! Did you hear about Raoul's painting?"

"Which one?"

"The one he did of me!"

"Of you?" Iason smiled, shaking his head. "I think you must be mistaken, pet."

"Daryl and Katze told me about it."

"Perhaps they're teasing you. I find it hard to believe Raoul would do a painting of you."

"It's true." Katze nodded at them as they entered the great hall. "I've seen it."

Daryl nodded. "I've seen it, too. There's an image of it circulating through the city."

"That's odd. He never mentioned it."

"It's from the day of the Whippings," Riki remarked. "When I saved your ass. Remember that?"

The Blondie, who was, at that moment, standing behind Riki, put his arms around him, squeezing him tightly. "Of course I remember that."

"Then how about you save my ass *now*, and let me go to the party without that stupid spanking machine," the mongrel suggested.

Lord Mink released him, smiling. "I haven't made my mind up yet about that."

Riki rolled his eyes. "Never do a favor for a Blondie."

"Toma and Tai have already left for the villa," Katze reported. "Odi drove them. So it's just us and the bodyguards. And Aki just called to ask if he can eat with Suuki."

"Tell him that's fine," Iason sighed, sitting down at the head of the table. "And call in the brothers."

"Where's Ayuda?" Riki wondered, suddenly realizing the bodyguard who always hovered silently near Iason was no longer there.

"I dismissed him for the evening."

Askel and Freyn joined them at the table, looking pleased to once again be allowed to eat at the table, especially with such an intimate group.

116

Freyn looked as though he were about to sit down, but at the last moment Askel slid into the chair.

"This one's mine," he announced.

"Askel!" Freyn muttered, sitting down beside him with obvious impatience.

"Odi says we can go to the party," Askel blurted out. "Is that right?"

Freyn nudged him in the side. "Moron," he whispered. "Wait until he tells us."

"Ow! You just bloody elbowed me!"

"Whether or not you two can go depends on whether you can get through this meal without annoying me," Iason replied.

Riki snickered at this. "Not too likely then."

"What's that supposed to mean?" Askel demanded. "Ow! Would you quit with the elbow?"

Freyn leaned over and whispered something in his brother's ear; Askel immediately fell silent, meekly staring at his plate.

Everyone looked to Iason, waiting for him to begin.

"Yes, we are all going to the party at Lord Ghan's villa tomorrow," the Blondie announced. "And I expect all of you to be on your best behavior. Be mindful of how much you drink. I'll not have members of my household bandying about half-drunk, singing bawdy songs and urinating in inappropriate places."

Riki and Katze both had trouble keeping straight faces at this, although Daryl looked a bit frightened, as he always did when Iason made his dinner announcements.

"Anyone who disobeys this mandate SHALL BE PUNISHED," Lord Mink finished, looking directly at Riki.

"What? I was just sitting here," the mongrel protested.

The Blondie then turned to the brothers, giving them a stern look. "The same goes for the two of you. I'm trusting you not to be an embarrassment."

"We won't," Freyn said quickly. "Right, Askel?"

"That's right," Askel agreed. "Erm…excuse me, but exactly how much can we drink?"

"I think I've made that perfectly clear. I'll bring my ruler if I have to, and start slapping hands with it."

Riki sighed loudly, eyeing the roast pheasant in the middle of the table. "Can we eat?"

"Pet, I'm giving my announcements."

"Well, why do you have to give them, like, right when we're about to eat? I mean we're all here staring at the food!"

"Riki, come here."

"Why?"

Katze nudged him, giving him a warning look.

With a loud sigh, the mongrel slammed his napkin onto the table, rising and then marching over to stand before Iason's chair.

The Blondie seized the king-sized wooden salad spoon from the table and then whacked Riki on the bottom with it a few times.

"Ow! Hey! That hurts! YaOWWW!"

Daryl, Katze and the brothers tried desperately not to laugh. Katze had to look away from the table, and was biting his lip so hard he almost drew blood.

"Now, go sit down and be quiet," Iason ordered, putting the spoon back on the table.

The mongrel rubbed his bottom grumpily, returning to his seat. He sat down, slouching dramatically in his chair.

"Now, as I was saying, I expect all of you to be on your best behavior."

"You already said that," Riki pointed out.

"Riki!"

"What?" the mongrel stared back as though perplexed, his eyes wide.

"Come here!"

"I just want to eat," Riki whined, remaining stubbornly in his seat.

Lord Mink stood up, looking decidedly annoyed. "Very well. Riki and I will join you all later. You may begin without us."

"Hey, that's no fair!"

The Blondie took a few steps and was at Riki's chair, yanking him out of his seat by the arm and then dragging him to the bedroom.

The door hummed shut behind them. Iason released Riki, hands on his hips. "What is the matter with you?" he demanded.

"What is the matter with YOU?" Riki countered. "I just wanted to eat like a normal person! And next thing I know you're beating me with a salad spoon!"

"Riki, I need you to obey me, especially in front of the household," Lord Mink explained, exasperated. He opened one of his drawers and retrieved a round hand paddle.

The mongrel eyed the paddle with alarm. "You can't be serious!"

Iason sat down on the bed, pulling Riki over his knees and then tugging on his pants until his ass was bared, although the mongrel fought him the entire time.

"If you had obeyed me, I wouldn't be doing this. Stop struggling!"

"Stop acting like you're going to paddle me!"

"I *am* going to paddle you."

"Then why would I stop struggling?!"

The Blondie put an end to the discussion by commencing with the paddling. He delivered a long series of stinging whacks to the mongrel's bared ass, much to Riki's profound annoyance. "And you'll be wearing the device to Omaki's party," he added. "You've ruined your chance to get out of that."

"Okay! You've made your point! Fuck!"

"Are you going to obey me?"

"Yes! I'll obey you—OW!"

"And act respectfully?"

"Yeah. OW! I said yes! FUCK!"

"And be well behaved at the party tomorrow!"

"I promise! I promise whatever you want, just—OW! Stop hitting me with that thing!"

Iason tossed the paddle aside, admiring his handiwork. Both cheeks were apple-red, and the blush extended down to his thighs.

"Can we eat now?" Riki grumbled, reaching back to rub his ass.

"No. Stand up."

The mongrel scrambled to his feet, reaching down to grab his pants.

"Leave them down," Iason commanded. "Turn around, facing away from me." Paddling Riki had aroused him. He unfastened his trousers, releasing his erection, and then fondled himself for a moment, enjoying the view. At one point he leaned forward and kissed one of the mongrel's red cheeks.

"Huh?" Riki peered behind him, and then, realizing the Blondie's intent, groaned. "You said we could wait until after dinner!"

"Hush." Iason stood up, turning the mongrel around and repositioning him over the bed. "Bend over." He retreated to the drawer where he'd gotten the paddle and retrieved a vial of oil, covering his cock with its warm wetness.

Riki waited impatiently, reluctantly bent over the bed, his hands on the mattress. "Can you make this quick?"

"I'll make it however long it pleases me," came the Blondie's immediate reply, though he knew privately he would not last long.

Lord Mink removed his other glove and then pressed his hands against Riki's ass, smiling when the mongrel yelped.

"Ow! I'm still sore there, ya know! My ass feels like it's on fire!"

"Oh, pet," he whispered, pressing his cock up against his portal. "Stay just like that."

He eased in, delighting in the view of his organ disappearing between the two reddened cheeks. Iason had a soft spot for a well-spanked ass; he didn't know why, only that spanking Riki always excited him.

"Ohhh," he groaned, pulling out and then sinking in again.

"That feels good," Riki admitted. "Oh! Mmmm."

"Good boy," Iason praised, when the mongrel arched his back to make himself more accessible. He thrust in again, hissing his pleasure.

"Oh! You hit my spot! Fuck yeah...keep doing that!"

"Like this?" Lord Mink pulled out a bit and then gave a few quick, short thrusts, intentionally bumping against the mongrel's pleasure area.

"Holy fuck! You're gonna make me come!"

"Isn't that the idea?" Iason whispered, continuing to stimulate him ruthlessly.

The mongrel almost immediately orgasmed, panting as Iason began pounding him hard. The Blondie spread his own legs wide, thrusting his pelvis wildly, his fingers digging into the mongrel's hips. He arched his back and threw back his head, thrusting with abandon.

"Pet," he cried. "Oh, Riki, Riki!"

The Blondie ejaculated, his body shuddering as he released his seed. He continued to thrust slowly for a few more seconds before he finally pulled out.

"They probably didn't hear that," Riki teased.

As if just realizing how vocal he'd been, Iason reddened.

"Hey! You're blushing!"

"Hush," the Blondie scolded.

"You are! Aww...that's really cute." Riki gave Iason a kiss on the cheek. "That was a super great orgasm so I guess I'll forgive you for the paddling. Can we eat now?"

Lord Mink nodded, wiping himself with a cloth and then offering it to Riki.

"Eww! That has your semen kooties on it," the mongrel protested. "Give me a fresh one."

Iason tossed him another towel, rolling his eyes.

"Speaking of kooties," Riki continued, as he wiped himself up, "I hope someone got a new salad spoon."

Chapter 05 ~
Games, Gags, and Gamians

"RIKI, FOR HEAVEN'S SAKE!" IASON CALLED. "We're all waiting for you." The Blondie was standing in the great hall, and Daryl and Katze were both at the kitchen table. All of them looked as though they had been waiting for a long time.

"I'm not going," Riki answered, from the guest wing.

"You most certainly ARE going, so let's get moving. We're going to be late."

"Go without me!"

"Riki! Come here this instant!"

The mongrel peeked out from around the corner to the great hall, sulking. "I don't want to go. Can't I wear something else?"

"Hurry up, pet. Don't make me tell you again." The Blondie stood up, chains ready, tapping his foot impatiently.

"Come on out, pretty boy," Katze teased. "Let's see your outfit."

"At least let me take off this stupid spanking device," Riki whined.

"Someone is getting a taming if he doesn't come here NOW." Iason pressed his glove-tipped fingers to the taming stick he wore at his belt, giving Riki a meaningful look.

"Oh, bloody hell." The mongrel trudged out into the hall, his face reddening.

Katze snorted and Daryl giggled, bringing a hand to his mouth. Even Lord Mink couldn't help but smile. The mongrel was wearing practically nothing at all, his outfit held together by the merest pretense of a design, the slender chains hanging low on his hips. But the spanking device strapped around his waist, the two paddles poised and ready to strike at his side, made the otherwise sexy outfit comical.

"Omaki is going to love this," the Blondie murmured, looking very pleased with himself. He held out Riki's chains, motioning to him. "Let's get these on."

Sighing dramatically, Riki held out his arms to receive the chains, rolling his eyes when Iason fastened the golden collar around his neck as well.

"Don't roll your eyes at me," Iason warned, slipping his hand into a pocket to retrieve the remote for the spanking device. "Perhaps I'll test this, just to be sure it works." With that, he pushed a button on the remote, which immediately caused the paddles at Riki's sides to move into striking position and whack him on the ass.

"Yow!" Riki yelped.

Katze laughed so hard he nearly fell out of his chair. "Holy shit," he gasped, wiping the tears from his eyes.

Daryl laughed as well, delighted with Iason's sense of humor. It was unusual for the Blondie to dream up something like the spanking machine, and he was truly looking forward to the evening.

"It's not funny!" Riki protested, rubbing his ass.

"Oh, but it is," Katze answered. "It's a fucking riot. Iason, you are a complete genius."

"Thank you," Lord Mink replied with a bow.

"Yeah, go ahead, kiss his ass. I'll remember this! I'll get my revenge!" Riki shook his fist threateningly at Katze, and then his eyes widened. "Hey! We never had that competition!"

"That's not my fault," Katze replied. "You forgot about it."

"You could have reminded me!"

"What's this?" Iason asked.

"Riki challenged me to a sit up competition. The winner gives the loser a massage."

"Hmmm." The Blondie looked decidedly displeased at this, shooting Riki a disapproving look.

"With your permission, of course," Katze added quickly.

"I'm not sure I like the idea of either of you giving the other a massage," the Blondie announced.

"Why not? We're not going to fuck this time," Riki protested.

"Riki!" Daryl hissed, jabbing Riki in the side with his elbow.

"Ow! What?"

Katze and Daryl watched Iason anxiously, wondering how he would take the reminder of their rather ill-conceived threesome.

The Blondie arched a brow, turning to look at Katze. "You may proceed with the competition upon our return. However, the winner gives *me* a massage."

"Of course," Katze murmured, blushing at the thought of rubbing oil over the Blondie's naked body.

Daryl shot him a jealous look, frowning.

"Come here," Katze whispered, sliding his hand down Daryl's back to grab his ass.

Daryl gave a little yelp and then smacked Katze on the arm. "Katze!"

"What a rip off," Riki remarked. "What's the point of the competition if *you* get the massage?"

"Watch your tone, Riki," Lord Mink warned.

"What's that supposed to mean?"

WHACK! WHACK!

The spanking machine whirled into action again, delivering two more smacks to the mongrel's ass.

"Ow! Dammit, Iason!"

WHACK! WHACK!

"Fuck! I can't say anything!" Riki wailed. "This party is going to SUCK!"

Suddenly Katze and Daryl burst out laughing. They were behind Riki, both of them suddenly noticing the words NAUGHTY PET spelled out on his ass.

"What?" Riki tried to look behind him, annoyed.

"Nothing. We're just admiring your ass," Katze replied.

"I beg your pardon?" Iason gave Katze a stern look.

"Forgive me, Sir. I meant…we were admiring the *words* on his ass."

"What words?" Riki once again attempted to look behind him, but couldn't quite get a view of his own ass. In his mortification over the spanking machine, he had failed to notice that the device offered the additional humiliation of imprinting a message on his punished flesh. "What does it say?" he demanded.

"It says…Sir Riki," Katze replied, his face completely deadpan.

"Oh. That's not too bad, I guess."

Daryl slapped a hand to his mouth to keep from giggling, and even Iason pressed his lips together to hide his smile as he headed for the door.

"How long do we have to stay at this party?" Riki moaned.

"WHAT SHALL I USE NEXT?" VOSHKA MUSED, as he studied the array of disciplinary implements laid out on the table next to the bed. He picked up a paddle, testing its weight in his hand. "A paddle, perhaps?"

Aranshu made no answer, simply closing his eyes and waiting for the punishment to begin.

The Commander proceeded to give his pet a few solid whacks with the paddle, enjoying the sound it made when it hit Aranshu's flesh. The pet clenched his buttocks, his head reeling from the impact.

"I imagine that burns," Voshka remarked. "But I don't want to numb you. Perhaps I'll switch to the cane."

He put the paddle down and picked up a long, slender cane, examining it for a moment.

"Yes, this should do nicely."

Aranshu, who hated the cane, instinctively flinched when Voshka placed the cool wood against his thighs.

"Ah, you remember this, do you?" the Commander taunted, rubbing the cane teasingly over his skin. "This has more of a bite to it, I think." With that he raised his arm brought the cane down with a loud THWACK!

Aranshu tensed, unable to help straining against his chains.

"You felt that, I think? How about this?"

THWACK!

"Or this?"

THWACK!

As strike after strike made its mark on the pet's buttocks and thighs, Aranshu began to reach a point at which he could no longer remain silent. He cried out, struggling to hold back and yet simply unable to, his voice a strangled, tortured cry.

"Yes," Voshka hissed triumphantly. "I want to hear you suffer, just as you made *me* suffer."

The Commander continued the caning, pushing Aranshu past his limit. Finally, the young man began to openly weep.

Upon securing Aranshu's tears, Voshka put the cane aside and left the room. Punishing his pet had made him break out into a fearsome sweat, and so he made for the showers. The cool water seemed to wash away his anger as well as his sweat. He felt relieved of a great burden. He felt cleansed, almost elated.

He dried himself and returned to his quarters, wearing only a towel around his waist.

124

Aranshu had quieted, though he immediately tensed when he heard the Commander enter the room. He was prepared for another round of punishment, so he was surprised when he felt, instead, Voshka's warm, naked body pressing on his back.

"Aranshu," Voshka whispered, sliding his hands under his chest and kissing his shoulder. "Why did you leave me? Why?"

"Because you lied to me," Aranshu replied.

"What did I lie to you about?"

"You told me my mother might still be alive. And you said you'd let me return home if I did as you said. Those were lies."

Voshka fell silent, enjoying the warmth of Aranshu's body beneath him. His cock was already solid as a spear, ready to penetrate. "Those were lies," he agreed. "But can you blame me for telling them? I wanted you to be happy. I wanted you to try to enjoy being with me."

"You don't care about my happiness. If you did, you'd let me go."

"You don't want me to let you go. Admit it. You want to be exactly where you are, beneath me right now. That's why you came back to me, isn't it?"

As if to prove his point, Voshka slid a hand under his pet, seeking out the small gland just above his navel. He rubbed it expertly, knowing exactly how best to stimulate him.

Aranshu made a sound, a shudder moving through his body.

"You see? You were already aroused, even before I touched you."

"I came back to kill you," Aranshu asserted.

"I don't believe you."

"Believe what you like! If I weren't in chains now, you'd be dead."

"Is that so?" Voshka kissed his shoulder again, snuggling up against him. He had already lubricated himself, and now he slid inside Aranshu, groaning when he felt his pet clench his cock.

Aranshu gasped, opening his eyes wide. It had been a long time since he'd felt his Master inside him, so long that he'd almost forgotten what it was like. Their fit was perfect; it had always been so, almost from the very beginning. He loved the way Voshka felt inside him, and he hated himself for this. It was an old struggle, one that Aranshu had grown weary of—his fight not to love the man who had enslaved him.

"Why would you want to kill me?" the Commander whispered, nibbling his ear and thrusting deep inside him.

"Because I hate you."

"Now which of us is the liar?"

"It's not a lie."

"Are you saying you don't enjoy this?" Voshka proceeded with a slow, sensual fuck, thrilled to once again have his pet beneath him.

Aranshu was quiet, his eyes closed, but his breathing had increased. He felt sapped of strength, of all his abilities to resist the Commander's charm. Voshka felt marvelous inside him, his body pressed against his; he longed to arch his back and offer deeper penetration, but he managed to lay still, resisting his urges.

Then, Aranshu did something he'd never done before. It was so surprising that for a moment Voshka stopped thrusting, simply remaining deep inside him. The man had begun to contract against him in an impossible way that the Commander had felt only once before—from the Amoian Blondie Iason Mink.

At that moment, Voshka knew that what he had long suspected was now proven, at last, to be true.

Aranshu was a Blondie.

"WELCOME, WELCOME!" LORD GHAN ANSWERED the door himself, bowing as he waved in his guests. "Ah, Iason! The guest of honor!"

"Excuse me?" Lord Mink entered, looking a bit confused.

"Oh, nothing, nothing. I meant, my honored guest. Come right in. You must excuse me, I've already been sampling the punch. Katze, Daryl." He nodded at the two eunuchs, and then his gaze shifted to Riki. "Oh my. What do we have here?"

"Fuck off," Riki replied, marching grumpily into the villa.

WHACK! WHACK!

"Ow! I mean… errm… excuse me, your majestic highness, um, Sir."

"Oh, Iason. You have truly outdone yourself. Do my eyes deceive me? Is this a spanking machine? How delightfully genius!" Omaki walked around Riki as though enamored, bringing a hand to his mouth. "Oh, my. My, my."

"Yeah, yeah. Where's the bar?" Riki replied, scowling.

Iason rewarded his rudeness with another two whacks, which Riki bore through clenched teeth.

"Oh dear. You'd better watch yourself, Riki, I think. The bar's in the corner of the room." Lord Ghan motioned toward the other end of the main hall, where the pets and attendants had gathered.

"Can I go, please?" Riki demanded, tugging on Iason's cloak.

"I have a bone to pick with you," Iason remarked, leaning forward to whisper in Omaki's ear.

"What's that you say? You have a boner for me? Oh, Iason. How thoughtful of you."

"Omaki! I must tell you I'm…I'm quite upset over the little prank you played on me!" Iason said loudly.

"You found out already, did you?" Lord Ghan blinked, looking surprised.

"What? What do you mean? I'm talking about…the," Iason leaned closer, his voice lowering to a whisper, "the collar. With the bell. The one you loaned to Riki."

"Oh, that." Lord Ghan grinned. "I'm sure that made quite a pretty picture. Wish I could have been there to see it." The Blondie winked at Riki, who only stared back at him suspiciously. "Iason, do let me take your cloak. The party can now officially begin." Omaki slipped the cloak from the Blondie's shoulders, daring to give him a kiss on the cheek.

"Omi!" Iason protested.

"Oh, forgive me. I'm just so happy to see you," Lord Ghan apologized. "Enyu! Take Lord Mink's cloak."

"Yes, Master." The pet happily assisted the Blondie, glad to be included in the festivities. Although it was not typical for a pet to take on the duties of an attendant, Enyu was not a typical pet and was always eager to do whatever his Master asked of him.

"Hello, Enyu," Iason said softly.

"Lord Mink," Enyu nodded, bowing.

The two of them exchanged a brief look. Iason arched a brow, a slight smile at his lips.

"Are you flirting with my pet?" Omaki demanded.

Lord Mink ignored this, pretending to remove a stray thread from his spotless dark blue bodysuit.

"Cat boy," Riki murmured, with a slight nod of acknowledgment.

"Riki," Enyu nodded, with a teasing smile. "That's a…um…very nice outfit you have on."

"Can I go?" Riki pleaded, turning away from the Xeronian and back to Iason.

"Very well," Iason nodded, removing the clasp from his arm. "Be on your best behavior, Riki. Come back to check in with me every half hour."

"Every half hour! I mean," Riki quickly caught himself, instinctively jutting his pelvis forward as though afraid the spanking machine would deliver another round of blows, "I mean, okay. Sure. Every half hour."

The mongrel rolled his eyes as he walked away, ignoring the gasps and snorts that followed him as he made his way across the immense main hall to the area where the pets and attendants had gathered.

"But where is my Aki?" Lord Ghan asked, looking around.

"He'll be here momentarily. He's arriving separately, with his friend Suuki. Sir Elusiax is bringing them."

"Ah, very good. Then, come in, my dear Iason, and help yourself to some punch." Omaki smiled mysteriously, and then held out a small object that appeared to be a bell attached to a stick, hung with ribbons. "Don't forget your party favor."

Iason took the party favor a little reluctantly, finding it a bit odd and childish, though he supposed Omaki was handing them out to make the party more amusing for Aki and Suuki.

As he made his way out of the foyer into the main hall, his entrance was greeted by a rather enthusiastic shaking of the bell party favors. The Blondies all seemed to be looking at him. Were they laughing at him?

"Iason!" Heiku called out, shaking his bell a bit obnoxiously. "The Blondie himself!"

"A toast to Iason!" Xian announced, raising a glass of punch.

"Here, here!" The other Blondies all cheered, raising their glasses and laughing.

Iason turned to Raoul, who looked a little uncomfortable.

"What are they going on about?" he demanded.

"The punch bowl," Lord Am answered, motioning toward the large crystal bowl that was prominently displayed in one corner of the room.

Iason turned and then gasped. Above the punch bowl was an image of Iason, displayed as a holopic. He was naked, lying in bed with a look of surprise on his face, the bell collar around his neck.

"Omaki!" the Blondie gasped, mortified. "Shut it off at once!"

"Oh, no," Lord Ghan replied. "It's been the hit of the party. Everyone loves it." He shook his party favor, the meaning of the tinkling bell suddenly all too clear.

"I insist! Shut it off!"

"Oh, very well. If you insist." Omaki replied, reaching into his pocket to retrieve a remote. He fumbled with it as though unsure of how it worked. "Let's see. Is it this button?"

128

Now a new holopic appeared, this one in the center of the room. It showed a Blondie, from behind, one hand on his hip, cracking his whip smartly and startling another Blondie, who was face down and tied to a bed, his backside covered with the marks of discipline. Although neither face was shown, everyone knew the pair was Iason and Raoul.

"Oh, that's the wrong button," Omaki announced.

"What's this?" Heiku cried, delighted.

"Oh, this is even better," Xian remarked.

"Yes, indeed," Megala murmured.

"Omaki," Lord Mink hissed. "How dare you...."

The Blondie regarded him with a look of innocence. "What is it, my friend? You seem a bit upset. It's a shame we can't actually see the faces of these two lovely little dishes. Are they friends? Lovers? What did the naked one do, to deserve such punishment? No one's quite sure. Although the punished one has a remarkably nice ass." Omaki's eyes shined mischievously as he enjoyed Iason's mortification.

"Cease...turn it off at once," Lord Mink whispered.

"Now, if I did that, it would only confirm certain speculations." Lord Ghan leaned forward to whisper in his ear. "Relax. No one knows for sure whether it's you or Raoul. I'll shut it off in a bit."

Iason shook his head. "Omaki. You're...incorrigible."

The Blondie grinned, seeming proud of this appellation. "Ah yes. I am indeed. But no hard feelings, I hope."

Iason glanced over at Raoul, who nodded at him, looking equally perturbed over Omaki's little joke. Iason offered him a slight smile, as if to apologize.

"Now, now, Iason," Heiku chided. "Why spoil the fun? Come over here and sit by me. I have something I want to talk to you about. It will cheer you up, I promise."

Lord Mink rarely showed his true feelings in public, but on this occasion, his face was red as a beet. He made his way over to Heiku, unsure what else to do.

Lord Quiahtenon leaned forward, grinning. "I have a marvelous plan for some payback," he said, then whispered something into the Blondie's ear.

Iason listened to his plan and then smiled, nodding.

"What's this you're talking about? Payback? It's Raoul you ought to be angry with," Omaki protested, scooping a generous portion of the punch into a cup for Iason. "He's the one who first painted you naked for all the world to see. Can you blame me for wanting another look? Although I must confess, even his painting didn't do you justice."

"Which image are we talking about?" Megala asked.

"Yes, that's you with the whip, isn't it, Iason?" Xian pressed.

Iason refused to answer, smoothing out the fabric of his tunic.

"Well, the punch bowl image is certainly you. How on earth did Omaki manage to get it, I wonder?" Lord Sami asked.

Iason frowned. He reached into his pocket and pulled out the remote, pushing the button several times.

Riki had already endured the humiliation of being laughed at for his outfit as he approached the other pets and attendants at the other side of the room in the area that had been obviously designated for them. Already at the party were: Regiland, Lord Am's pet, and Yui, his attendant; Shimera, Lord Chi's pet, and Nomi, his attendant; Sarius, Lord Quiahtenon's attendant; Yousi's pet Arian and his attendants Quin and Yura; and Lord Sami's new pet Enshu, along with his attendant Juthian. Daryl and Katze were also there, though Tai, Toma and Kahlan were in the kitchen helping Ru. Almost immediately the room grouped off according to position—pets on one side, and attendants on the other.

Riki had managed to secure a drink and was delighted to discover that smoking was not prohibited, so he was smoking a nice, especially mellow Dark Baccalias, leaning against the bar counter and surveying the room when his spanking device suddenly sprung to action and began smacking him.

He yelped, dropping his smoke and spilling his drink. Everyone began laughing at the mongrel's plight and the way he danced forward on his toes to escape the wrath of the machine.

Katze, who was standing near him at the bar, laughed his ass off. "That's got to be the most fucking brilliant thing I've ever seen."

"Dammit, Iason," Riki grumbled. "What's he spanking me for now? I didn't even do anything!"

"I imagine that's for the punch bowl image," Ru answered, as he brought in a tray of hors d'oeuvres and set it on the bar counter. "The one of Lord Mink with the bell."

"Well, fuck! I should have known better than to trust that Omaki!"

"What's this?" Katze perked up, looking towards the main hall.

"In the corner of the room, above the punch bowl, there's an image of Lord Mink wearing only a collar with a bell. I guess Riki took the picture," Yui explained.

"Ooo, I'll have to take a peek at that."

Daryl gave him a disapproving look, and Katze laughed. "I'm sorry, love."

"Do you need some help in there, Ru?" Daryl asked, ignoring him.

"Yes," Ru nodded, looking a little frazzled. "I can use some help. Tai and Toma have been wonderful, but those Blondies eat faster than we can bring out more trays of food. This is the first tray I've had a chance to bring out for all of you."

"I'll help, as well," Katze offered.

"Me, too," Juthian nodded.

"I'll help as long as it doesn't involve serving Puki," Yui announced.

"So, what's it like, Yui?" Daryl asked. "Being fully restored, I mean?"

"It's wonderful," Yui admitted. "Only Puki is making my life miserable. At least he got a good strapping yesterday."

"What for?" Juthian asked, smiling.

"I'm not even sure, but apparently he really enraged Master Raoul. He really let him have it. It's the happiest I've been since the Public Whippings!"

"What about you, Juthian? Are you happy to be back with Lord Sami?" Daryl asked.

"Oh, yes," Juthian said, nodding. "I have no complaints either, except for his stupid pet Enshu."

The group all turned to look at the two pets, who were both sitting at a table some distance away, looking annoyed that no one had come to wait on them.

"Oh fuck!" Riki went white as a sheet, staring over at the corner of the room as Ima walked over and sat down at a table there. The female pet had spent the first few minutes of the party primping in the bath closet and only now was joining the others.

"What is it, Riki?" Daryl asked.

"That's...that's Ima! What's she doing here?"

"Oh, didn't you hear? Sir Heiku bought her back!" Ru leaned forward, happy to impart this bit of gossip, turning to make sure Sarius was out of earshot.

"Really? Do they know who the father is?" Juthian whispered.

"No. That's the interesting thing. They couldn't find a match. Which means the father isn't Amoian."

"Either that or he's a mongrel," Katze added, giving Riki a pointed look.

Riki made no reply, but his look said everything.

"Shit. I was only teasing," Katze exclaimed. "Don't tell me you have something to do with it?"

The mongrel shrugged. "I'm not sure."

"What do you mean, you're not sure? Did you…did you sleep with her?"

"Maybe," Riki admitted. "When Iason let me go for that week."

"Oh, Riki!" Juthian gasped, horrified.

"You idiot," Katze proclaimed, sighing. He took a deep drag of his smoke, shaking his head. "Iason's going to kill you when he finds out."

"But I don't know for sure it's mine," Riki pointed out.

"Well, who else would be stupid enough to sleep with another pet?" Katze demanded.

"I don't know! But I mean, look at her! She's hot as hell!"

Katze looked over at her, unimpressed. "You'd risk Iason's fury just for a piece of ass?"

"Well now, look who's talking," Riki shot back, arching a brow.

The two of them shared a meaningful look.

"Fair enough," Katze nodded, remembering. "You want my advice? Stay away from her tonight."

"Yes, Riki," Daryl pleaded. "Don't make Master Iason angry. He's probably already upset about the image."

"I have to talk to her," Riki protested. "This is probably my only chance. I need to find out what the deal is."

"Well, don't let Iason catch you," Katze warned.

"What are we talking about?" Sarius demanded, joining the group.

"Riki's in trouble because of Iason's holopic," Juthian said quickly. "But he wanted to go take a peek at it."

"I wouldn't do that if I were you," Sarius laughed, pointing to his spanking machine. "That's pretty cute, by the way. Hey! Where's everyone going?" Sarius looked mystified when the group all headed to the kitchen.

"We're going to help Ru," Yui explained.

"Oh. I guess I can help," Sarius said a little unenthusiastically, following them with obvious reluctance.

The attendants left were Quin, Nomi and Yura, none of whom Riki knew, so he took the opportunity to approach Ima.

Ima looked up, surprised when she saw Riki walking toward her. Then she brought a hand to her mouth, giggling at the mongrel's appearance.

"Yeah, yeah. Go ahead and laugh." Riki rolled his eyes, sitting down uninvited in the seat across from her. He turned to Shimera, who had been talking with Ima. "Hey. Would you mind giving us a moment, please?"

"Why?" Shimera demanded suspiciously.

"Just go, would ya?"

"Why should I go? I was here first."

"Look, I need to talk to Ima. So? Do you mind?"

"Yes, I do mind," Shimera replied, crossing his arms on his chest. "You think you own the whole universe, Riki. Well, guess what? You don't."

Riki rolled his eyes at this. "That's the best you can come up with? That I don't own the universe? How about you get the fuck out of that seat before I shove this beer bottle up your ass!" He waved the bottle in front of the pet's face.

Shimera stood up, looking offended. "Humph! Wait 'til my Master hears what you just said to me!"

"Yeah, go running to your Master, I don't care," Riki answered. "Just get the fuck out of my sight."

"Riki," Ima scolded, as Shimera went huffing off to the main hall. "He *will* tell his Master."

"I don't care. I need to talk to you."

"Riki, do you have my barrette?" she demanded.

"What? I told you no," the mongrel replied, flustered. "Why are you asking me about your dumb old barrette at a time like this?"

"It's not a dumb old barrette. It has gamians in it! It's worth a fortune! Master Heiku wanted me to wear it tonight and was angry when I said I couldn't find it. He told me I'd better find it or he'll spank me."

"Is that all you care about? I'm trying to ask you something important, here."

"Do you have it?"

"I told you, no! Quit trying to avoid the subject." He leaned closer, lowering his voice to a whisper. "I need to know. Is it mine?"

"I don't know," she answered.

"How could you not know?"

"Because you weren't the only one I was with."

"Who else were you with?" Riki demanded, suddenly feeling a little jealous.

"Hush! You'll get us both in trouble."

"Who else were you with?" Riki repeated, this time in a whisper.

"I can't tell you."

"Why not?"

"Because I promised."

"Well, does he know about me?"

"I can't tell you that either."

"Who is he?"

"Riki! I just told you I can't say."

"Tell me. Is it someone I know?"

"Stop asking me. I'm leaving." Ima made as if to stand up, but Riki grabbed her wrist.

"Don't go. All right, so keep your big secret. Sheesh. I guess this means there's a chance it's not mine, then?"

Ima nodded. "Yes."

"Well, that's actually good news, as far as I'm concerned. Iason's going to throw a fit if he finds out about us."

As if on cue, the Blondie was suddenly standing at the table, his gaze immediately locked on Riki.

The mongrel startled, looking up in surprise. "What do you want?"

"Get up," Iason demanded.

"Why?"

"Riki!"

"Okay, okay! Sheesh! I was just sitting here." The mongrel stood up, wise enough not to offer Ima a parting look.

Lord Mink seized his wrist and led him across the room.

"Why were you talking to that pet?" he demanded in a low voice.

"Why not?" Riki shot back.

"There are plenty of other pets to fraternize with. Why her?"

"What are you going on about?" the mongrel sighed. "We were just talking."

Iason fell silent, though his dark look conveyed his jealousy. Riki knew he wanted to discuss the matter a bit more and was relieved when it looked as though he was going to let the matter drop. "I told you to behave. Is that really so difficult? Why did you insult Megala's pet?"

"Because he wouldn't move!"

"That's no excuse for threatening him."

"I didn't threaten him!" Riki protested, cowering a bit when Iason gave him an angry look. "I just told him I'd shove my beer bottle up his ass. That doesn't really count as a threat, does it?"

"Riki," Iason sighed.

134

"Are you in a bad mood because of the image? Because honest, I didn't know Omaki was going to do that."

"We'll discuss that later."

"Great," Riki mumbled.

Lord Mink led him across the room, pointing to the floor next to the chair where he'd been sitting. "Sit."

Sighing unhappily, the mongrel sat down on the floor. At least when he was sitting, there was no chance he could be paddled, which was something of a relief, since his ass was already a bit sore. He looked up and scowled at Shimera, who was sitting next to his own Master, looking pleased with himself.

"Nice job," he muttered under his breath. "Now you ruined it for both of us."

"Hush, pet," Iason scolded.

"I told you my Master wouldn't stand for you talking to me that way," Shimera replied, shaking back his hair arrogantly.

"Quiet, Shimera," Megala said sternly. "Quit egging him on."

Riki couldn't help but smile triumphantly at the pet's reprimand. Shimera could only glower at him, furious to have been chided in front of his new rival.

"Ah, Iason," Omaki exclaimed suddenly. "I really must commend you for that marvelous device you've made your pet wear. Riki, stand up so everyone can see it!"

The mongrel looked decidedly disinclined to move, pretending not to have heard Lord Ghan's request.

"Riki," Iason prompted.

Sighing loudly, the mongrel stood up, one hand on his hip. The Blondies all laughed, complimenting Iason on his device.

"How does it work?" Heiku asked. "Give us a demonstration."

"Yes, a demonstration," Xian agreed, raising his punch cup as if toasting the notion.

Iason held up the remote. "It answers to this." He pushed the button, and the spanking machine discharged another round of disciplinary action on the mongrel's bared backside. The Blondies all nodded their approval, chuckling.

Riki rubbed his ass, scowling.

"You haven't seen the best part! Turn around, Riki," Lord Ghan directed.

With reluctance, the mongrel turned. Xian snorted when he saw the words NAUGHTY PET stamped on Riki's rump, nearly inhaling his punch.

"Iason, I never knew you had such a sense of humor," Heiku remarked.

"Naughty pet," Yousi read aloud.

"What? That's not what it says!" Riki once again attempted to look behind him.

"You must allow me to borrow that sometime," Megala commented.

Shimera, who had been smirking at Riki's humiliation, looked suddenly distressed at this.

"We're here!" Aki came running into the villa, followed by Suuki and Sir Elusiax.

"Ah, my little love! Come here!" Lord Ghan scooped him up, planting a kiss on his cheek. "Are you ready to see your surprise?"

"Yes, please!"

Omaki set him back on the floor. "Then, follow me." The Blondie nodded at Sir Elusiax. "Welcome. Help yourself to some punch."

Sir Elusiax looked over at the punch-bowl, noting the image of Iason, his gaze then shifting to the second holo-projection in the center of the room. "That's quite all right," he murmured politely, one hand stiffly on Suuki's shoulder.

"You mustn't mind Omaki's sense of humor," Iason remarked. "The punch is quite good, and not too strong."

"I'll pass, all the same," Sir Elusiax replied.

"I'll have a tea-tray sent up to you, then," Lord Ghan announced.

"Thank you," the Blondie murmured.

"What's the surprise?" Aki demanded, as he followed Omaki up the stairs.

"At the top of these stairs, you shall see," Omaki replied mysteriously.

Excited, Aki raced up the stairs, waiting expectantly before the door there. Omaki opened it, and Aki looked inside the room, astonished.

The entire second floor of the villa had been converted into a giant playroom, complete with winding slides, moving jungle gyms, and robotic animals saddled for riding. The floors were all padded for safety, and there were stands built into the walls, manned by robotic attendants, for mustard dogs, gauze candy, popped corn, lemonade, sweet ice cones, and frozen creams. There were giant gumball machines and confetti launchers, but best of all, in the center of the room was a miniature replica of Commander Khosi's ship, the Emperor-VI.

"Goodness," Sir Elusiax remarked.

"It's a paradise!" Aki exclaimed.

"Holy shit," Suuki remarked.

"Suuki! That is *not* appropriate language for an Elite!" Sir Elusiax scolded sternly.

"Sorry," the boy murmured, glancing at Aki, from whom he had picked up the expression.

"So, do you like it?" Omaki asked, his eyes shining as he bent down to look at Aki.

"I love it," Aki replied, hugging the Blondie's legs furiously.

"Go ahead and explore it, then. Have fun."

The boys took off toward the room at full speed, running around in random circles as though unsure of what to do first. They both shrieked their delight as they discovered one surprise after the next. There was a trunk filled with costumes, and both of them immediately donned military garb, their capes swirling behind them as they rushed around the room.

Omaki turned to Sir Elusiax. "You'll be watching them, then? That's very good of you."

"Yes, well. My job should be pretty easy. They'll be occupied for a few hours at least."

"There's a seating area over there." Omaki pointed out the comfortable-looking chairs in the corner of the room. "There's a holoflic-player there with an immense database of viewings of all types, mostly legal—including some good imported Quadrant documentaries, if you're interested—and quite a few magazines and books on the table and on the bookshelves on the walls just beyond. You'll be served by a robotic host. He's top of the line, and he'll bring you whatever you want—drinks, tea & biscuits, food—you name it and he'll return with it. That's him right there, standing in the corner. To get his attention, just say, 'Server!'"

"Goodness," the Elite replied, shaking his head. "This must have cost a fortune."

"It was worth every credit for the look on Aki's face," Omaki replied.

"Did you say you have Quadrant documentaries?" Elusiax asked, unable to conceal his interest in the much sought-after, though decidedly rather dry, holoflics which Lord Ghan had correctly guessed were much more to the Elite's tastes than many of his other more controversial choices.

"Yes, yes, I have a nearly complete collection of those," Omaki replied with a friendly smile. "You might enjoy the one about Alpha Zen and Commander Khosi's rise to power."

"Oh yes," Sir Elusiax agreed. "Indeed I would."

Satisfied that Aki and Suuki were happily occupied, and Sir Elusiax was making himself comfortable with a selection of holoflics and some tea, Lord Ghan returned to the main hall. The Guardian was busily whirling about the room, identifying all those who were not yet in its system.

"That thing certainly is annoying," Heiku remarked. "But thankfully it's ignoring me this time."

"We made something of a discovery," Iason replied. "It actually implants a small tracer in the retina and therefore knows the exact location of everyone it's encountered."

Lord Quiahtenon shook his head. "Is that true? Remarkable."

"What's its range, I wonder?" Raoul mused.

"I imagine anywhere in the Quadrant. We were able to determine the Aristian pet Commander Khosi was looking for—Aranshu—was already aboard his ship, when he was on route to Aristia."

"How did it manage to scan the pet's retina?" Xian asked.

Lord Mink sighed. "We had a small breech of security. The Aristian broke into the penthouse."

"What!" Xian exclaimed.

"That's a *serious* breech of security, Iason," Raoul asserted. "I hope you fired your Head of Security."

"In fact, I did not," Iason replied, "although I probably should have." He looked toward Megala. "He used the secret passageways you built into the Tower."

"Then he was the one who stole the blueprints," Megala exclaimed.

Lord Mink nodded. "Probably so."

"Where are your bodyguards, by the way?" Raoul asked, scanning the room. "I don't see them."

"They're here somewhere. They're officially off-duty."

"So the unit can give the location of anyone it scans?" Heiku repeated. "Oh, this could be interesting! Guardian! What is the location of Headmaster Konami Sung?"

"Lord Sung is presently at Minas Qentu," the Guardian replied.

The Blondies exchanged baffled looks.

"What's he doing there?" Xian wondered.

"An excavation, perhaps?" Iason guessed.

"Seems a bit chilly for that," Lord Quiahtenon remarked.

"Good. Maybe he'll freeze to death," Raoul said under his breath.

"Raoul," Omaki laughed. "Don't play coy with us. We all know you enjoyed getting caned last week."

"I most certainly did *not*," Lord Am replied. "And if we don't find those logs, I'm not going to the next lecture."

"You have to go, just like the rest of us," Heiku remarked.

"Perhaps the Aristian pet took the logs," Yousi suggested.

There was a brief moment of silence as this idea sunk in.

"That's true, actually," Raoul murmured. "That would explain why you can't find them."

"And he was in the penthouse. Was it around the time that they disappeared?" Omaki asked.

"I believe so. It was during the Whippings."

"Yousi, you're brilliant," Heiku praised. "Perhaps we've just solved our mystery."

Iason nodded. "I'll contact Vosh about it. He'll know whether or not they're in his possession."

"Don't you think he would have contacted you, if he had found them?" Xian pointed out.

"Perhaps he has them but doesn't know what they are."

The Blondies discussed this possibility for awhile and amused themselves asking the Guardian about the location of various Elites until finally Omaki moved to the middle of the floor, shutting off the holograph projection and clearing his throat.

"May I have everyone's attention, please?" he announced.

The Blondies all groaned.

"Not another speech," Heiku teased, for the previous year Omaki had made a rather long, ridiculous speech at his annual bash, declaring his friendship for them all and announcing that he would do anything for each of them, as long as it didn't cost too much, and as long as he didn't have something better to do.

The pets, suspecting that a pairing might be wanted, instinctively gravitated to their Masters. Most of them sat on the floor next to their chairs, following Riki and Shimera's example. Yui, who felt his rightful place next to Raoul was usurped by Regiland, sat some distance away, sulking. Juthian sat down next to him, offering him a small smile.

"Omaki. Can I get a copy of that projection?" Megala purred, and everyone laughed, except Iason and Raoul, who both attempted, rather unsuccessfully, to look unaffected.

"Now now," Omaki replied, ignoring this remark. "No, I'm not going to make a speech."

"You're not going to sing, are you?" Xian quipped.

"No," Lord Ghan replied, raising his voice to be heard over the laughter. "I'm not going to do that either. Probably because I've managed to stay *mostly* sober…this year."

This brought another loud laugh, as everyone remembered the previous year's bash, when Omaki had been so drunk he had started singing Jupiter's Mass, rather badly, before ejaculating into a potted plant.

"I brought you a gift, Omaki," Raoul called out. "A blooming nysthia. But I left it outside, just in case."

The Blondie took all this teasing in good stride, waiting for the jeers and laughter to stop before continuing.

"That was probably wise," he answered, bowing. "Now, earlier today at my household, the topic of the ancient Midwinter's Day's festival was brought up. I had this idea," he began, smiling.

"I'm not fucking you, Omaki," Heiku piped up, sending the hall into a clamor.

Unable to resist laughing at this himself, Lord Ghan tried his best to quiet his guests, who were now in such high spirits, it seemed the slightest thing set everyone off.

"I'm rather relieved to hear it," Omaki shot back. "No, I'm not proposing any illicit coital activity, much as that might surprise you. However, I thought it might be interesting to play an old game I'm sure you all remember from the Academy. Midwinter's Day Kiss."

"But it's not Midwinter's Day," Yousi remarked.

"It's Late-Spring," Omaki replied. "We'll call it Late-Spring's Day Kiss."

"Lately Sprung, you mean," Heiku quipped. "Omi, I can see your erection from here."

"I'm not playing," Raoul announced.

"Nor, I," Iason added.

Omaki stood with his hand on his hip. "Oh, come now. You've all played this game."

"I assure you, I have not," Lord Mink said, his voice low and refined.

"No, that's true. You were off playing games with Raoul."

Iason looked mortified at this, and Raoul blushed furiously as the hall erupted into laughter once again.

"And we all know what sort of games they play *now*," Xian added, flipping his wrist and imitating the sound of a whip cracking.

Though the Blondies roared at this, the pets were quiet, enjoying the spectacle of their Masters teasing one another.

"All right then. It's settled. I'll begin. For my kiss, I choose…Iason Mink." Omaki sauntered toward Iason, amidst the cheers of the onlookers.

Lord Mink, who had been looking rather relaxed in his chair, sipping a glass of punch, now froze as the Blondie approached him.

"What's wrong, kitten?" Omaki whispered. "You never knew I had a crush on you?"

"Please tell me you're joking," Iason replied.

"Throw your punch on him, Iason," Heiku advised.

"Now now. No need for insults or beverage assaults." Omaki bent down, placing his hands on the armrests of the chair as he bent closer for his kiss. He managed to prod Iason's rather reluctant mouth open, sliding his tongue into the warm wetness within. As the kiss continued, the Blondies began clapping and cheering, until finally Lord Ghan broke away, backing off with a little bow.

"Your turn, Iason," Xian called out.

The Blondie, looking rather unenthusiastic about the game, looked around the room, deciding finally that he was best off with someone whose kiss was familiar. Setting down his punch glass, he rose, walking slowly toward Raoul.

This set off an ungodly clamor, as the Blondies clapped and cheered to see the two renowned lovers about to kiss publicly for the first time. Raoul looked rather shocked to see Iason approaching him and found, despite himself, that his heart had started to pound rather dreadfully.

Riki crossed his arms on his chest. "This game sucks," he announced, and he was not alone among pets and attendants in this assessment. Yui watched jealously as Iason stopped before his Master, and then leaned forward to kiss him.

Lord Am, rather unprepared for this stimulation, found his arms instinctively encircling Iason's back, pulling him closer as he returned the kiss, as though unable to help himself. When Iason made to move away, Raoul stayed him, kissing him deeply.

The hall grew quiet.

Iason pulled away. "Raoul," he whispered, a little angrily.

Yui's face was dark, his eyes flashing with anger and jealousy.

"Raoul's turn," Yousi yelled, merrily, breaking the ice.

Now the Blondie, feeling suddenly a little self-conscious over what had just transpired, not to mention confused, found his eyes straying to Yui, who glared at him.

"Now you do realize, Raoul, it's Blondies only," Xian remarked, with a wicked little smile.

"You should talk, Xian," Heiku teased.

The Blondies snickered at this, while Raoul stood, rather indecisively, looking around the room.

"Come on, Raoul. Make up your mind," Omaki said, shaking his bell party favor.

"I don't want to kiss any of you," Raoul protested.

"Kiss Iason again," Heiku suggested.

"No kisses between the same persons," Lord Ghan asserted.

"What? You didn't state that clearly at the beginning of the game," Heiku pointed out.

"Well, that's the rule."

"Give Megala a kiss. Make his fantasy come true," Xian teased.

Although the Blondies all snorted and hooted at this, Raoul considered Megala, deciding that, of all those there, perhaps the blushing Blondie was the least offensive choice. When he moved toward Megala, however, the room erupted in a fit of clapping and cheering.

Megala was blushing furiously as Lord Am approached him, looking almost as if he might pass out. Raoul leaned down and offered him a kiss—one that lasted a bit longer than everyone expected. Megala uncrossed his legs, unable to hide his erection.

"Megala's Lately Sprung!" Xian announced, amidst the laughter and cheers.

"Megala, you can't just sit there fantasizing. You have to pick someone," Heiku prompted.

The poor Blondie was so humiliated over his arousal that he continued to sit for a moment, staring down at his lap.

"Pick someone, Chimi," Omaki said softly.

Megala looked up into Omaki's kind eyes, and immediately gravitated toward him. After all, he'd already kissed Omaki once before—years ago.

"The old lovers reunite," Xian proclaimed, as Megala and Omaki kissed.

Megala broke away and returned to his chair, still blushing furiously.

"Omi's turn again," Yousi announced.

"This isn't fair. Omi's been kissed twice and I haven't even been kissed once," Heiku complained.

"I hope that wasn't meant to seduce me into kissing you," Omaki replied, walking toward Raoul.

Raoul looked alarmed at Lord Ghan's approach, having only just recovered from his turn with Iason and then kissing Megala. He had been surprised most over Megala's kiss, finding the Blondie's lips unexpectedly sweet and yielding, the taste of it still tingling deliciously in his mouth. He would never have picked out Megala as a lover, particularly after all that had happened, yet he couldn't deny that, if given the opportunity, he wouldn't mind exploring the Blondie a bit more. And now Omaki was approaching him for a kiss, smiling at him with a mischievous glint in his eyes.

"Pucker um, Am," Xian snickered.

Omaki reached Raoul's chair. "Would you mind standing up? My back is killing me."

Raoul stood up with obvious reluctance. Omaki then put his arms around Raoul, holding him close for a long, slow kiss. Lord Am broke off the kiss, pushing against Omaki's chest.

"For heaven's sake, Omi," he whispered. He could feel the Blondie's erection pressing against his own groin, and there was no mistaking Lord Ghan's passion.

"Goodness. It's suddenly rather warm in here," Lord Quiahtenon remarked, fanning himself.

Omaki returned to the side of the circle, where he stood, looking rather pleased with himself.

"Who's next?" Xian wondered.

Raoul wiped his mouth, looking around the room at his choices. Then he made his way toward Yousi.

"Hold on a minute here," Heiku protested.

"Yousi's fair game," Omaki argued. "Go ahead, Raoul."

Yousi looked up at the Blondie with wide, fearful eyes. He'd never kissed anyone besides Heiku—at least, not that he could remember—and the prospect of being kissed by the fearsome Lord Am was almost too much. Before he could really protest, Raoul was kissing him. He kept his eyes open, looking a bit disoriented when the great Blondie moved away.

"He's taken Yousi's breath away," Xian teased. "Watch out, Heiku."

Heiku frowned, crossing his arms on his chest.

"Yousi, it's your turn," Omaki prompted.

Yousi immediately turned to Heiku, smiling.

"Remember, all you have to do is kiss," Xian quipped. "Spare us the graphic sex scene, please."

Yousi gave Lord Quiahtenon a nice, long kiss, managing to bring a smile to the Blondie's face again.

"How long is this game going to go on?" Raoul demanded, when Heiku looked tentatively toward him.

"Yes, I say it's time to move on to something else," Iason agreed.

"That's not fair. I never got kissed!" Xian protested.

"Well, I wasn't planning on kissing you, anyway," Heiku replied. "And after Yousi, I don't really feel like kissing anyone else."

"What do you say we have a pairing now, instead?" Omaki suggested.

This proposition was met with nods of approval.

"Who shall it be?" Omaki asked.

"Riki!" Lord Sami called out, loudly. "We've never seen him pair."

The others were all in agreement, as Iason had been stingy about showing Riki anywhere, and had never once had him pair.

"Absolutely not," Iason announced.

"You can't hold out forever," Omaki protested. "Why not show him? We're all friends here."

"No."

"It would probably please Jupiter," Heiku pointed out. "We could make it known that you finally showed him."

"That's true," Raoul agreed.

"I said no, and I mean it," Iason now looked a little angry, his eyes starting to flash.

"Why not?" Xian pressed. "We'd like to see him. Are you going to refuse your friends?"

The Blondies continued to badger Iason, refusing to let up, until finally Lord Mink felt forced to consent, though he looked decidedly displeased.

"Bloody hell," Riki whispered, when he realized what was about to happen.

"He doesn't look too happy about it, though," Heiku remarked.

"And his partner?" Omaki asked.

"Heiku's pet!" Megala called out, having observed the flirting between Riki and Ima earlier in the evening.

Riki perked up at this, looking over at Ima with wide eyes.

"He looks a little happier now," Xian commented, eliciting more laughter.

Iason, however, was visibly unhappy with this selection.

"Now hold on," Heiku protested. "My pet is in a delicate condition. And she's...well, she's special."

"You're saying your pet is more special than Iason's?" Xian challenged.

"I'm just saying," Heiku replied, raising his hand as if to calm down the masses, "that she's considered, right now, rather exceptional."

"What do you mean by that?" Lord Sami demanded.

"Yes, Ku-ku, whatever do you mean?" Omaki remarked.

"Omi! Don't call me that!"

"He doesn't like to be called Ku-ku," Yousi announced, nodding.

The Blondies immediately jumped on this, yelling out the unwanted appellation and laughing at Heiku's growing chagrin.

"Ku-ku doesn't want to let Ima fu-fu," Xian teased.

"So explain exactly what you mean about Ima being *exceptional?*" Omaki pressed.

Xian nodded. "Yes, do, Ku-ku."

"I only mean that she might be considered something of a medical miracle," Lord Quiahtenon answered. "And that's all I'm going to say about it."

The Blondies exchanged looks, delighting in Heiku's ridiculous assertion.

"You're not saying that she got herself pregnant without a partner, are you?" Xian demanded.

"I'm not saying anything."

"That *is* what you're saying!"

"Let's save this argument for another day," Lord Ghan suggested. "What about that pairing?"

"It can't hurt to have her pair," Raoul remarked.

Xian was rolling his eyes and shaking his head. "He's completely clueless about his own pet," he murmured.

"What's that supposed to mean?" Heiku demanded, looking offended.

"It means you don't even know about the pet magazine, and now you're under some delusion about her chastity," Lord Sami answered. "I'm honestly surprised Jupiter didn't strip her of her Alpha status long ago."

"How dare you!" Heiku looked about ready to explode, a vein in his neck starting to protrude.

"Gentlemen, let's keep things civil," Omaki directed.

"He just insulted my pet!" Lord Quiahtenon exclaimed. "This is insufferable!"

"Settle down, Heiku," Raoul soothed. "We're here to relax, remember?"

"That's right," Omaki nodded. "This is all just good fun. So, what about that pairing? Will you show Ima?"

"The mood's spoiled now, I think," Raoul remarked.

"I agree," Iason said quickly.

"None of us are surprised to hear *you* say that, Iason. But perhaps you're right. Let's save the pairing for later. Come, come. I insist you all drink more of the punch. Raoul's right, as well—we're here to relax."

"I have an idea for another game," Heiku announced.

The Blondies all groaned.

"Not one of *your* games, Ku-ku," Omaki teased.

"Whatever do you mean? I come up with marvelous games!"

"I'm not playing," Raoul announced.

"Of course you're playing. You're all playing. The name of this game is: Paddle the Host."

The Blondies all smiled at this, turning to look at Omaki.

"I like the name of it," Iason asserted. "Is this the payback we discussed?"

"Yes," Heiku replied, raising his eyebrows.

Lord Ghan frowned. "You can't be serious."

"Indeed I am. In fact, I have the paddle right here." Heiku jumped up and rushed across the room to retrieved his cloak, pulling out the Xtreme Punishment 9800 Spank-Cam and holding it up for the others to see.

Omaki eyed the paddle and then looked at the Blondies, and then, quick as lightning, he took off running.

146

Chapter 06 –
Unexpected Guests

VOSHKA LAY ON ARANSHU FOR A FEW MOMENTS, savoring his release. "I know you're aroused," he whispered. "And I know what you want."

Aranshu closed his eyes, fighting back an involuntary shiver. Why was it so hard to resist Voshka? And why did he love the Commander's touch so much? In all the years since he'd last been with his Master, he'd never stopped thinking about him. Not a day went by when he didn't wonder where the man was. He craved his touch, more than anything else in the world. For this, he hated himself. How could he enjoy intimacy with the man who was responsible for his mother's death?

"Anders!"

The bodyguard entered the room as the Commander rolled off his pet and stood up, not even trying to hide his nakedness. Although it was not the first time Anders had seen him naked, he couldn't help but catch his breath. Voshka Khosi was undeniably gorgeous—fit and trim, with muscles and hollows in all the right places. It was no wonder he was practically worshipped on Alpha Zen, no wonder that the harem boys got into fights over him; no wonder, indeed, that whoever Voshka set out to seduce was unable to resist him.

"Help me flip him onto his back."

"Yes, Commander."

"We'll use the thigh spreader." Voshka opened a cabinet and pulled out the restraint, which Aranshu remembered all too well. It fit around the waist and then wrapped around the thighs, pulling the thighs back and apart.

The two men spent a few minutes situating Aranshu on his back and into the restraints; the angry young man resisted the entire time, making them work to accomplish what should have been an easy task. Both Anders and Voshka had to use all their strength to force Aranshu into the restraints.

"Why are you resisting? It's obvious you want this," Voshka scolded, nodding toward his erection.

147

"My body may want you, but my heart doesn't," Aranshu shot back. In truth, he was so eager to be serviced he could hardly wait; it was only out of pride that he resisted. Having his legs spread again in the familiar restraint, his arms chained overhead, was thrilling; in fact, just seeing Voshka take the restraint out of the closet had made him almost groan with eagerness. It was a continual war Aranshu had with himself—wanting Voshka's touch and then hating himself for it.

Voshka felt the sting of this remark, though he kept a smile on his lips. "Is that so?" he murmured.

"Yes. Yes, it's most definitely so!"

"Is that all, Sir?" Anders asked.

"Yes. Leave us."

"Yes, Sir." Anders left the room, allowing himself one final glance at the Commander before he closed the door.

Voshka climbed back onto the bed, running his fingers down Aranshu's thighs. "If your heart doesn't want me, then why were you so jealous of the other harem boys?"

Aranshu refused to answer, looking away.

The Commander laughed softly. "Azka," he commanded.

Azka, who had been watching the scene with interest and a bit of awe over Aranshu's defiance, startled when his Master called him.

"Yes, Master?"

"Come here."

The red-haired, slender boy immediately approached him, excited to have been summoned. He had assumed that the Commander would no longer be interested in him, now that he finally had his long lost pet again.

"Get undressed," Voshka ordered.

Azka immediately removed his flimsy loincloth, standing before his Master eagerly. He had an erection in progress that quickly matured, his cock standing out from his body in full readiness within a matter of seconds.

"Would you like me to pleasure you, Azka?"

"Yes, Master!" Azka cried.

The Commander turned to Aranshu, giving him a wicked smile as he knelt down on one knee and slid his mouth over Azka's cock. Aranshu tried not to watch but couldn't help himself; he felt both angry and aroused, as well as extraordinarily jealous of Azka.

When it came to the art of lingual pleasure, Voshka Khosi was unparalleled. He knew exactly how to begin, with his mouth slowly closing over the head, how to move his tongue while he sucked, how to alternate between licking and sucking, how to take a cock deep into his mouth and hook it in his throat, how to groan in just the right way and just the right amount of vibration, when to move lower, and what each pet or lover liked best.

Azka panted and moaned, sometimes almost squealing.

"Oh, Master, *Master!*"

Aranshu watched with jealous eyes as the new young pet was brought to his climax. He hated Azka, hated the familiar way the pet put his hands in Voshka's hair, hated how attractive he was, hated his little moans and cries. He hated, most of all, when Azka finally released and Voshka drank him.

The Commander stood up, wiping his mouth and looking over at Aranshu, his eyes shining. "Did you enjoy watching that?" he taunted, though Aranshu refused to answer.

"Thank you, Master," Azka whispered.

"Of course, my pretty little pet." Voshka kissed Azka on the forehead, much to Aranshu's displeasure. "You may go sit now."

"Yes, Sir."

Voshka laughed at Aranshu's expression as he got back onto the bed. "Your jealousy betrays you," he remarked, once again running his hands down his pet's thighs. Aranshu's cock twitched and rose up with undeniable eagerness in response to his touch. "Ask me to pleasure you."

"No."

"No? Shall I torment you?" Voshka flicked his tongue across the tip of Aranshu's cock, and then stopped.

Aranshu grimaced, desperate for him to continue but too proud to ask for it.

"Ask me," Voshka pressed. "I know what you want." He licked a finger seductively, holding it up for him to see. Then he slowly slid it inside his pet, finding the place he knew Aranshu couldn't resist.

Aranshu gasped and closed his eyes.

"You see? Why must you resist me?" The Commander watched him for a moment as he fingered him, hoping Aranshu would finally give in and ask to be pleasured. When the young man remained silent, he decided to proceed anyway. Aranshu would be begging for his attention soon enough.

He flicked his tongue over Aranshu's special gland, which was located near the navel. It was a gland that only Aristians had and was highly sensitive to touch. His pet moaned in response, unable to help himself. Then Voshka began his lingual exploration of the entire groin region, starting slowly and then becoming progressively more enthusiastic, just as Aranshu liked it.

Aranshu was beside himself with pleasure. Voshka's tongue was everywhere, moving wildly against him; his cock was dripping with pre-cum, about ready to burst. He gave up trying to suppress his groans—it felt so perfect, so absolutely heavenly, that he no longer cared. All he could concentrate on was the glorious rush of pleasure that centered around his groin, a mounting tension that promised an exquisite conclusion, once his release was accomplished. When the Commander finally removed his finger and replaced it with his tongue, he was unable to contain himself. He ejaculated, his eyes rolling back from the intense waves of pleasure that shuddered through him.

Though Aranshu had enjoyed sex with several others since he had last been with his Master, none of them came close to the Commander. Only Voshka could make him lose himself completely in the moment or bring him that level of pleasure. It was magnificent—even more so than it had been ten years ago, when he had first become the Commander's pet.

Voshka was thrilled with Aranshu's reaction, with his every gasp and cry—he noticed the difference in his pet's response right away. Aranshu was more sexually mature now, able to last a little longer and, somehow, even more sensitive than he had been before. He moved up next to him, giving him a kiss on the cheek. "I missed hearing that, so very much. You hurt me terribly when you left, Aranshu. I never stopped searching for you."

Although Aranshu did not reply, there was a softening of his features, of the hard, angry lines around his eyes and mouth. Voshka sensed his reception and began to stroke his hair, an intimacy that Aranshu allowed without resisting.

OMAKI RAN FROM ONE ROOM TO THE OTHER, PURSUED by all the Blondies. Even Iason and Raoul, normally inclined to refrain from such silliness, joined in on the chase, both of them still rather annoyed over Omaki's holo-projection of their afternoon at the Taming Tower.

The pets and attendants watched with delight, laughing at the sight of the dignified Blondies behaving in such a childish fashion.

Eventually Lord Ghan was caught and held down as each of the Blondies gave him a few hard whacks with the paddle.

"I hope you realize this is arousing me," Omaki announced, smiling mischievously. Although he had pretended not to want to be paddled, it was actually exactly the sort of thing he loved. To be held down and punished was like something out of a fantasy, especially when Iason and Raoul each held the paddle.

"You won't be aroused by the time we're finished with you," Heiku asserted cheerfully. He proceeded to give the paddle a mighty swing, the loud THWACK! frightening some of the watching pets.

"That one did sting a bit," Omaki admitted.

"And so will this."

THWACK!

"Ouch. All right, that's enough."

"We'll decide when you've had enough," Heiku replied, whacking him again.

"Blast it all, Heiku! That's enough!"

"You're hurting him!" Yousi exclaimed, tugging on Heiku's sleeve.

"That's the point of the game!"

"Perhaps it *is* time to stop," Raoul agreed. He had been holding Omaki and he released him, as did Xian.

Lord Ghan straightened up, rubbing his ass and scowling at Heiku. "I'll think twice before I invite you to a party again."

"Oh, come now. It was just a game," Lord Quiahtenon protested, putting the paddle down on one of the tables.

Lord Ghan immediately broke into a smile. "I'm just teasing you, Ku-ku. I adored the game. Only now I've got an erection."

"Only you," Heiku replied, rolling his eyes. "You weren't supposed to enjoy it."

"So, who's going to help me out?" Omaki demanded, as the Blondies once again took their seats.

"Where's that plant Raoul brought? You can ejaculate into that," Xian suggested.

"Perhaps I'll just relieve myself right here," Omaki announced, unzipping his pants.

"For the love of Jupiter, Omaki," Raoul protested. "Please spare us."

"Yes, Omi," Heiku agreed. "I'm all for a pet pairing, but I'd rather not be forced to watch you."

"You don't have to watch," Omaki replied, pulling out his cock.

"Omaki!" The Blondies all cried in unison, some of them shielding their eyes. Only Megala was quiet, watching with delight as Lord Ghan began stroking himself. The pets and attendants all watched in a shocked silence while the Blondies continued to berate Omaki.

"Really, Omaki, I must protest," Iason murmured. "At least excuse yourself to the bath hall."

"Too late for that. The flight is about to depart. Oh yes," Omaki moaned, as his semen pumped out and over his glove.

"My eyes," Heiku groaned, feigning great offense at Lord Ghan's performance.

"You ought to be ashamed of yourself," Lord Am scolded.

"You all loved it. Admit it." Omaki removed his glove and tossed it toward the Blondie, who put his arms up in defense.

"Omaki!" Raoul bellowed. "You just threw your smut juice at me!"

"I thought you might want to keep it as a trophy," he replied, zipping up his pants. "You know, to enjoy at a more private moment." His eyes sparkled playfully, for he loved getting Raoul all riled up.

The flustered Blondie opened his mouth to speak and then simply shook his head, rolling his eyes. "Intractable scoundrel," he sighed, finally.

"Thanks for the wonderful game, Heiku," Xian said dryly.

"Oh, come now. You enjoyed the paddling part, at least. Admit it."

"I did enjoy the paddling," Lord Sami confessed. "Though I would have enjoyed it even more if it had been *you*."

"Megala enjoyed the paddling *and* the free performance. Didn't you, Megala?" Omaki winked at Lord Chi, who reddened a little, sinking down in his seat and trying to cover the bulge in his pants.

Xian snorted, spitting out some of his drink when he caught sight of Megala's predicament.

"Some things never change," Heiku remarked.

"I bet he would have enjoyed it more if it had been Raoul," Lord Sami added, snickering.

Heiku laughed. "Remember the time he bribed Raoul with those krevlians in the coatroom, and got him to expose himself?"

"And then we got in trouble, too," Xian remembered.

The Blondies all smiled at this. Although Yousi and Iason hadn't been involved in the episode, they remembered well the sight of the rest of them hauled in front of the classroom for a thrashing.

Raoul shook his head. "I couldn't sit down for about a week after that."

Megala's face was now a deep crimson. He hated finding himself the center of attention and having everyone laugh at his proclivities.

"It didn't stop there, did it, Megala?" Xian teased. "Is that why you became an architect? To build secret passageways and peepholes?"

Lord Chi was so ashamed that he hung his head.

"We've forgiven him for that," Iason pointed out gently. "He's going to build us seaside estates."

Raoul nodded. "Quite right. Leave the poor devil alone. Speaking of those estates, when can I see the blueprints?"

Megala perked up at this, smiling. "I brought them with me, if you'd like to see them."

"Of course I want to see them!" Lord Am replied.

"As would I," Iason agreed.

"I'll get them." Megala rushed off to retrieve the blueprints, which he had left with his cloak.

"Will they be adjoining estates?" Omaki asked mischievously. "Or perhaps just adjoining bedrooms?"

Though the other Blondies snickered and snorted at this, Iason and Raoul looked decidedly uncomfortable with the teasing. At one point the two exchanged a look, and Iason, feeling sympathy for Lord Am's obvious suffering, offered him a small smile. Raoul returned the smile, his heart so full of longing he feared it might burst.

ONCE OMAKI'S PERFORMANCE WAS OVER, the pets and attendants all gravitated to the other side of the room, to the area that had been designated as theirs for the duration of the party. Riki and Shimera both took the opportunity to slip away, as neither of their Masters seemed to notice their departure.

"Lord Mink and Lord Am are flirting again," Shimera announced, as he walked up to the area where the others had gathered.

Riki, realizing that Shimera was only trying to fluster him, shrugged. "Like I give a fuck. Would you mind stepping away from me? You smell."

"Humph!" Shimera turned his nose up at him, joining the other pets who were gathered around several tables near the small band that played in the corner of the hall.

Yui, however, looked rather dismayed at Shimera's report.

"Don't listen to him, Yui," Daryl said soothingly. "Everyone knows Lord Am loves you. Think about how much he risked to have you restored."

"He still loves Lord Mink. I know it," Yui asserted dejectedly.

Katze lit up a cigarette, dismissing this remark with a shake of his head. "Those two go way back. It's natural there would still be feelings. But I think Raoul just wants what he can't have."

"How is that supposed to make me feel better, knowing he still wants Lord Mink?" Yui protested.

"We had a saying in Ceres: Lovers are like planets. Just because you're visiting Aristia doesn't mean you don't want to return to Amoi," Riki remarked. "I think it's possible to love several people at once, but in different ways."

"And I think that if you really love someone, you wouldn't have feelings for anyone else," Yui replied.

"That's a sweet thought, but I don't think it works that way," Juthian said. "I know my Master loves me now. But I also know that he has a crush on Lord Sung. He has, for as long as I can remember."

Katze nodded. "I agree. You can't turn feelings on and off like a faucet. Things take time to die down, even when a new relationship has begun."

Kahlan, who had been silent for most of the party, now spoke up. "On Aristia it's common for there to be three people in a relationship."

Daryl looked surprised at this. "Seriously? Seems like that would cause a lot of problems."

"Sometimes it does, but most times it works out," Tai confirmed. "Usually the way it works is one of the lovers brings home someone new. Rather than make a fuss and split up over it, the older lover makes love to him or her first. Then the three of them simply stay together."

Juthian shook his head. "I can't imagine that."

"Me either," Daryl agreed.

"I would hate that," Yui asserted.

"I don't know. It could be interesting," Riki remarked, taking a long drink of his stout.

"Bullshit," Katze argued. "You wouldn't go for that, and you know it."

"How do you know?"

"What, are you saying you'd allow Raoul in the relationship?"

Riki shrugged. "Would I really have a choice? Iason gets to do whatever he wants. Besides, I've already been in bed with both of them at the same time."

The attendants gasped at this, exchanging astonished looks.

"Liar," Katze snorted.

"It's true," Daryl said, nodding. "Master Iason called Lord Am over to help punish Riki after he broke a Vergatti."

"What's a Vergatti?" Kahlan asked.

"Zavo Vergatti. He's a famous sculptor from Alpha Zen," Sarius answered. "His vases and statues are worth millions. They're called Vergattis." He turned to Daryl, his eyes wide. "Did Riki really break one?"

"He did," Daryl replied.

Riki grinned as though proud of his accomplishment.

"Oh, Riki," Juthian murmured. "Was it an accident?"

"Nope. I threw it off the balcony."

"What!" Juthian exclaimed.

"Sir Raoul had sent it to Master Iason as a gift," Daryl added.

Katze laughed at this—a low, sensual laugh. "I'll bet they whipped your ass raw."

"They did," Riki agreed. "But they used a paddle."

"And afterwards they went into Master Iason's bedroom," Daryl finished.

"Bloody unbelievable." Katze took a deep drag on his cigarette, eyeing Riki with a bit of admiration. He couldn't believe the things the mongrel did sometimes.

"So what was it like, Riki?" Sarius pressed.

Riki was silent for a moment, not sure if he wanted to admit the truth of what happened that day.

"I don't believe it," Katze murmured. "You got off on it!"

"Did you?" Sarius asked excitedly.

The mongrel lit up a smoke, smiling mysteriously. "I'll never tell."

Disappointed, Sarius tossed a rolled-up paper napkin at him. Juthian and Kahlan both did the same. Riki laughed, warding off the assault with one hand.

"Anyway, when you mentioned threesomes, I wasn't talking about Raoul," Riki began, and then he stopped.

"Oh? Are you finally going to tell us about Vosh?" Katze asked, arching a brow.

"Yes, Riki. Tell us!" Sarius pleaded.

"Well," the mongrel replied, taking another drag and then blowing it out before continuing, "as it happens, we *did* have a threesome. Iason, Vosh and me."

"You had sex with Commander Khosi?!" Kahlan exclaimed loudly.

The others all hushed him, looking over to see if the Blondies had heard, but they all seemed engaged in an intense discussion of some kind.

"What are they talking about?" Juthian wondered.

"The debates, I think," Ru reported, as he walked toward them with another empty tray.

"Oh, Ru! We should be helping you more," Daryl said.

"I'm going back to the kitchen now," Tai announced, looking a little guilty for having visited with the others.

"It's okay," Ru replied. "They're finally starting to slow down a bit on the hors d'oeuvres. I have four more trays ready, thanks to all of you helping out before."

"What are the debates?" Kahlan asked.

"There's a huge fuss over Jupiter's new citizenship law," Katze answered. "Many of the Elites say they won't tolerate mongrels in the city. They don't care if Jupiter makes them citizens or not."

"Assholes," Riki muttered.

"They don't really have a choice, do they?" Juthian remarked. "If Jupiter wants to make them citizens, they're going to be citizens."

"It's a mess," Katze sighed, shaking his head. "The Elites were all raised to think that mongrels were the scum of the earth. No offense, Riki."

Riki nodded slightly as if to acknowledge his concession.

"Now they're suddenly being told mongrels could be citizens. So, well," now Katze stopped, unwilling to articulate his point.

"So Jupiter fucked up," Riki finished.

"Shhhh, Riki," Daryl cautioned.

"What? That's the truth, isn't it? Jupiter's contradicting herself. And if these Elites are gathering to debate the issue, doesn't that mean they've lost a bit of respect for her?"

Katze nodded. "Riki's right."

"Has anyone listened to the Channel lately?" Sarius whispered. "The word is that our Masters, 'The Rebels,' are being seen as heroes. There's a secret anti-Jupiter movement at the Academy, apparently."

"It's not so secret, if it's on the Channel," Juthian pointed out.

"That's incredibly stupid. Have people forgotten about the Public Whippings already?" Katze exclaimed. "If Jupiter ferrets out whose involved in that, they'll be punished for sure."

"I'm surprised Jupiter even tolerates the debates," Yui murmured.

"Technically, it's a public forum 'to discuss the integration of former non-citizens into Tanagurian society'," Sarius reported. "Although everyone knows it's going to end up being a debate over whether it should even be done or not."

"Not to change the subject, but did you really sleep with Commander Khosi?" Kahlan asked, looking at Riki with awe.

Everyone laughed, relieved for the change of topic. It made most of them uncomfortable to even say the word Jupiter. Daryl, in particular, was squirming in his seat the entire time, looking as though he wanted to get up and run away.

"I'd better get back to the kitchen," Ru said reluctantly.

"I'll go with you," Tai said.

"Hey, where's Odi and the other bodyguards?" Riki asked.

"I think they went outside to make sure the villa was secure," Katze reported. "Odi said something about picking up lot of chatter on the airwaves."

"Chatter? What's that?" Ru asked.

"It just means there's an increased volume of unidentifiable communication on the Independent channels," Daryl answered. "I guess there's some concern there might be another strike against Tanagura or Lord Mink."

"You mean like the time Iason was poisoned?" Riki asked, looking concerned.

Daryl nodded. "Yes."

"Well, fuck. That's not good!"

"It actually happens a lot," Katze said reassuringly. "Chatter, I mean. Usually nothing ever happens. They're just being cautious."

"They've been out there a long time," Tai remarked. "They're missing the party."

"I'll go find out what's going on," Riki announced, putting out his smoke and then unfastening the spanking device from around his waist. "But first I'm taking this bloody thing off."

"You'd better not, Riki," Katze said in a warning voice.

"That's right, Riki," Daryl agreed. "Master Iason didn't give you permission."

"Master Iason can go fuck himself. I'm not wearing this for one more minute!" Riki removed the device, letting it fall to the floor in defiance.

Katze shrugged, laughing. "It's your ass. Personally I'd take the spanking machine over Iason's arm."

"Excuse me, Riki?"

Riki turned to see Arian, Yousi's pet, who was standing a few feet away from the group as though afraid to approach them.

"Yeah?"

"Ima said to give you this," Arian said, handing him a folded up piece of paper.

"What is it?"

"A note, I think." Arian blushed, a little shy to suddenly have the attention of all the attendants. Unlike most pets, Arian didn't like to be looked at, except by his Master. He was frightened of attendants, for his own attendants punished him regularly for the slightest infraction. His attendants, Quin and Yura, had separated themselves from the others there and sat at a table with Nomi, Megala's attendant. He glanced over at them fearfully, as though afraid of a reprimand for delivering the note, and then slunk back to the table where Ima sat.

"A note, huh?" Riki replied, trying to suppress a smile. He opened the note, which had been folded a dozen times into the smallest possible configuration. The note read,

> Riki,
> Why are you over there with those dumb old attendants? Come sit with us. Anyway, I want to tell you something.
> Smoochies,
> Ima
> P.S. I think you have my gamian barrette. Give it back, pretty please? I'll give you a special surprise if you do.

"What does it say, Riki?" Daryl asked.

Riki looked up and realized everyone was watching him. "Ima wants me to go over there."

"You're a fool if you do," Katze remarked.

"You'd better not, Riki," Daryl agreed. "Master Iason didn't look too happy last time he found you with her."

"He won't even notice," Riki replied, gesturing to the Blondies. "Look at them."

Everyone looked. The Blondies seemed to be having a good time, laughing and making toasts. Heiku, Xian, and Omaki had formed a sort of kick line and were putting on an impromptu performance, while Raoul, Iason and Megala looked on, shaking their heads.

"They're drunk," Kahlan exclaimed.

"They always get drunk at these bashes," Sarius said, nodding.

"Master Iason isn't drunk," Daryl observed.

Riki looked over at him, studying him for a moment. "But he's distracted. And he's definitely had a few. Anyway, he's looking at a map or something."

"Those are blueprints, I think," Sarius informed them. "For the estates Lord Chi is going to build him and Lord Am."

"Like Iason really needs another house," Riki laughed. "Do you know, he once told me he has a house on Aristia, one on Alpha Zen, a third on Icaria, a fourth on Gardan, and yet another one on Xeron. That's in addition to the penthouse and villa he has here."

"He also has an apartment in Apatia and a house in Urus," Katze added.

"Goodness," Kahlan murmured. "He must be loaded."

"He is," Daryl confirmed.

"I guess I'll go over there," Riki said, glancing over at Ima.

"Are you at her beck and call?" Katze demanded, taking another approach. "Make her wait a bit."

"That's true," Riki agreed, stuffing the note in the small, pocket-like metal compartment that hung between the chains at his waist. "I'll have another smoke."

"I thought you were going to check on Odi and the others," Katze pointed out. "I could use a bit of fresh air myself."

"Yeah, all right."

"I'll go help Tai and Ru," Daryl announced.

Katze grabbed Daryl's arm, leaning over to kiss him. "Hey! No kiss goodbye?"

"I'm just going to the kitchen," Daryl giggled.

"Even so, you're not allowed to leave my presence without kissing me first," Katze insisted.

Riki rolled his eyes at this, shaking his head. "You two."

"I PROPOSE A TOAST," HEIKU SAID, LIFTING his punch glass, "to Omaki for his marvelous party."

"Here, here!" The other Blondies all raised their glasses in salute of Lord Ghan, who bowed deeply before joining them in the toast.

"A toast to Iason, for his festive punch bowl nakedness," Xian said, raising his glass.

Iason rolled his eyes to the heavens, but the other Blondies all laughed and drained their glasses.

"More punch, Omi," Xian demanded.

"Yes, more for me, too," Heiku agreed.

"I'm out of punch as well," Yousi remarked.

"For Jupiter's sake, are the lot of you so lazy that you can't get your own punch?" Raoul demanded, standing up. "Walk over to the punch bowl and get it yourself! Give poor Omaki a rest."

"Thank you, Raoul," Lord Ghan said, sitting down and crossing his legs in a leisurely fashion, a smile at his lips. "Now, does this mean we've come to an understanding, you and I? Will you be sharing my room tonight, finally?"

Raoul pretended not to have heard this remark, though the others all laughed. He turned to Iason. "More punch, Iason?"

"I would prefer wine, if he has it," Lord Mink murmured.

"There's plenty of wine, to be sure. Perhaps not Red Emperor, at a billion credits a bottle, but some White Moon, at least," Lord Ghan said.

"White Moon would be lovely."

Heiku leaned over to Xian, holding his hand up as though to shield his remark, though he spoke loudly enough for everyone to hear. "Raoul is getting Iason's drink. What do you suppose that means?"

"Hot sex later in Raoul's room, no doubt," Xian replied.

"I thought Raoul was coming to *my* room," Omaki protested. "Shall we make it a threesome?"

The two Blondies endured the teasing, exchanging a look of mutual annoyance when Raoul handed Iason his drink.

"Thank you, Raoul," Iason said softly.

160

"That's code for I want your big cock up my ass, loverboy," Xian translated.

"Now, how do we know Raoul was on top?" Heiku mused. "Couldn't it have been Iason? After all, he *is* Head of the Syndicate."

"Iason's a bottom where Raoul's concerned. I'd wager the Taming Tower on it," Lord Ghan remarked.

"I don't know, he looked rather domineering in that holo-projection, with the whip and all," Xian pointed out.

Heiku turned to Yousi. "What do you think, love? Is Iason underneath Raoul, or is Raoul on the bottom?"

"Right now they're both sitting in chairs," Yousi answered innocently.

The Blondies smiled at Yousi's sweetness.

"But once I saw Iason mounting Raoul in the planetarium," Yousi continued.

This announcement caused a commotion, especially when both Raoul and Iason looked a bit uncomfortable and surprised.

"It's true!" Lord Quiahtenon proclaimed. "Look at Raoul! His face is probably redder than his ass was when Konami caned him last week!"

Raoul was, in fact, mortified that his interlude in the planetarium with Iason back in the Academy days had been observed.

"I can't believe you can remember that, Yousi," Xian remarked.

"I just now remembered," Lord Xuuju replied.

Heiku nodded. "His memory has been coming back to him."

"That's strange," Raoul murmured. "That's never happened before."

"I know. It's very curious," Heiku agreed.

"You'd better not let Jupiter find out about it," Megala whispered nervously.

Raoul nodded. "That's true. She'd wipe his mind again."

"What?" Yousi exclaimed anxiously. "What do you mean? What would Jupiter do to me?"

Heiku put his arm around Yousi, pulling him close. "Don't you worry about a thing, love," he whispered. "But just be careful who you tell about your returning memories. Don't mention it to anyone except us, all right?"

"All right," Yousi agreed. "But what would she do?"

"She'd probably take your memories away again."

"No!" Yousi cried. "Please don't let that happen!"

"Hush, love," Heiku soothed. "I won't let Jupiter do anything to you."

The other Blondies grew quiet, wondering how Heiku could really honor that promise.

"A toast, to Yousi," Raoul said suddenly, raising his glass.

"To Yousi!"

The Blondies all drank to the surprised Blondie, who smiled at the gesture and seemed to forget his previous worry.

"I'm starting to get a little tipsy," Raoul confessed.

"As am I," Xian agreed.

"What do you say we play another game?" Heiku suggested.

The Blondies all groaned.

Heiku frowned. "Now, I'm not going to take offense at that, although I find it odd you all always have that reaction, when I provide such outstanding entertainment for our parties."

"We hate your games, Heiku," Xian protested.

"You'll love this one. It's called Confess or Undress. You have to answer a candid question or else remove one article of clothing."

"I'm not playing," Raoul announced, per usual.

"Of course you're playing; everyone is playing," Heiku replied.

"I'm not," Iason asserted.

"You're playing, Iason, and you're going first. We'll go in a clockwise circle."

"Why clockwise? Why not counterclockwise? And I think *you* should go first, Heiku, since you're so anxious to play this game," Xian declared.

"Very well. I'll go first, and we'll go counterclockwise. That means *you* will be next, Xian."

"Who gets to ask the question?" Omaki asked.

"You decide that among yourselves."

"Ask him if he ever cheated on one of Konami's exams," Raoul suggested.

"Who cares about that?" Xian protested. "Ask him who he's had sex with!"

"We already know that," Omaki interjected. "Ask him who he'd *like* to have sex with."

"How does this game work, exactly?" Raoul wondered. "Who wins?"

"It's not about who wins, it's about who loses," Lord Quiahtenon explained. "The first one to be completely naked has to, well, let's see here...."

"Has to what, Heiku?" Omaki pressed.

"I'm thinking. Ah! I have it. The loser has to wear Riki's spanking machine," Heiku finished.

The Blondies laughed and nodded, agreeing that this was a fitting punishment for the loser.

"Then confess or undress, Heiku: who would you like to have sex with, *besides* Yousi?" Xian asked.

Yousi frowned at this question, looking at Heiku anxiously.

"What's it going to be, Heiku?" Raoul pressed. "Are you going to confess?"

Heiku answered this by standing up and removing his tunic, so that his chest was bare. The Blondies clapped and cheered at this, although Yousi looked a bit confused about what had just happened.

"Xian's next," Heiku announced. "And I think we should ask him if he plans to have Juthian restored."

"No, ask him if he still has a crush on Konami, now that he's had his ass caned," Raoul suggested.

"I vote for Raoul's question," Megala said.

"Confess or Undress, Xian. Do you still have the hots for the Headmaster?" Omaki asked, arching a brow.

"I'll confess. The answer is: yes." Lord Sami blushed a bit at this admission, and the Blondies went wild, laughing and stomping their feet.

"I wonder if Konami knows?" Omaki mused, once the laughter had died down.

"I think we should tell him," Heiku asserted.

Xian looked horrified at this. "You wouldn't."

Heiku's eyes twinkled. "Oh, we most certainly would."

"There's still time to invite Konami to the party," Lord Ghan remarked.

"Jupiter help us," Raoul muttered. "If the Headmaster is coming, I'm leaving."

"Speaking of the Headmaster, I heard a very juicy rumor from Sarius, who heard it on the Channel," Heiku reported.

The Blondies all turned to him, interested.

"Oh? Do tell us," Omaki pressed.

"Apparently there's some talk that the Headmaster has been showing special favor to a young Blondie on the Syndicate track. I think his name is Aertis something-or-other."

"Aertis Jin," Raoul confirmed, nodding. "I've heard of him. He's at the top of the graduating class."

"So now is he on the top, or the bottom?" Xian quipped.

"Do you think they're actually pairing?" Megala mused.

"I wouldn't put it past old Sung. He's a rascal, make no mistake," Omaki said.

"Now, I object to this discussion," Iason protested. "Headmaster Konami is above such salacious conduct, surely."

"Once again, Iason comes to Konami's defense," Xian remarked wryly. "You know, there was a time when we all speculated a bit about the Headmaster and *you*, Iason."

"That's outrageous! I'll not have you slander Lord Sung! He is a decent, upstanding Blondie. Might I remind you all that he is Head of the Eos Disciplinary Committee? Besides that—"

"Settle down now, Iason," Heiku laughed. "We won't say any more about the blasted old fart if it upsets you so much."

"I agree with Iason. I think the Headmaster is above such conduct. However, I'd give my right hand to have a go at him with that cane of his," Raoul remarked.

"The canings really are unacceptable," Xian agreed. "We shouldn't have to put up with being treated like first-years! We're not children!"

"That caning did sting," Heiku said, nodding. "Although I would have thought *you* might have enjoyed it, Xian."

"I might have enjoyed *one* strike, but he nearly made me wet my pants. I couldn't believe how much it hurt."

"I wonder how much trouble we'd get in if we *did* abduct him and have our way with him?" Omaki mused.

"Don't even joke about such things," Lord Mink scolded.

"Count me in," Raoul announced.

"Me, too," Xian asserted, raising his punch glass. "To the abduction and violation of Headmaster Konami!"

"Here, here!"

Everyone but Iason joined in on the toast.

"Now, I really must protest," Iason murmured, frowning.

"Don't worry, Iason, we won't have you do anything. You can just watch," Heiku said soothingly.

"I wouldn't mind watching," Megala piped up, not fully understanding that the Blondies were only speaking in jest.

"You hear that? Megala wants to watch!" Heiku exclaimed, snickering.

"Maybe we *should* do it," Omaki remarked. "How much more trouble could we be in than we are already?"

164

"We'd have the perfect opportunity at our next lecture," Xian pointed out.

Iason stood up. "I'm leaving. I'll have no part of this."

"Now, now, sit down, Iason," Omaki laughed. "We're just having a bit a fun. We're not serious." Lord Ghan put his hands on the Blondie's shoulders, persuading him to sit down again.

"I was serious," Raoul remarked wryly. "I'd shove that cane up his ass."

"Careful, Raoul, you're arousing Megala," Omaki teased.

"I think we need more punch," Heiku said, standing up. "I'm making a trip to the punch bowl. Refills, anyone?"

The Blondies all raised their empty glasses, with the exception of Iason, who was still sipping his wine.

"What about the game?" Yousi murmured. "It's Omaki's turn."

"Ah, Omaki's turn!" Heiku gathered the glasses and went to the punch bowl, returning with the filled punch glasses balanced on his bionic arm rather precariously against his bare chest.

"Ask him how many Blondies he's had sex with," Xian suggested.

"Is every question going to be identical?" Iason sighed. "How tedious."

"Ah! Now we know what question Iason doesn't want to be asked!" Heiku exclaimed.

"A toast, a toast," Megala suggested, when Heiku handed him his punch glass.

"To what, Megala?" Omaki asked.

"I don't know. A toast to something," Megala replied sheepishly.

Xian snorted at this, leaning back in his chair and kicking the air for no particular reason.

"I like that. A toast to the Random Something," Omaki proclaimed, raising his glass.

"Here, here!" The Blondies all raised their glasses, with the exception of Raoul and Iason, who had both tired of the constant toasting.

"Some of us have already had a bit too much punch," Raoul remarked.

"What question shall we ask Omi?" Heiku pressed.

"Ask him if he was the one who put red dye in the faucets at the Academy," Megala prompted.

"Don't waste the question with that," Raoul protested. "Everyone knows that was Yousi."

"It was?" Megala looked surprised, as did Yousi.

"What did I do?" Yousi asked, perplexed.

"It was in the lotion," Heiku laughed. "You and I put gradual resolution red dye in the hand lotion at the twelfth-year residence hall before the yearly physicals. We were just second-years, if I recall correctly. The red dye only gradually appeared over the course of about a day. Anyone who'd used the lotion to masturbate was in for a surprise."

"Yousi said we'd caught them red-handed," Xian remembered, laughing.

Yousi furrowed his brow, trying to remember.

Omaki nodded. "That was one of your best pranks, Yousi."

"Headmaster Konami was so angry he spanked us in front of the entire section."

"Oh! I do remember that," Yousi said excitedly.

"I'm sure you do. I know I do," Heiku remarked, shaking his head. "It's hard to forget having your ass bared before the entire section and sobbing over the Headmaster's knee.

"I never saw those spankings!" Megala exclaimed.

"No, you were too busy peeping, no doubt," Omaki teased.

"What's Omi's question?" Xian asked. "His most erotic encounter?"

"That will do. Confess or undress, Omi. What was your most erotic encounter?" Heiku asked.

"That would be the time Yousi, Iason and I took that Aristian virgin," Lord Ghan replied.

"What's this?" Raoul, who had been deep in thought, was roused by the mention of Iason's name.

Iason looked mortified, uncrossing and crossing his legs.

"I answered the question," Omaki replied. "You didn't ask me to relate the encounter, just to name it."

Heiku turned to Yousi. "Do you remember that, Yousi?"

The Blondie shook his head. "I don't think so."

"Well, I know what Omi's next question is going to be," Xian said.

"It's Raoul's turn," Megala announced.

"I think we should ask if he enjoyed kissing Megala," Omaki said softly, his eyes shining impishly.

Megala looked horrified at this, looking toward Raoul as though afraid he would answer and say that he had *not* enjoyed it.

"Is that your question?" Raoul demanded.

"Yes. Confess or undress!" Heiku shouted, raising his glass as though toasting the notion.

166

"Confess or undress!" Xian, Yousi and Omaki raised their glasses in unison, draining them again, while Megala sat still, watching in wide-eyed horror.

Raoul untied a scarf that was fastened neatly around his neck, pulling it off and dropping it on the floor, a mysterious smile at his lips.

The Blondies cheered, though Heiku looked a bit grumpy. "I don't think his scarf should count as an article of clothing," he protested.

"Iason's next," Yousi called out merrily.

"Have him tell us about the Aristian," Xian suggested.

"I'd rather hear about Vosh Khosi," Omaki murmured.

"I have a better question," Heiku asserted. "Remember when the Commander's brother was visiting? Ambassador Anori Khosi? He stayed with Raoul at your penthouse while you were off in Urus. Of course we all know what they were probably up to. And then he was in that mysterious, fatal accident. So confess or undress, did you kill Anori Khosi?"

Although Heiku was mostly teasing, the look on Iason's face told him, and everyone there, the truth of the matter.

There was a moment of stunned silence as everyone exchanged curious glances.

Iason stared at his wine, frowning.

"I think I've had about enough of this game," Raoul remarked.

"Goodness," Omaki exclaimed. "Does Vosh know about that?"

"Of course he doesn't know," Xian guessed. "He wouldn't have been nearly so friendly with us if he had known."

"There's no reason why he should ever find out about it," Heiku pointed out.

"I'm sure I don't know what you're talking about," Lord Mink stated firmly.

Heiku nodded. "Yes, of course not."

"So this discussion is over," Raoul added.

"Quite right." Omaki stood up. "Perhaps I shall sing."

The Blondies groaned, some of them tossing their party favors at him in protest.

"Perhaps I shall dance, then."

"What about those blueprints, Megala?" Raoul asked.

"Oh! They're right here." Lord Chi reached down next to his chair and retrieved them, unrolling them. "This one is yours, Raoul. And this one is Iason's." He handed one of the blueprints to Lord Mink.

"Ah! I see fountains! These circles are fountains, am I right?" Raoul exclaimed happily.

"Yes, yes. There are twelve fountains in all in a huge outdoor/indoor garden."

"Splendid." Lord Am nodded his approval.

"What are these spirals?" Iason asked, pointing to his blueprints.

"Those are towers. I know how much you liked the Observatory I built for you."

"Very good," Iason nodded, pleased.

Omaki, Heiku and Xian had formed a kick line, all of them so drunk that they were snickering and giggling like schoolboys.

"Ow! You stepped on my foot, Ku-ku!" Xian complained.

"Omi," Heiku announced, "this is the best party ever."

"Here, here," Yousi said, raising his punch glass in a lone toast.

"THAT'S STRANGE," AYUDA REMARKED. "I'M PICKING UP an old Federation vehicle signal."

"Are you sure?" Odi asked, frowning. "I thought they got rid of all those."

Ayuda nodded. "They run on solar and irimathium. See?" He pointed to the readout. "That's definitely irimathium."

"There are other things that run on irimathium, aren't there? Like portable heaters and torches?"

"Yes, but not at these levels."

"That *is* odd," Odi agreed.

"The signal is increasing, which means it's getting closer."

"Which direction is it coming from?"

"I can't tell that. This unit only picks up the level of emission, not the location."

"I'll bet the 8900-X units do," Odi remarked. "We should have upgraded."

"That won't help us now."

"What's going on?" Freyn asked, as he and Askel approached them.

"We're picking up a Federation vehicle," Odi reported. "Did you find anything?"

"The villa seems clean," Askel answered. "We checked for cams and bugs and didn't find anything."

"A Federation vehicle?" Freyn frowned, bringing his hand up to his chin. "I didn't think there were any of those still around."

"Where would they even get the irimathium to run it?" Askel wondered. "It's illegal except in extremely low quantities."

Ayuda shook his head. "I haven't any idea. It must have been fueled ages ago and then just hidden somewhere for all these years."

"The signal is getting stronger," Odi murmured, pointing to the screen.

"It sure is," Ayuda agreed.

The bodyguards scanned the lake and the horizon but didn't see anything.

"This is getting worrisome. I'd better alert Iason." Odi pulled out his communicator, frowning when the unit failed to respond. "The bloody thing is jammed!"

"Mine is, as well," Ayuda reported.

"And mine," Askel confirmed.

Freyn shook his head, flipping his communicator closed. "This isn't good. I'll go inside and alert Iason and the others."

Ayuda pointed to the readout on his scanner, perplexed. "At these levels, it's practically on us!"

"I don't see anything," Odi replied, looking around him.

"Shit. It's freezing out here," Riki grumbled, shivering when he and Katze stepped outside.

"You got that right," Katze agreed.

"Riki, Katze! Get back inside!" Odi commanded, pointing towards the door.

The mongrel stopped, looking surprised. "Why? We were just coming to see what you all are up to."

"Just do it! We're having a security issue!"

"What sort of issue?" Katze asked, concerned.

"It's got to be here somewhere!" Ayuda shouted.

Suddenly a hovercraft appeared directly above them, settling down on the ground before them.

"A cloaking device," Ayuda hissed.

"Riki, go back inside!" Odi commanded.

"Come on, Riki," Katze urged, pulling his arm.

The bodyguards drew their weapons, aiming toward the hovercraft and firing the moment the door opened. Several individuals dressed in police-issue body armor and helmets jumped out of the vehicle, immediately returning fire.

Askel and Odi were both hit.

Riki stopped and turned back when Odi cried out.

"No, Riki," Katze ordered. "Leave him!"

"He's hit!"

"Riki. His mongrel pet," one of the strangers said, motioning toward Riki. The group moved toward Riki but Ayuda stopped them, managing to hit one of them with a laser through the throat. The man fell to the ground, dead.

The remaining men fired at Ayuda, bringing the bodyguard to his knees.

"No!" Riki cried.

"The mongrel, the mongrel!" one of the men shouted.

Katze stepped in front of Riki and took a laser through his chest, falling to his knees. The men seized Riki, injecting him with something.

"Not all of it!" one of the men hissed, knocking the injection to the ground.

Riki immediately fell unconscious and was carried back to the vehicle.

Odi, who had blacked out after being shot, now came to, just in time to see Riki put inside the vehicle and the hovercraft lift off and disappear.

"Riki," he whispered.

Chapter 07 – Qentu

"YOU STEPPED ON MY FOOT AGAIN," HEIKU complained, giving Xian a shove.

"You keep putting your foot in the way," Xian argued.

"What's that supposed to mean? I'm just putting it on the ground, where it's supposed to be!"

"But you're putting it on my side."

"Your side of what?!"

"My side of…of…the universe."

Omaki snorted at this, losing his balance and almost pulling Heiku and Xian down with him. The three Blondies had their arms around each other at the shoulders, attempting a sort of pathetic kick line that had degenerated into a comical rotation, with Heiku at the axis and Xian and Omaki on either side of him.

"For the love of Jupiter! Would you three please sit down?" Raoul growled.

"But we're performing," Lord Ghan protested, offering a feeble kick in the air that served to remind Heiku and Xian (who, being drunk, had both mostly forgotten why they were standing up together) that they ought to join in on the performance. Heiku, in an attempt to offer a synchronized kick, lifted his leg clumsily and succeeded in engaging the back of Raoul's chair, while Xian stepped on Heiku's other foot.

"Dammit, Xian!" Lord Quiahtenon yelped.

"They're drunk," Iason remarked.

"What a brilliant observation," Raoul snapped, crossing his legs grumpily.

Iason, a bit surprised at the Blondie's jab, gazed at him. "I beg your pardon?"

"Sorry," Lord Am muttered, looking away. He felt embarrassed to have lashed out at Iason, but as the party wore on, he found himself feeling increasingly uncomfortable. It was always this way when he was around Iason, but especially during gatherings like this, when he was reminded of the old days and how, at a party such as Omaki's infamous bash, he was guaranteed to have Iason in bed by the night's end.

He was aroused, and all he wanted was to drag Iason off to one of Omaki's bedrooms and give him the fucking of his life. He longed to feel his old partner quiver beneath him, to hear his breathy moan when the waves of consummation shuddered through him—to be alone with him, just for one more night. And it didn't help that Iason looked heavenly: as usual, dressed to the nines, in a tunic and pants cut tantalizingly, annoyingly close to his body, revealing his every muscle when he moved. The Blondie's soft white hair cascaded down his dark blue tunic, taunting him with its shiny softness. He wanted to run his hands through that hair, to breathe into it and let its scent wash over him—that wonderful, exquisite scent that only belonged to Iason Mink.

It didn't help, too, that Omaki had broadcast that holopic of Iason sprawled out naked on the bed, with that delightful little bell collar at his throat. He found he could not get the image out of his mind, much as he tried, and for once in his life he felt rather grateful to Lord Ghan for his incorrigible mischief.

Once, his thoughts drifted to Yui, and Raoul felt a momentary rush of comfort knowing that he would at least be able to expend his pent-up sexuality with his enthusiastic attendant-pet. But for all the fondness he felt for Yui—perhaps even a deeper stirring of his heart, something that bordered on a sort of love, even—he could not think of anything but Iason when he was around the Blondie. His body responded to his mere presence reflexively—his heart pounding faster, his stomach clenching, his groin demanding his attention and pushing the restraints of his trousers. And even more than the intense physical frustration he felt when around his old lover, Raoul felt the hollow ache of his heart. He still loved Iason. It would always be so. And knowing that Iason did not regard him in the same way—that his heart was, undeniably, wrapped around Riki—was his great torment.

"Are you ignoring me?"

"Hmmm?" Lord Am looked up, feeling the heat rush to his face when he realized that Iason was addressing him.

"I asked you what you thought of the blueprints."

"Oh! Yes, the blueprints," Raoul murmured, uncrossing and crossing his legs again. This movement caught Iason's notice and the Blondie lowered his gaze to Raoul's crotch, an amused smile quivering at his lips.

"Still worked up a bit over Megala's kiss, are we?" he teased.

"What! Of course not!" Raoul protested, his face reddening even more.

"Hmmm." Iason arched a golden white brow, giving Raoul a knowing look.

The look only served to unsettle poor Raoul further. "Blast it all, Iason! Quit toying with me!"

"I'm sure I don't know what you mean," Lord Mink protested, his eyes widening with genuine innocence. "How am I toying with you?"

"You…you keep…well, you know what you do! Quit giving me that look!"

"I assure you, I am not giving you any special look that I'm aware of. What sort of look do you mean, precisely?"

"The blueprints," Raoul said loudly, ignoring Iason's question entirely, "are most…most…acceptable."

"Ah. I agree entirely. Megala has outdone himself, I think."

"I especially like…the erm…the…the fountains."

"He says it shall take a year to complete," Iason remarked.

"A year! That long?"

"That's hardly surprising, I should think? They're both quite elaborate."

"I beg your pardon, Lord Mink?" Freyn stood waiting a few feet away from where Raoul and Iason were sitting, looking a bit troubled.

Iason turned to him, frowning. "Yes?"

"I think I should tell you that we're picking up some strange signals. High levels of irimathium. We believe it may be a Federation vehicle."

"I'm sorry, you'll have to speak louder or come closer. I can barely hear you over all this noise. I thought you said something about a Federation vehicle."

"That's right," Freyn confirmed, stepping forward anxiously. "We believe one is approaching the villa."

"What's this?" Raoul seemed to snap out of his reverie, his attention focused entirely on Freyn. "Did you say a Federation vehicle? And it's approaching us?"

"Yes, Lord Am."

"Omaki! Stop that blasted music! We've got a security issue here!"

Lord Ghan immediately saw from Raoul's tone of voice and expression that the Blondie wasn't joking. The music came to an abrupt end at Omaki's command, and everyone at the party turned to Freyn, who repeated his message.

"Our scanners indicate the vehicle—or whatever is—is approaching us."

"What makes you think it's a Federation vehicle?" Raoul pressed.

"High levels of irimathium, Sir. That's what we're picking up."

"How can that be?" Raoul and Iason exchanged puzzled looks.

In the next instant, a commotion was heard from outside—screaming, and the unmistakable hum of lasers firing. Iason leapt to his feet, his wine glass crashing to the floor. "Where's Riki?" he bellowed. "Daryl!"

Daryl came running across the floor, a look of pure terror on his face.

"Where's Riki?" Iason repeated.

"He went outside with Katze to look for Odi!"

Iason retrieved a laser from a concealed holster beneath his tunic and raced outside, Raoul just behind him with his own laser in hand.

"Wait, Iason!" Raoul pleaded, trying to slow Iason's pace. "You're the one they're after, surely! Don't walk into their trap!"

"That's right," Heiku said breathlessly, trying to catch up with them and shake off his intoxicated state.

Lord Mink, suddenly feeling instinctively that something was gravely wrong, ignored the Blondies and stepped outside, stopping in his tracks when he saw the scene before him. There were bodies on the ground—Katze, Askel, Ayuda, and Odi—and a fifth man he didn't recognize.

"Askel!" Freyn cried, running past him to his brother, who lay in an unnatural position on the ground as though he were dead.

"Riki?" Iason called, scanning the scene with a look of horror on his face. "Riki! Where are you?"

Daryl was already running to Katze, sobbing when he found his lover lifeless on the ground. "Oh, Katze!" he cried, falling to his side and putting a hand to the wound on the eunuch's chest in an attempt to stop the bleeding.

Odi groaned, his eyes fluttering open.

"Odi," Iason whispered, rushing to the guard and dropping to his knees.

"Ri...Riki," Odi murmured weakly.

Iason leaned closer, his eyes wide. "Where's Riki? Where is he, Odi?"

The bodyguard struggled to regain consciousness, looking at Iason intently, his mouth parting. "Took...took him," he gasped.

"Who? Who took him?" Iason cried, shaking him when Odi's eyes rolled back again.

"Don't....know."

"Here's one of them," Raoul remarked, giving the dead man a kick.

"Ayuda's dead," Omaki said, nudging the fallen bodyguard.

"No! No!" Toma collapsed at Ayuda's side, looking at the man's face with alarm and grief. All the pets and attendants, with the exception of Tai, had followed the Blondies outside, looking on at the unfolding scene with shock and confusion.

"He's not dead," Heiku announced, after scanning Ayuda's body. "But he's not far from it. We've got to get them all some medical attention NOW."

"I'll call Tanagura," Raoul offered, flipping open his phone.

"No. We don't have time to wait for them. We've got to take them directly to the hospital."

Iason, after trying unsuccessfully to rouse Odi again, stood up and rushed back inside the villa.

"How are we going to do that?" Omaki argued. "None of us can possibly drive. I can barely walk."

"I could try," Raoul offered.

"I can drive," Yui said, stepping forward. "Just put it on automatic."

"Any of us could drive on automatic," Raoul remarked. "So I'll drive."

"But if something goes wrong, you wouldn't be sober enough to switch to manual," Heiku pointed out. "You'd better let Yui do it. Besides," now Heiku's voice lowered as he gave Raoul a meaningful look, "Iason needs you."

A look of comprehension and urgency crossed Raoul's face. "Yes, of course," he murmured. "I'll go after him." He rushed back inside, leaving Yui staring after him.

Tai, who had come out of the kitchen with another tray of hors d'oeuvres and, finding the villa emptied, now appeared outside, his eyes wide with alarm when he saw his lover on the ground. "Odi! Odi!" He dropped the tray and hurried to him, turning to Yui. "What happened to him?"

"We don't know exactly," Yui answered. "We're getting ready to take them all to the hospital."

Tai looked around and saw the others on the ground but his attention almost immediately shifted back to Odi, who was mumbling something. He leaned close. "What? What is it?"

"What's he saying?" Xian asked, crouching down next to him.

Tai shook his head. "I don't know."

"He's delirious," Heiku commented. "Come on, let's get them all inside one of the vehicles. I'll need everyone's help."

IASON MADE FOR OMAKI'S TERMINAL, PUNCHING in Riki's identification and waiting impatiently for the locator to respond. When he saw the blinking light on the grid, he frowned, watching as it swiftly approached the Kattahar Mountains, the southern boundary of the territory monitored by Jupiter.

"You've got a reading?" Surprised, Raoul came up behind Iason, staring at the moving cursor in disbelief. "They didn't bother with an Interceptor. They're heading off the grid, though."

"I've got to go after them," Iason whispered, though he continued to gaze at the identifier, hoping it would not move off the grid as Raoul had predicted.

"How are you going to do that? They'll be in the Forbidden territory in a matter of seconds. You can't go after them."

"I'm going," Iason replied firmly.

"Even if you're not afraid of disobeying Jupiter, you wouldn't know where to go. And that's just what they want, Iason. They're baiting you. You won't be able to see them, but I'll wager they can see you. They'll be waiting for you."

"They have Riki," Iason whispered. "I have to go after them."

"They're not going to kill him," Raoul reasoned. "They're using him to get to you. They'll contact you with their demands soon enough."

Iason shook his head. "This is my fault. I was too lax with security."

"We all were. Blaming yourself isn't going to change anything."

"Raoul," Iason whispered, turning to the Blondie with a pleading look in his eyes. "Please help me. Please help me get Riki back."

Raoul gazed at the Blondie's face, contorted with grief and fear, and nodded. "I promise I'll do...whatever is possible."

Lord Mink looked away, then back at the grid. Riki's signal had disappeared. He slammed his fist onto the terminal, cracking the glass that covered the grid viewing area.

The other Blondies joined them as soon as the wounded were on their way to Tanagura Medical.

176

"Didn't get a reading?" Omaki asked, nodding toward the cracked terminal.

"We got one," Raoul answered. "But he's off the grid now. They're heading toward the Kattahar Mountains."

"Kattahar? Why would they go there?" Xian murmured, perplexed.

"I'll wager they're heading back into the old Federation territory," Omaki remarked. "Didn't Freyn say they were picking up irimathium signals, and that they thought it was a Federation vehicle?"

"I'm going after them," Iason announced.

"You can't go after them," Raoul repeated. "It's too dangerous. That's exactly what they want you to do."

"Jupiter won't like it if you cross into the Forbidden territory," Omaki added.

"I have to do something!" Iason snapped.

"None of us is in a state to do anything at the moment," Heiku argued, striding into the room. "We're lucky our attendants drank less than us. I can barely clear my mind enough to think about this."

"Perhaps we should call Headmaster Konami," Yousi suggested.

Heiku looked at him, nodding. "That's not a bad idea. We could use the voice of reason just now."

"I don't want him involved," Iason protested.

"You don't want him involved because you know he'll prevent you from doing anything to jeopardize your position," Raoul argued, putting his hand on Iason's shoulder. "Heiku's right. We'd better call him."

"You can't stop me from going after Riki," Iason hissed, shrugging off Raoul's touch angrily.

"Perhaps not, but the rest of us can," Heiku answered, motioning to the other Blondies. "You can't fight all of us, Iason."

Lord Mink looked at Heiku and then at the others, and then back to Raoul. Finally he sunk down in his chair, closing his eyes and bringing a hand to his forehead.

Raoul crouched down, putting a hand on the Blondie's knee. "We're trying to help you, Iason. We'll do everything we can to bring Riki back. I promise."

Heiku flipped open his phone, preparing to send an outgoing emergency beacon to Lord Sung.

"Are you encrypting that?" Omaki asked, motioning to his phone.

"No. The Headmaster never uses Independent channels, so I can't make a connection with an encrypted signal."

"It's just as well," Xian remarked. "This shows we're not trying to hide the situation from Jupiter."

"Perhaps we should inform Jupiter directly," Megala suggested, feeling a bit nervous about any situation that might not please Jupiter. Though he had only received a few lashes at the Public Whipping, he had found the whole affair excruciatingly painful and had no desire to provoke her wrath again.

"We can't," Raoul answered.

"I know we can't," Megala clarified. "I meant Iason. Iason should contact Jupiter directly."

"He can't either. Not directly, that is."

"Why not?" Heiku flipped his phone closed, frowning.

"Because of the Sentinels."

"The Sentinels?" The Blondies all exchanged confused looks.

"What in the hell is a Sentinel?" Omaki asked, voicing what all the others there were thinking.

Lord Am hesitated for a moment and then decided it was time to tell them. "We're not exactly sure. They seem to be some sort of...new Guardians for Jupiter."

"New Guardians? What do you mean?" Heiku pressed.

"Iason wasn't able to get through to Jupiter. There was...well, we thought it was an earthquake. At the Tower. Iason tried to contact Jupiter about it, but his access was blocked by a Sentinel."

"I felt that earthquake," Megala confirmed, nodding. "I spent the whole day making inspections, just to be sure the Tower was still stable. I was worried that—"

"Tell us about the Sentinel, Raoul," Xian interrupted.

"There's not much to tell. It—he—whatever it was, called himself Armeus, Sentinel One. He said there were five of them, in all, and that they were in charge of protecting Jupiter."

"But," Omaki protested, "that's what *we're* supposed to do."

Raoul shrugged. "You know as much as I do about it now."

"It's hardly surprising," Xian remarked. "I mean, after what happened. Jupiter doesn't trust us now."

"I'm calling Konami," Heiku announced, flipping his phone open again.

RIKI TRIED TO OPEN HIS EYES, BUT THE ROOM seemed to be spinning. He closed them again, wondering why he'd gotten so drunk. *I'd better get up. Iason will be pissed when he finds out I drank this much.*

Groaning, he forced his eyes open again, and then peered around the room in confusion. He was in a dark chamber, lit only with an eerie green light. It reminded him of Dana Burn, in some ways. Was he back at Dana Burn?

What was going on?

He tried to move, and immediately discovered that his wrists were manacled at his sides, and his ankles to some unseen restraint beneath him. He was lying face down on a thin mattress or bedroll of some kind, elevated off the floor.

"Ah. You're finally waking up. Good. I was worried they'd given you an overdose."

Riki jerked his head up, startled by the voice, and then simply opened his eyes wider, transfixed.

The man that stood before him was unlike any man he had ever seen before. He was as tall, and well-built, as a Blondie, but he was no Blondie—he had long, jet-black hair that hung past his waist, pale skin, and dark, gleaming eyes. He was dressed head-to-toe in black and silver, with a long dark cape and black gloves. His black, silver-trimmed thigh-high boots reminded him of the expensive, outlandish boots the Blondies often wore—only these seemed almost a parody of such footware; indeed, his whole ensemble seemed to resemble, or perhaps mock, the Blondie style of dress. If Riki had been in the state of mind to appreciate it, he would have also found the man quite attractive.

But he was not in that state of mind.

"Who the fuck are you?" Riki demanded.

"I am Amon Qentu. Perhaps you've heard of me?"

"Who?" Riki struggled against his restraints. "Hey! Let me go!"

"No? How disappointing. However, I'm certain you'll know my name by the time I'm through with you." Amon walked closer to him, and then slipped off one of his black gloves, running a warm finger down Riki's nearly naked body.

"Don't touch me," Riki hissed.

"There's not much you can do to stop me, is there?" Amon taunted. "It's been a long while since I had a truly good fuck. I hope you'll oblige me."

"Iason will kill you if you touch me!"

"Who? Iason, did you say? Ah, wonderful. So you are, in fact, Riki the Black."

"It's Riki the Dark, you idiot," the mongrel muttered and then fell silent. Suddenly he realized that it was Iason who Amon was after, and he had a horrible feeling that he'd just helped him, in some way, by confirming his identity.

Amon leaned against Riki's bed in a relaxed, comfortable fashion. He smiled down at the mongrel, running a hand down to his bared bottom. "I adore the message on your rump, Riki. Naughty pet. How charming." He gave him a slap on his ass.

"Fuck you," Riki growled.

"You're quite the rebel. Just as I've heard. Perhaps you'd like to be my pet. I've always wanted one, you know." Amon reached out and stroked the side of Riki's face. The mongrel responded to this by snapping at him, though Amon jerked his hand away, narrowly escaping a nasty bite.

"Naughty pet, indeed." With that, Amon gave Riki a rather hard backhand, so hard that it left Riki reeling. The mongrel tasted blood in his mouth and he closed his eyes, sighing. He wasn't looking forward to whatever was in store for him.

"Of course, I'll be filming everything we do," Amon continued. "I can't resist teasing Iason a bit. You're sure he never mentioned me?"

Riki refused to answer, trying to remember if he ever had heard the name Amon Qentu before. Something about it was familiar....

"Minas Qentu," Riki answered finally. "I've heard of that."

Amon seemed legitimately pleased with this answer. "Yes, that's right. That was named after my grandfather, who discovered it. Perhaps you've heard of the Qentu Mountains?"

"No."

"The Kattahar Mountains, then? You've heard of them, surely?"

"Yes," Riki answered, after a pause.

"The Kattahar Mountains used to be called the Qentu Mountains. They still are, as far as I'm concerned."

"Whatever," the mongrel shrugged. He wasn't in the mood for the discussion, and he was starting to panic. He knew he was in trouble. And if Iason came after him, the Blondie would be in trouble, too.

"The Federation was run by the Qentu family. That was before Jupiter shut us down. You're a mongrel. Surely you remember that Davith Qentu led the revolt against Jupiter."

"Thanks for the history lesson. Can I go now?"

Amon smiled, crossing his arms on his chest. "You don't seem to understand. You won't be going anywhere, at least until your Master comes to get you."

"He won't come," Riki asserted quickly.

"I think he will," Amon replied. "From what I've heard, he's willing to risk everything to keep his little mongrel, including his position as Head of the Syndicate."

"What do you want?"

"I thought I made that clear. I want Iason Mink."

"Why?" Riki pressed.

"That should be obvious. He's Jupiter's favorite, is he not?"

Riki snorted. "You're an idiot. Either that or you don't have good informants."

Amon narrowed his eyes at this. "What do you mean?"

"Are you kidding me? You don't know about the Public Whippings?"

Amon shrugged as though uninterested, though he frowned, wondering what the mongrel was referring to.

"Iason was publicly whipped for sedition against Jupiter," Riki answered.

"You're lying."

"I'm not! I can't believe you don't know this! All of Tanagura and Midas has been in an uproar since it happened!"

Amon fell silent, considering. He knew something had been going on in the cities lately, but he—or at least his men—had assumed it was Jupiter's Festival and the Trade Convention with Alpha Zen. It had been impossible until recently to even approach Tanagura, there had been so much heavy security. And before that there had been the visit from Commander Voshka Khosi of Alpha Zen, which had made it impossible to get anywhere near the Eos Tower. All their signals had been jammed because the airwaves were being monitored by the Tanagura Police, who put out a large-scale signal barrier around the city limits to avoid interception from foreign airspace. And recently there had been a new signal barrier, one that confused Amon. The signal carried a message: Access Forbidden by the Sentinels.

It was only by pure chance that his men had tried to penetrate Tanagura from the west, just as Iason's vehicle was making for Lake Erphanes. They'd planned an impromptu attack without even knowing exactly what Iason and the other Blondies were doing there. Nearly all of his men had been wounded, though not seriously—though one unfortunate man had been killed. Again, by sheer luck, they'd managed to identify and capture Iason's infamous mongrel pet, Riki, escaping before they lost any more lives.

But Riki, he knew, was a trouble-maker. Most likely he was lying to him. Even if he wasn't, Iason was still Head of the Syndicate, wasn't he?

"You can't outwit me, mongrel," Amon answered, finally. He unclasped his cloak-pin, letting the dark cape swirl to the floor. He unfastened his pants, drawing out his cock, and then with Blondie-like grace, he straddled Riki, grabbing a handful of his hair with his hand.

"Get off me!"

Amon penetrated, giving a low laugh as he did so. "Ah, I can see why Iason keeps you. What a nice, tight hole you have, Riki. Tight, but accommodating, I should say. The Blondie has certainly broken you in."

"Bastard!" Riki gasped, wincing when Amon slid completely inside him without hesitation. Amon clenched his buttocks and thrust his pelvis forward, forcing himself in even deeper.

"Don't try to pretend you're not enjoying this." Amon turned to the side, as though addressing some unseen audience, undulating his body slowly as he forced his cock deep inside the mongrel and then out again, in and out, a smile at his lips. "I'm enjoying your little mongrel, Iason. I'll be fucking him, just like this, until you're ready to come and get him. Surely you know where I am. But in case you don't, I'm at the Qentu estate, west of the Qentu Mountains. I'll send along the coordinates for you, if you like. But don't try to bring anyone else along. If you do, I'll be forced to kill Riki. I'll torture him first, of course."

Riki bit his lip to keep from crying out. Why did it hurt so much? Surely this man was no bigger than Iason. But it felt as though his entire backside was filled with Amon, and Amon's cock felt hot, unnaturally so. And it burned.

Amon leaned forward, lowering his voice. "That's one hundred percent real man you're feeling. No genetic manipulation. I may not be as long as a Blondie, but I'll wager I'm twice as wide. Stings a bit, doesn't it?"

The mongrel made no answer, trying desperately to relax his muscles to ease the pain. He felt torn, and the warm wetness he felt was probably his own blood.

Amon leaned forward again, this time whispering in his ear. "Now I've got you, Riki. I'll make you come for me. Feels better now, I think?" As if to prove his point, Amon moved slowly against him, the lubrication of Riki's blood now making the movement decidedly erotic.

Despite himself, Riki shivered, annoyed when he felt a flush of interest in his groin as his own cock sprang to life. He swallowed, closing his eyes.

Amon sat up, laughing again. He turned back toward his unseen audience. "I wish you could see this. He's positively quivering beneath me."

The man threw his head back, his long dark hair brushing against Riki's thighs.

I won't come, Riki told himself. I can control this. He tried to think of unappealing, horrible things, tried to ignore the rising pressure inside him. He gasped when Amon pulled his head back again by the hair, this time forcing his head to turn. Riki then saw the small holo-recorder mounted on a tripod. That was the first time he saw that there was another man in the room, as well.

He strained, trying to hold back.

Amon snaked his body artfully against him, seeming to be perfectly in control of his every movement. He was smiling, watching the mongrel try to fight the inevitable. "Closeup on the mongrel's face," Amon commanded.

"Yes, Sir," the man answered, zooming in to Riki's face.

Riki tried to mask any sort of reaction, but there was no hiding completely the moment of his release. His lips twitched and his eyes involuntarily closed as pleasure shot through his body.

Amon thrust a few more times, eagerly. "Yes. Do you see your pet responding to me, Iason? He likes me, I think." He made a long, breathy hiss, ramming his cock once more deep inside the mongrel as he ejaculated. After a long moment, he turned back to the holo-recorder, grinning. "You'd better hurry, Iason. I have quite an appetite for sex. I'll be ready again in less than an hour." Amon nodded at the man behind the recorder. "Cut the transmission."

Lord Sung smiled as Aertis talked excitedly about the dig. His enthusiasm was infectious; indeed, not since Iason Mink had attended the Academy had the Headmaster been so interested in archeology.

"I can hardly wait for morning. Can we get up right away?"

"Somehow I doubt I could stop you," Konami laughed.

"I'm getting hot. That tent heater is really powerful," Aertis remarked.

"I'll turn it down," the Headmaster answered, reaching over to switch the heater to low.

"I hope you don't mind if I take my tunic off." Without waiting for an answer, the beautiful young Blondie stripped off his tunic, revealing his delightfully sculpted upper body.

The Headmaster could hardly take his eyes away from the sight of young Aertis, though he finally forced himself to concentrate on the map that the Blondie had sprawled out on the floor of the tent. He felt his face flush crimson when his groin instinctively tightened in response to the Blondie's bared upper body. He felt ashamed of himself.

"Is something wrong, Headmaster?" Aertis frowned, studying him.

"No," Konami lied, embarrassed.

"I'm keeping you up. You must be exhausted." Aertis stood up, unfastening his pants and slipping out of them before the Headmaster could protest. "I hope you don't mind, but I prefer to sleep in the nude."

Lord Sung stared at him, his gaze running up and down the Blondie's naked body. He almost winced, Aertis was so handsome.

"Aertis," he whispered.

"Hmmm?" The Blondie looked at him with wide, completely unknowing eyes, unaware of the effect he was having on the Headmaster.

Lord Sung opened his mouth to ask Aertis to put his clothes back on, but somehow he couldn't bring himself to do so. He nodded toward the lantern. "Turn it off. We have a long day ahead of us tomorrow."

"Yes, of course, Headmaster." Aertis lay down on his bedroll, and then held up a small pen-light. "Would you very much mind if I continued to look at the map? This won't make much light."

The Headmaster grunted his assent, pretending to straighten his sleeping place. Unlike Aertis, he chose to remain fully clothed, except for his cloak, which he had discarded when they first entered the tent. He pulled the covers over himself and then closed his eyes, pretending to sleep.

It wasn't long before he peeked at Aertis, his heart beating fast when he realized he could still see the Blondie's nakedness in the blue glow of the pen light. Aertis had put on a pair of headphones and was listening to music, nodding his head to the beat of a song.

184

Konami's hand slid to his pants instantly, and in the next instant he had unfastened them, gently coaxing his cock out. He allowed himself the luxury of imagining himself between the Blondie's legs, giving him a deliciously forbidden suck. He felt guilt and excitement at his fantasy, stroking himself faster.

He almost groaned with disappointment when Aertis shifted position onto his stomach, but when the Blondie positioned his pen light in a pocket up high in the tent, he nearly lost his seed at the sight of the young student's ass. Aertis was facing away from him, his legs slightly spread. Lord Sung could see every curve of his ass, and a part of him—a deviant, usually well-repressed part—had an urge to mount him right then and there. He stifled an instinctive moan, though he couldn't quite control his breathing, and he was glad Aertis was listening to music, or he would have certainly heard the Headmaster's hand pumping vigorously beneath the covers.

I should stop, he told himself. But he couldn't stop. His eyes were open wide as he imagined himself sliding inside Aertis, giving him a good, hard fuck. He imagined Aertis resisting him, having to slap a hand over his mouth, and this thought stimulated him even further.

I must have him! Konami was beside himself with lust. And he was burning up. He flung the covers from his body, forgetting his need to hide what he was up to, and, unable to stop, even when Aertis turned toward him with a questioning look, he ejaculated, his semen arching to his thigh.

Mortified, he stared back at Aertis. The Blondie looked surprised, his gaze lowering to the Headmaster's groin.

Konami grabbed his covers and quickly covered his body. "Jupiter help me," he whispered.

Slowly Aertis removed his headphones, his eyes wide with confusion.

"Please forgive me," Konami whispered. "I beg you to forgive me. I hadn't intended for you to see that."

It took a moment for Aertis to fully comprehend what had just taken place. "It's all right," he said softly. "We all have needs."

"We do, but I have crossed the line, Aertis. I confess, I'm rather...dangerously attracted to you. That is why I almost refused your request to come here with you."

"Oh," Aertis breathed. "I see."

"And then when you...undressed...I'm sorry, I just couldn't resist."

Aertis sat up, pulling his covers over his nakedness. "How foolish of me! I should have realized!"

Lord Sung closed his eyes, bringing a hand to his head. "I should be punished."

The young Blondie was silent for a moment, the full implications of the situation starting to sink in. "You're...attracted to me?"

"Yes, I'm afraid so. This is madness! I shouldn't have agreed to come here!"

"But you didn't really do anything," Aertis protested softly. "You just relieved yourself. There's no law against that."

"If I hadn't done that, I don't know that I could have controlled myself."

"You would have," Aertis said solemnly. "Everyone knows that...about you." Aertis smiled gently at the Headmaster, finding the Blondie's confession of his attraction to him strangely flattering.

Konami shook his head. "Before you, I would have agreed. But...there's something about you, Aertis."

Aertis, for all his obedience to Jupiter, was so moved by Konami's confession that he almost felt like giving himself up to the Headmaster. He clutched the covers around his body but wanted to let them drop away. He couldn't help but wonder what it would be like to lie with Lord Sung. At the thought, his cheeks flushed pink.

"I've embarrassed you," Konami whispered.

"No," Aertis protested. He looked down at the Headmaster and then made a decision. He let his cover fall away. "Take me, if you like." He was kneeling, his thighs apart and his buttocks resting back on his heels, his cock not altogether flaccid.

A flash of excitement and disbelief filled Lord Sung's eyes, followed quickly by anger. "What are you saying? Don't debase yourself because of my folly. Shame on you, Aertis!"

The Headmaster was glad he'd just released, or he would have found the Blondie's offer irresistible.

"But I thought," Aertis whispered, his brow furrowed with confusion. "I thought...this is what you wanted."

"It doesn't matter what I want! Jupiter's Sake, cover yourself, Aertis!"

But Aertis, who had always thought of Headmaster Konami as a mentor, underwent a sort of transformation there in the tent on Minas Qentu. If Lord Sung was capable of unspeakable, carnal desires, than he need not hide his own any longer. He'd been tormented with his own shameful thoughts for years now. And he could think of no one else that he'd rather share his lust with than Konami Sung. He reached down and began stroking his cock.

"St...stop that," Konami pleaded, his gaze lowering.

"No one will know," Aertis answered, a small smile quivering at his lips. "You didn't bring the robotic chaperone, I noticed."

"No, I didn't," the Headmaster admitted. Had it been intentional? Had he secretly been hoping for such a moment with the young Jin? Aertis was right. Technically, no one would know what they did together on Minas Qentu, even if some might speculate about the two of them being alone together on an excavation. "But we shouldn't. You know we shouldn't."

"We're the only Blondies in all of Eos who don't fornicate, Headmaster."

"That's not true," Lord Sung protested, though he had a feeling Aertis was right.

"I know we should obey Jupiter. I know you want to as much as I do. But now that you've confessed your desires to me, I have a confession of my own. I long for sex. I dream of it, every night. I want to penetrate, and to be penetrated. I want to feel a hot mouth around my cock. I want to taste salt...your salt, Headmaster. I want—"

Konami bolted upright, and in the next instant the Blondies were kissing, then rolling down around the floor, their passion escalating. Aertis helped Lord Sung out of his tunic, kissing his chest and suckling his nipples while the Headmaster removed his pants with shaking hands.

"This is wrong, this is wrong," Konami moaned, when Aertis flipped him onto his stomach.

"I know it is. We shall punish each other...later."

The Headmaster clung to this thought, that they could perhaps redeem themselves for their transgressions through a sound discipline session later. "Yes," he whispered. "We must be punished for this."

"I want to be inside you," Aertis hissed, spitting on his hand.

"Aertis," Lord Sung pleaded. "Please don't."

"You want it. I'll fuck you, and then you can do as you will with me." Aertis inserted a finger inside the Headmaster's rectum, slowly thrusting.

Unaccustomed to the stimulation, Konami gasped, closing his eyes. He knew he should make Aertis stop. But he just couldn't.

"What does that feel like?" Aertis whispered.

"Good...Jupiter help me, it feels so good."

"And this?" Aertis kissed his shoulder as he penetrated him.

Konami shuddered, as did Aertis.

"I can't stop now," Aertis warned, thrusting. "Oh, Konami. Oh! Great Mother!"

"Go ahead. Fuck me hard," the Headmaster encouraged, finally giving into the moment. "Fuck me, Aertis!"

"Mmmm, Headmaster! What are you doing? That's...that's...oh, it feels so good!"

Konami's head was swimming. He couldn't believe he was indulging in such forbidden pleasures, but at the moment he didn't care. He loved the sound of the Blondie's cries of pleasure. And despite having released just moments before, he was aroused again.

As soon as Aertis climaxed, the Headmaster bucked the young Blondie off him and then flipped him onto his stomach, penetrating him while Aertis was still recovering. His own cock was still wet from his own semen, and slid quickly into the Blondie. Konami groaned as he felt the tight resistance giving way to his demanding entry.

It was a moment he'd fantasized about so many times that he almost knew exactly how it would play out. Aertis cried out as Konami pumped him hard—far harder than he should have, he knew—and in that moment the Headmaster lost all control of a lifetime of teachings that had been drilled into him since birth—teachings that warned him what he was doing was absolutely, incontrovertibly wrong.

He didn't care. He glorified in the pleasure, thrusting like a wild animal, grunting and hissing and, finally, calling out the young Blondie's name as he ejaculated, his entire body shuddering with the waves of pleasure that came with it.

He lay on top of Aertis, breathing hard, suddenly aware of a strange sound. Was it a beeping?

His gaze moved toward the entrance to the tent, where he'd left his phone. The device was blinking red with an emergency incoming beacon.

Chapter 08 ~
Jason's Decision

LORD SUNG FUMBLED WITH HIS PHONE, HIS mind racing. At first, he assumed the worst: Jupiter knew what he was up to, and was summoning him! She was probably watching them both in the tent at that very moment! He was to be publicly whipped for fornication; he would be disgraced before all of Tanagura, for his unforgivable indiscretion with a student....

He let out a sigh of relief when he saw the call was from Heiku Quiahtenon. "Yes?" he answered, glancing nervously at Aertis, who smiled back at him reassuringly.

"Headmaster. Sorry to disturb you, but we have a situation. There's been a strike against us, here at Lake Erphanes. Riki—Iason's pet? He's been abducted. We're not sure by who, but we think it may be Federation-related. The truth of the matter is, we're out here at Omaki's villa, and none of us are in a state of mind to think clearly about this. We've all been drinking. Could you come and help us out?"

Konami almost instantly switched into full Headmaster mode, standing up in the tent and pacing, his eyes narrowing as he digested the situation. "What do you mean, a strike? And why are you all drinking, for heaven's sake? You're saying you're all too drunk to deal with this? And who, exactly, is there?"

"Our security was attacked outside the villa—Iason's bodyguards, I mean. They slammed us hard—all the bodyguards, but for one, were hit. We sent them to Tan Med. We were...just unwinding a bit, having a small bash. The gang, that is."

"The gang? Meaning?"

"Omaki, Iason, Raoul, Megala, Xian, Yousi...and myself."

"Leave it to the lot of you to come up with a ridiculous way to spend the evening, drinking and carrying on like you were still at the Academy!"

"Yes, Headmaster," Heiku murmured. "We know it was foolish. We all just needed an evening away from Eos."

189

"I see." Lord Sung sighed, running a hand through his hair. "What were you saying, then? They've taken Riki?"

"Yes. We tracked them on the grid—via Riki's tracer. They were heading over the mountains into the Forbidden territory. Of course, Iason wants to go after them."

"I hope you dissuaded him of that ridiculous notion!"

"Yes, yes. He's very upset with us. You know how he is…about Riki."

"All right. I'm on my way now. I'm coming from Minas Qentu and," now the Headmaster paused, glancing at Aertis, who was leaning back on his elbows, making no effort to hide his admiration of Lord Sung's nakedness, "I'll be bringing a student with me. We're…here on an excavation."

"Yes, Sir. Thank you, Headmaster."

"Right." Lord Sung terminated the call, turning to regard Aertis for a moment. "There's an urgent situation I must attend to."

"Yes, I gathered that. How disappointing. I was rather hoping for another round." Aertis smiled, gesturing with his head to his groin, where a second erection was obviously maturing.

"Aertis," the Headmaster sighed. "This…this was a horrible mistake. I was very wrong to take advantage of you."

"You didn't take advantage," the young Blondie protested. "I wanted you to fuck me. I want you to fuck me again. Right now."

Lord Sung shivered, drinking in the sight of his favorite student. Aertis looked so beautiful, his long blond hair trailing behind him, his perfectly sculpted, naked body sprawled out suggestively, his cock springing to life again. The Headmaster felt a tightening in his own groin, just looking at him. This was a moment he had been fantasizing about for ages, and now he was being called away from it. Even though he knew how very wrong their sexual congress had been, in truth, he felt like pouncing on Aertis again. They had already stepped over the line; why not fornicate all night long? And then they would most definitely stop. He would absolutely insist on it. Then, they would have to discuss what disciplinary action would be taken for their shameful liaison.

But no; they couldn't do that. Heiku and the others were waiting for him.

He shook his head. "We should go."

Aertis sensed his ambivalence, a slow, provocative smile creeping onto his face. He reached down and coddled his erection, slowly, noting

190

Lord Sung's burgeoning arousal as he did so. "We'll be fast," he whispered. "Suck me, Headmaster."

Lord Sung swallowed hard, shaking his head. "No."

"Suck me, and I'll suck you."

"Aertis," the Headmaster scolded, biting his lip. "Stop that."

Aertis ignored him, flipping over onto his hands and knees and spreading his legs apart. He looked back over his shoulder. "Fuck me, then. I know you want to. Come on. Give it to me good. Ram me."

The Headmaster caught his breath at the sight of Aertis so enticingly positioned. His heart was beating hard. His organ, which had been slowly betraying his renewed interest, now went completely rigid, jutting out from him in undeniable readiness. But he remained standing, frozen with indecision.

His mind told him a second round wasn't even an option—he needed to leave at once. But he had never before faced such temptation. And Aertis was…simply irresistible.

"Stick your tongue up my ass," Aertis demanded. "Please, Headmaster."

Lord Sung closed his eyes, fighting back the carnal impulses that threatened to break his composure once again. He reached down and snatched his tunic from the floor of the tent. "I'm getting dressed now."

But Aertis was not so easily put off. He stood up, grabbing the Headmaster's wrist as he attempted to kiss him.

Lord Sung dropped his tunic but turned his head to the side, wincing. "No, Aertis. Please."

Aertis slipped a hand around the Headmaster's engorged cock, his fingers squeezing and rubbing over the taut skin. "How about that?" he taunted. "That feels good, doesn't it?"

Lord Sung was silent, his eyes closing as powerful sensations slammed through his body. Just that small bit of erotic touching was enough to nearly drive him wild with carnal need. Aertis was merciless in his artistry, fondling him intimately in a manner suggestive of his own experience, his manipulations hinting at a deep familiarity with the pleasures that could be garnered from a cooperative and skilled hand.

He realized then that Aertis, like himself, had spent many an hour in masturbatory exile, and knew exactly how to work an erection to achieve maximum pleasure, slowing down every now and then to thwart a premature ingress toward his ascent.

The Headmaster now felt paralyzed, completely unable to stop the young Blondie's overtures. When Aertis dropped to his knees, his eyes flew open. He watched with unblinking eyes, instinctively panting when the young student nuzzled affectionately against his cock and then worked his tongue down Konami's length, drawing a wet, erotic design along his engorged flesh.

Then Aertis looked up at him, his seductive, vibrant blue eyes glimmering with lust, and opened his mouth, admitting his cock with deliberate leisure. He suckled him and then took him into his throat, the Headmaster's length disappearing into the young Blondie's mouth.

"Ohhh," Lord Sung moaned, his hands on the young student's shoulders. He intended to push Aertis away, but instead he found himself arching into his mouth, unable to resist the pleasurable sensations that such instinctive positioning afforded him.

He spread his legs a little further apart, thrusting his pelvis forward as he offered himself without reservation, sinking a bit deeper into the hot, welcoming wetness of his mouth. He wiggled a bit when he hit the back of Aertis' throat, probing excitedly with his cock, his need to fuck now overtaking him, compelling him to move, to explore, to thrust.

He had handfuls of the young Blondie's silky-soft hair in his hands, as he fucked him full in the mouth. His entire body was quivering as the handsome young Blondie serviced him. Konami found that he could not stop, could not extricate him from the situation as he knew he should.

He was breathing hard, dangerously close to losing control.

"Lie back," he commanded finally, withdrawing abruptly and giving Aertis demanding push.

Aertis did so immediately, offering his own erection eagerly as Lord Sung repositioned himself and began suckling him.

"Oh, Headmaster!" Aertis cried. He was far more vocal in his appreciation of the pleasures of fellatio than Lord Sung had been, gasping and whimpering with every circuit, every wiggle of Konami's tongue.

The Headmaster relished the moment, giving Aertis a very slow, sensual exploration with his mouth and tongue. He no longer was even thinking about Heiku's call or the urgent matter that awaited him at Lake Erphanes. All he cared about, at that moment, was pleasuring Aertis.

"I'm on fire!" Aertis exclaimed. "I'm about to ejaculate!"

Lord Sung immediately pulled away, gifting him with a smoldering look. "Not yet. Get on your hands and knees. Exactly as you did before, with your legs spread wide apart."

Aertis bit his lip, trying to rein in his impulse to release, and then obliged him, turning over onto his hands and knees and happily offering

192

himself, his thighs spread apart wide, as Lord Sung had commanded. He started to look behind him and then gasped, losing all sense of place and time when the Headmaster began his lingual explorations.

Konami buried his face in the young boy's ass, his tongue squeezing up inside him with merciless enthusiasm.

"Jupiter help me! Oh, Headmaster!" Aertis arched his back and wiggled back eagerly against Lord Sung's tongue, his eyes rolling back as he enjoyed the ecstasy of the Blondie's pleasuring arts. "I can't wait anymore, please! I'm going to come!"

"Not yet," the Headmaster hissed. He repositioned himself again, entering Aertis from behind, one hand reaching under the boy to give his cock some much-appreciated attention.

"Oh, yes! Fuck me! Fuck me, Headmaster!"

The Headmaster did so with relish, releasing a long, anguished groan as his massive organ sunk into the submissively-positioned Blondie.

"Now Aertis," he commanded. "*Now* you can come."

Aertis immediately began crying out, a high-pitched, desperate sound that in any other situation would have been mistaken as a cry of pain. But at that moment, the young Blondie felt nothing but pleasure, the sound of his rapture filling the Headmaster with a deep sense of satisfaction.

"Yessss," Lord Sung whispered, as he snaked his body against him. "I love the sound of your pleasure. Don't hold back, Aertis."

Aertis could only offer a strangled cry in response as his semen burst from him, shooting onto the covers beneath them. At that moment he began twitching against the Headmaster, rhythmically squeezing his cock.

"Aertis, Aertis," Lord Sung murmured. "I'm in complete heaven! Get down on your elbows! I'm going to give you a hard fucking now."

Aertis allowed the Headmaster to do just that, breathing deeply and erratically as he recovered from his own release, his face resting on his arms, which were completely on the floor of the tent, his ass high in the air behind him.

Konami rocked against him violently, delighting in the exquisite pleasure of the young Blondie's twitching grip, which only seemed to increase in intensity the harder he fucked him. So he thrust with all his might, lifting his hips and setting him down again as he repositioned himself and pulled back impatiently on the Blondie's hips.

Aertis' submission was perfect; he allowed Konami to do as he would, without resistance.

He was searching for something without even knowing exactly what, but once he'd shifted to a certain position, the Blondie's grip suddenly intensified, squeezing him mercilessly and magnifying his enjoyment beyond bearing.

Konami slowed, feeling his ascent, held back for so long, finally break free. It spiraled up in him quickly, flooding him with glorious sensations, sensations unlike anything he had ever felt before. It was building, pushing him toward an even greater pleasure, one that he could not, now, deny himself.

"Jupiter forgive me," he whispered, and then he let loose another groan, one of intense pleasure as he enjoyed the unparalleled satisfaction of sexual rapture.

Afterwards, he collapsed next to Aertis, his arms finding the young Blondie and pulling him close.

"We must never do that again," he said sadly, his voice breaking with emotion.

"I know," Aertis answered. "I'm sorry, Headmaster. I know I seduced you."

"Yes, you did," Lord Sung sighed. "But I'm much more to blame. I'm in a position of authority. I should have restrained myself."

"Headmaster?" Aertis whispered, after a long moment.

"Yes?"

"I'm not so sure we can stop this, now that we've started."

Lord Sung closed his eyes, the same thought already in his mind. "We must stop, Aertis. This could ruin us both."

"Suppose no one ever found out? It could just be...our little secret."

"No," the Headmaster answered firmly. "It would be risking far too much. And we'll have to be punished, for what we've done."

"How can we be punished without telling anyone?"

"We'll go to Xanthus Kahn. I won't relate all the details, but I'll let him know we both must take some physical discipline for a serious transgression. He may guess what it's all about, but he won't tell anyone about it. I've been to him once before."

Aertis was surprised. "You have? For...this same thing?"

"Oh no. Goodness, no. I went to him," now Lord Sung hesitated a moment, for he had never shared this secret with anyone else before, "about a year ago. It had to do with a matter of...deception, actually. Something I was hiding from Jupiter. Xanthus didn't know the exact reason I needed to be punished, but he obliged me, and gave me 50 strikes with a cane."

"Ouch."

The Headmaster turned to Aertis, looking serious. "You know we're in for far worse punishment than that, for what we've done."

The young Blondie stared back at him, fear in his eyes. "Must we be punished?"

Konami nodded. "Yes, we must. You know we must. It must be severe enough that neither of us will want to risk ever doing this again."

Aertis frowned, sliding a hand down the Headmaster's chest to his abdomen. "I'm afraid I'll still want to be with you again. Now that I know what it's like."

Lord Sung took hold of Aertis' hand, shaking his head. "This ends now, Aertis. Right now. We're both getting dressed now. I'll have to find another sponsor for you, for your dig. I can't be trusted alone with you again. And from here on out…I must insist you not come to visit me in my chambers."

"But…I have feelings for you," Aertis protested.

"Hush. Don't say such things."

"But it's true. And I know you feel the same way."

The Headmaster shook his head. "This is impossible. Surely you know this. It was very wrong of us to give into such wayward desires."

"I'm going to seduce you again," Aertis threatened. "I'll come to your office and close the door behind me. You won't be able to resist me, when I show myself to you. I know your weakness now."

Lord Sung quickly sat up, pushing him away as he reached for his clothes. He found he was trembling. "That's enough. This conversation is over. Now, get dressed," he said sharply.

Aertis slipped on his tunic, slowly buttoning it. "You can have me punished and try to push me away, but I'm not going to be able to just forget what we just shared, as though it didn't even happen."

"I forbid you to bring this up again, Aertis!"

"But—"

"Enough! Hurry up, we need to go, now!"

The Headmaster dressed hurriedly, refusing to look at the young Blondie, who watched him the entire time, a look of despair on his face. He stood up, unfastening the door to the tent. The cold air whipped inside, chilling them both.

"But, Headmaster—"

Lord Sung turned and gave Aertis a hard backhand across the face. "I told you, enough!"

Stunned, Aertis brought a hand to his cheek, though he said nothing.

The Headmaster felt foolish for having struck Aertis, after everything they had just shared, but he was at his wit's end, and the Blondie's threat to seduce him again had him worried. He knew he wouldn't be able to resist his advances again. He had to put an end to the matter, then and there.

He took a deep breath, setting his jaw with resolve. "I realize you may harbor feelings for me. You're young. But I assure you, I feel nothing for you, other than a strong physical attraction. I was momentarily distracted by your sexual appeal. But what happened tonight will never happen again, Aertis."

Aertis listened to these words in shock, his hurt written clearly on his face.

Lord Sung turned away, stepping out of the tent into the cold of the night. He felt horrible for what he'd just said, and for striking Aertis, but he felt it was absolutely necessary. He couldn't give the Blondie any encouragement, not even the slightest bit. It didn't matter what was truly in his heart; he knew, without the smallest shadow of a doubt, that he was in love with Aertis. But he could never let him know that.

Aertis followed him outside, his face burning, and his mind a turmoil of emotions. He felt confused and rejected. After a few hours of wondrous intimacy, the Headmaster had suddenly shut him out. He could feel a great wall rise up between them, something that had never been there before. Lord Sung's threat that they had to cease all contact filled him with despair. Especially now, after they had spent such an amazing night together on Minas Qentu, now he was barred from even stopping by his office?

Hurt, and now a little angry, the young Blondie stared at the Headmaster's back, deciding that he was not going to be so easily put off. So what if Lord Sung forbade any future contact? Aertis would visit him anyway. Even if his hurtful remarks were true and the Headmaster didn't have feelings for him—other than sexual feelings—Aertis intended to take advantage of his obvious inability to resist him. He would seduce Konami again. It was only a matter of time…and place.

"COMMANDER?"

Voshka, who was dressed head to toe in his finest military garb and on his way to the bridge, turned to Anders without slowing his pace. "Yes?"

"Might I have a moment, Sir?"

"Can it wait? We're about to approach Alpha Zen. I don't want to miss it. We should be there within the hour."

Anders fell into step with him, frowning. "It's about the book that Aranshu was carrying. You ordered a translation? I thought we might discuss the matter in private."

The Commander stopped in the middle of the corridor, looking around him to be sure they were alone. "You found something?"

"Yes. Our original assessment was correct. These logs detail a way to deactivate Jupiter." Anders held out the translation, along with the original log book.

Voshka took the translation, thumbing though it. "Are you sure?"

"I only had one of the University scholars look at it, because of the sensitivity of the issue. But he said there was no doubt about it. The logs are very specific. They were written five years ago by someone with access to the Amoian security grid. His name is Yousi, and he has an interesting letter in the front of the book, but we're not sure who is the recipient. But here," now Anders pointed to the bottom of the letter, "he mentions Iason."

"Hmmm. So he does," Voshka murmured. He furrowed his brow, thinking. "I seem to remember meeting a Yousi, briefly, when I was staying with Iason. It was just before we left. But he didn't strike me as possessing the sort of the intellect capable of producing something like this. He was something of a simpleton, if I recall, unless I am gravely mistaken."

"Yousi suggests, in the letter, that if the logs were discovered, Jupiter would have punished him, perhaps tampered with his mind," Anders pointed out. "Shall I have another scholar take a look at this?"

"No. Let's keep this very quiet." He handed the translation back to Anders. "Take these to my quarters and lock them up in my desk."

"Yes, Sir."

"And see if Aranshu is finished in the bath hall. Put a neck-chain on him and have him brought to the bridge."

"What about the other one...Azka?"

"Send him to the harem when we arrive."

"Sir, I really must protest. Aranshu is far too dangerous to keep in your private chambers. Why don't you send him to the harem, and keep the other one instead? Azka is such a docile, obedient pet."

"Don't argue with me," Voshka sighed. "I know what I want."

"But he intends you nothing but harm! He's a renowned terrorist!"

"I told you, the discussion is over. Obey me," the Commander snapped, his eyes flashing. "I won't tell you again, Anders."

Anders made a face as he struggled to bring his emotions under control. He wanted to argue with Voshka, but it was clear the Commander was in no mood for his opinion.

"Yes, Sir," he murmured finally, though the tone of his voice betrayed his annoyance.

Voshka gave him a warning look before turning on his heel and continuing on to the bridge.

Anders sighed, clenching and unclenching his fists as he looked after the Commander for a moment. Then he reluctantly made his way back to Voshka's chambers.

He was so irritated with Aranshu and the Commander's infatuation with him that he felt his blood boil with an overwhelming surge of anger. He'd never liked Aranshu, not even when he was a boy. And now he despised him.

When he entered the Commander's chambers, all his frustration with the situation seemed to hit him at once.

Aranshu had already returned from his bath and was chained to the bed, snarling and snapping at a meek attendant who was attempting, rather ineffectively, to rub oil onto his naked body.

"If you insist on behaving like an animal, you'll be treated like one," Anders announced with transparent impatience. He wasted no time muzzling the angry pet, much to Aranshu's obvious annoyance. Azka was watching the entire affair from the corner of the room, his eyes wide.

The attendant shot Anders a grateful look and then proceeded to rub the remaining oil onto Aranshu's body.

"Leave us," Anders ordered, when the boy had finished. He motioned to Azka. "Have him taken to the harem, as soon as we arrive."

The boy nodded, relieved to be excused from attending the Commander's wild charge, who he found completely terrifying.

As soon as they were alone, Anders dropped the logbook and the translation onto the bed and then pulled out a knife, pressing the blade up to the Aristian's cock.

"I'm on to you," he whispered. "You may have charmed the Commander, but you haven't fooled me, not for one second. You fuck with him, and I'll turn you into a eunuch. Don't think I won't."

Aranshu became very still while Anders slowly moved the blade over his cock in a teasing, provocative manner. The two men eyed one another, each evaluating the resolve of the other.

"You're all mine now," Anders continued. "And I'm sick of your game. We're going to play my game now. Turn over."

The Aristian slowly obeyed, warily eyeing the blade that Anders kept pressed threateningly against the base of his shaft. Once he was on his stomach, Anders manacled his hands behind his back. Then he repositioned him so that Aranshu was lying half on the bed, with his legs bent over the side.

Anders stood for a moment with his arms crossed on his chest, staring down at him. Aranshu's ass-cheeks glistened from the oil that had been rubbed into his skin, the marks from his recent punishment still evident. Suddenly Anders had an overwhelming urge to give him a brutal fucking in repayment for the trouble he'd caused. He decided that was precisely what he was going to do—after he administered a bit of physical punishment.

"Don't move," he warned. Then he went to a cupboard and retrieved one of the Commander's paddles, holding it up when Aranshu looked back questioningly at him.

"Perhaps you've forgotten I have the authority to discipline you whenever I find it necessary," he announced. "And I find it necessary to discipline you now, for your behavior with that attendant. I seem to remember you disliked being paddled, years ago. Let's see what you think of it now."

With that, he gave Aranshu a ten hard whacks with the paddle in quick succession. The young man made a slight noise of protest, his ass warmed uncomfortably by the paddle. He felt ridiculous to be punished in such a fashion, his hatred for Anders reaching new levels. He turned his head, straining to look behind him and fully expecting to be helped to his feet.

"Oh, we're not finished," Anders warned, when he saw Aranshu's impatient look. He held the paddle up against the Aristian's ass, caressing his skin with the cool, smooth wood. After a long, teasing moment, he swung again, delivering another stinging blow. Aranshu winced; this last strike hurt more than all the previous, because now he was really starting to feel the assault on his bare flesh.

Anders seemed to feed on his growing agitation. He would keep the paddle pressed teasingly up against his skin for several minutes, patting him in a menacing fashion as he whispered all manner of threats to him. Then, with a mighty swing, he would whack him again, eliciting increasingly anguished groans from Aranshu with each strike.

The angry bodyguard proceeded, with methodical deliberation, to punish Aranshu for nearly half an hour. To Aranshu, it seemed like an eternity. He had no choice but to submit to his torture; he was muzzled, his arms were manacled behind his back, and his legs were chained together, about two feet apart. He was bent over the bed, vulnerably positioned for whatever the bodyguard had in mind.

He was still raw from his punishment at the Commander's hand and found the bodyguard's new approach to discipline an utter torment. He could not even beg for an end to the session, for he was muzzled. Anders seemed to take sadistic delight in his strangled cries, laughing whenever he made any sort of sound.

Finally Anders tossed the paddle onto the bed. Aranshu eyed it where it landed, wanting to look back but not daring to. He waited, his heart beating fast when Anders pressed his knife up against his throat, the weight of his body now full on his back.

"It's time for a little more intimate punishment," Anders whispered in his ear. "You fuck with the Commander, and I'll fuck with you. Remember that. Now. You want my cock up your ass, don't you? Huh? I know you're dying for me."

Aranshu felt a sharp, searing pain as Anders filled him without any sort of preparation. He opened his eyes wide, shocked that the guard had actually penetrated him. He made a sound, but the muzzle prevented any real vocal protest. Anders kept the blade pressed hard against his throat.

"I should slit you, ear to ear," he threatened, as he moved against him. "And I'm going to fuck you, just like this, whenever you misbehave. Voshka is too easy on you. I won't be. This is just between us, by the way. If you're stupid enough to say anything, I'll kill you. He won't believe you anyway."

Aranshu spread his thighs instinctively, allowing Anders to penetrate a bit deeper.

"Yes," Anders hissed, allowing one hand to slide down the side of his body to his hip, which he caressed briefly. "You want it, don't you? You want to be fucked! You'll spread your legs wide for anyone who mounts you! Fucking little whore!"

Aranshu closed his eyes, filled with shame. The bodyguard's taunt was true—he was enjoying being taken, even now, just as he enjoyed it when the Commander mounted him.

"You like to be fucked," Anders accused. "Isn't that right?"

Aranshu groaned, pushing his hips back from the bed to relieve the pressure against his cock, which was now quickly springing to life, much to his complete mortification.

Anders slid a hand around his hip and apprehended his erection. "You *are* enjoying this! You pets are all the same! Filthy trash!" He seized Aranshu's cock, yanking on him angrily. "Go ahead and come, pet! Show me what a predictable slut you are!"

Aranshu tried to hold back, tried to hang onto some shred of self-respect. But his body responded to the bodyguard's manipulations with disappointing eagerness; in the end he was unable to stop the spray of semen that dripped between his legs and down his thighs, humiliating him.

"You have no self-control whatsoever," Anders spat. "Disgusting animal!" He suddenly fell silent, breathing hard as Aranshu began to internally twitch against him. He was startled by the sensation and equally surprised by his own ascent, which crept up unexpectedly. He gave a few excited gasps and then he ejaculated, thrusting a few more times as he released the last remnants of his seed.

"Remember what I told you," he whispered, as he remained inside Aranshu for a moment. "If I see any hint of disobedience, you'll get a little visit from me again. Count on it. I'll fuck you like this, or maybe I'll ram a poker-hot iron up your ass. So I suggest you undergo a major attitude adjustment."

Anders then withdrew and pulled him roughly to his feet, turning him around to face him.

"If you want this to be over now, get on your knees before me and show your submission to me," he demanded.

Desperate for an end to the bodyguard's sadistic agenda, Aranshu immediately got down on his knees, bowing his head.

"Kneel down!" Anders shouted, grabbing Aranshu's hair and pushing him to the floor. "Lie prostrate before me!"

Aranshu choked back his shame and did so, submissively positioning himself before Anders as requested.

"Where's the great rebel now?" Anders taunted, looking down at him with a mixture of haughtiness and disgust. "Is that all it took, to make you humble yourself before me? A bit of punishment and a good fuck? I ought to piss on you. You deserve it."

Aranshu waited anxiously, half-expecting the man to make good his threat.

But Anders only stood over him, his hands on his hips. "We'll put an end to today's session. But I'll have my eye on you, Aranshu. I expect you to show this same deference to the Commander. We'll have a special time together, each day, just the two of us, until I'm convinced you know the meaning of obedience. Is that clear?"

Aranshu nodded.

After that Anders helped him back to his feet and into the revealing chain-mail shorts that was to be the entirety of his outfit. He collared him and then led him, still muzzled, from the Commander's chambers toward the bridge, smiling at the Aristian's changed attitude. Aranshu's cheeks were flushed red and he kept his gaze lowered, trudging submissively beside Anders.

⁂

"SO? IS HE COMING?" OMAKI DEMANDED, when Heiku flipped his phone closed and seemed to be lost in thought.

"Hmmm? Oh! Yes, he's on his way. He says he's bringing a student."

"What do you bet it's Aertis Jin? So, the rumors are true!"

"How long will it take him to get here?" Iason asked anxiously.

"They're at Minas Qentu. So it shouldn't take all that long," Heiku answered.

"What are they doing there?" Xian wondered.

"He said it was a dig," Heiku reported, unable to resist exchanging a knowing look with Omaki.

"Oh yes. I'm sure he's doing some very *special* exploration," Lord Ghan snorted.

The other Blondies, with the exception of Iason and Raoul, all snickered at this. Iason, however, could not be diverted from the matter at hand and turned to Raoul with a look of utter misery.

"All right now," Lord Am scolded. "Enough of this talk. This is hardly the appropriate time for this sort of revelry."

"Yes, of course. You're quite right," Heiku agreed, putting on a serious face. "Iason, do please forgive us. We're all still a little intoxicated. I know I'm not thinking clearly, at any rate."

"Nor I," Omaki agreed, with a shake of his head. "I keep thinking this can't be real."

"I can't just sit here and do nothing!" Iason exclaimed, standing up and starting to pace.

"Wait for the Headmaster, Iason," Raoul advised gently. "He'll know what to do."

"I can't wait! By then who knows where Riki will be!"

At that moment, Iason's communicator began to emit the signal for an urgent incoming message. The frantic Blondie whipped it from his tunic pocket, reading the identification with alarm. "Incoming holo-projection from Amon Qentu!"

"Amon Qentu? Impossible," Raoul murmured.

"But…he's dead," Xian remarked, with equal perplexity. "Isn't he?"

"Apparently not," Lord Quiahtenon whispered, as the three-dimensional projection of the notorious Federation leader appeared before them all. The image was a close-up of Amon's face, and he wore a strained expression, though his lip was curled into a smile. As the camera panned out, it became clear what Amon was up to.

"Riki!" Iason cried. He gasped, as did the other Blondies, as Amon undulated against the restrained mongrel.

"I'm enjoying your little mongrel, Iason," Amon said in a low voice. "I'll be fucking him, just like this, until you're ready to come and get him. Surely you know where I am. But in case you don't, I'm at the Qentu estate, west of the Qentu Mountains. I'll send along the coordinates for you, if you like. But don't try to bring anyone else along. If you do, I'll be forced to kill Riki. I'll torture him first, of course."

Lord Mink was speechless, staring at the projection in disbelief.

"This is only a recording," Xian remarked, pointing to the time coordinates at the bottom of the projection. "But it was just made a few minutes ago."

The Blondies watched the rest of the projection in stunned silence, but when the camera panned in close to Riki's face at the moment of his release, Iason dropped the phone and collapsed into his chair, his face ashen-white.

The communicator spun across the floor but continued to play.

"That's unconscionable." Raoul shook his head, placing a sympathetic hand on Iason's shoulder.

"It's an instinctive physical reaction for Riki to ejaculate when he's being stimulated," Heiku explained quietly, feeling as uncomfortable as everyone else when the mongrel climaxed. "It doesn't mean anything."

The Blondies watched the rest of the recording in silence.

"You'd better hurry, Iason. I have quite an appetite for sex. I'll be ready again in less than an hour," Amon taunted.

The holo-projection abruptly stopped, but then automatically began playing again, with the camera panned in close to Amon's face.

"Shut it off," Raoul hissed.

Omaki and Xian both scrambled for the communicator, managing to turn it off before Riki came into view again.

"What am I going to do?" Iason whispered.

Lord Am crouched down next to him, putting a reassuring hand on his thigh. "Konami will be here soon."

"Amon's not going to *seriously* hurt him," Heiku added. "He's using Riki as bait."

"But if I don't give him what he wants, he *will* hurt him, probably even kill him!"

"Now, you don't know that," Omaki argued, though he and Heiku exchanged worried looks.

"You heard what he said," Lord Mink continued. "He's waiting for me. I have to go to him."

"Obviously you can't do that," Raoul protested. "That's just what he wants. He has a fate far worse in mind for you, I'll wager."

"I wonder what exactly he *does* want," Heiku remarked thoughtfully.

"Well, that's obvious! He wants Iason's throat!" Raoul answered, standing up and pacing for a moment. He turned back to Iason, frowning. "He's the one behind your poisoning, make no mistake!"

"The Police claimed that Amon was killed during the Federation Strike, nearly ten years ago," Lord Sami remembered. "That was the end of the Federation, they said."

"Yes, Xian, we all know that," Heiku answered, making no effort to hide his annoyance.

"You don't have to get all snippy about it," Lord Sami grumbled. "I'm just commenting on the fact that this is all something of a surprise."

"Now that's an understatement," Omaki remarked wryly.

"He's certainly grown up into quite the man," Heiku said after a moment. "The last time I saw him, he still looked wet behind the ears."

"The last time you saw him? You knew him, Heiku?" Omaki pressed.

"Oh no. You mistake my meaning. I only meant his image, when all those alerts for his arrest were posted, years ago."

"He's very handsome," Yousi announced. "But he seems like a bad man."

"Yes, Yousi. He is, that." Lord Quiahtenon gave Yousi a reassuring smile and then glanced nervously at Iason.

Iason brought a hand to his head. "Forgive me. I'm afraid all this has…brought on one of my headaches. I need to lie down."

"Of course," Omaki said, rising. "Shall I show you to the rooms?"

"Don't trouble yourself. I know the way. Please, come get me when Lord Sung arrives."

"Would you like me to rub out your shoulders, Iason?" Raoul offered, frowning with concern.

"No. Thank you, Raoul. I just need to lie down for a moment."

"That's an excellent idea, Iason," Heiku said encouragingly. "Lie down and try to relax. We'll tell you the moment Konami arrives."

Iason nodded and retired from the great hall, walking slowly toward the corridor that led to Omaki's guest suites, and then entering one of the first rooms he came to.

"I hope he'll be all right," Raoul murmured, watching Iason for a moment before sitting down and then clenching and unclenching his fists. "I feel so helpless."

"We all feel that way," Heiku sighed. He shook his head, lowering his voice. "I didn't want to say this when Iason was here, but this situation…is not good. I'm afraid Riki may be doomed, and there's nothing any of us can do about it."

Raoul, despite knowing that Iason would be devastated if something terrible were to happen to his pet, couldn't help but almost hope that the mongrel would soon be out of the picture. Although he'd finally come to respect Riki for bravely stepping in for Iason at the Public Whippings, he knew that as long as Riki was around, he would never win Iason back. He immediately felt guilty for his secret hope, lowering his gaze to his hands and trying to dispel the thought from his mind.

"You really think Amon was behind Iason's poisoning?" Heiku asked, after a moment.

Lord Am nodded. "It seemed like an organized strike. That happened nearly the same time we started fearing an incursion on the grid. We didn't know who it was, but now that we know Amon is still alive, it seems obvious."

"Why does he want to hurt Iason?" Yousi wondered aloud, not at all following the conversation.

"It's Jupiter he's after," Raoul answered. "He blames Jupiter for the disintegration of the Federation. And he knows the best way to strike at Jupiter is through Iason."

Megala, who had been silent for much of the evening, finally spoke up. "He seems a bit out of the loop. Doesn't he know about the Public Whippings?"

"That's true," Heiku nodded. "He seems to assume Iason is still Jupiter's favorite. I'm not so sure that's the case anymore."

"I wasn't going to bring it up," Lord Sami remarked, "but it does seem a bit odd that after that conversation with the Headmaster and this transmission from Amon, Jupiter hasn't made any attempt to contact Iason."

"Perhaps Jupiter isn't even aware of the situation," Raoul pointed out. "What if the Sentinels are keeping all this from her?"

The other Blondies nodded their agreement, pondering the situation for a moment.

Raoul looked at his watch. "Blast! Where is Konami anyway? How long can it possibly take to get here from Minas Qentu?"

Quin, Yousi's attendant, approached the group of Blondies a bit fearfully. He had been listening, along with other frightened attendants and pets, to their conversation from just outside the great hall. All the more confident, vocal attendants had accompanied the injured to the hospital, leaving the quieter, more uncertain attendants in charge, and none of them wanted to interrupt the Blondies when they were obviously having a serious discussion. But Quin knew something had to be said.

"Excuse me, Master," he murmured, bowing his head.

Yousi looked up, surprised. "Yes?"

"I'm sorry to bother you, Master. But I thought you—and the others—would want to know," now Quin glanced nervously at Raoul, "that Lord Mink…has just left the villa."

Raoul leapt to his feet. "What?!"

Quin instinctively took a step back, looking up fearfully at the angry Blondie who towered over him. "We think perhaps he slipped out through the window. I just saw his vehicle lift off."

"No. No!" Raoul cried. He raced outside with the others on his heels, just catching a glimpse of the Blondie's hovercraft before it shifted into high gear and transformed into a retreating speck of distant light, heading south toward the Kattahar Mountains.

Iason inserted his communicator into his terminal, his hands shaking as he did so. "Reply to last incoming via Independent relay," he commanded.

The computer screen flashed with his identification sequence, and then Amon appeared.

"Ah, Iason. How good of you to call. And just in time…I'm just about ready for round two."

"Keep your hands off my pet," Iason hissed. "I'm approaching the Kattahar mountains now, just as you asked."

"I think you mean the Qentu mountains," Amon clarified, a slight hint of anger flashing in his eyes. "Send me a coordinate relay to verify."

The Blondie hastily punched in the relay command, anxiously scanning the screen for any sign of his pet.

"So. You *are* on your way. Excellent."

"I want to talk to Riki."

"Very well," Amon agreed. "I must say, I'm quite pleased you've decided to be so cooperative, Iason. It will make this so much easier for us all. Here's your pet."

Riki's face suddenly filled the visual screen. For a moment Iason was rendered speechless, the sight of his beloved pet filling him with worry and love. "Riki," he whispered. "Are you all right? Has he hurt you?"

"Don't come," Riki answered. "Please don't come, Iason."

"Of course I'm coming."

Riki shook his head, his eyes filled with urgency. "You can't come. He has an agenda for you. Promise me you won't come!"

Amon's face once again filled the visual screen and Iason, who had been instinctively leaning forward, jerked back, repulsed.

"How sweet," Amon purred. "Your little pet really does care about your well-being, Iason."

"If you dare lay your hands on him again, you will spend your last few moments of life screaming in agony," Lord Mink promised, his voice low with anger and hatred.

"My. Such drama. However, you're really not in a position to be giving out orders. I suggest you remember that when you arrive, if you care about what happens to your pretty little pet. You'll be brought before me in chains, Iason. You'll get down on your knees before me. And you'll do everything I say, no exceptions." Amon gave him a wink, a slow smile curling his lips. "I'm looking forward to it."

The transmission was cut and Iason was suddenly staring at the rotating glyph of his own identification sequence. Almost immediately, the incoming emergency beacon blinked and Raoul came on-screen, his anger evident in his strained features.

"Iason! What are you doing? Are you insane?!"

"Don't try to stop me. I'll take care of this."

"Turn around NOW, before it's too late!"

"Please respect my decision," Iason replied calmly.

"How can I respect a decision that will get you killed? If Amon doesn't kill you, think what Jupiter will do when she finds out where you've gone?" Raoul shook his head, his green eyes full of pleading worry. "Iason, please. You're not thinking straight."

"Raoul's right," Heiku said, his face crowding in behind Raoul. "All of us agree with him, Iason. You're letting your…attachment to your pet cloud your thinking. Turn around and come back and we'll discuss what to do."

"I know perfectly well that you intend to sacrifice Riki," Iason replied. "So I have no interest in what any of you have to say."

"Give me the phone!"

Iason instinctively cringed when he heard the voice of the Headmaster.

"Lord Sung is here," Raoul announced, his relief obvious. "Listen to him, Iason. He'll know what to do."

The Headmaster's fearsome face came on-screen. It was immediately apparent he was in no mood for arguments. Iason could never remember seeing him look quite so stern…or angry—not even very recently, when he had lectured Iason and the others ad nauseum on their foolish rebellion. "Iason Mink. Turn that hover-craft around THIS INSTANT and return to the villa!"

"I'm sorry, Headmaster," Iason answered. "I can't do that."

"You WILL do it, and you'll do it NOW!"

It was so ingrained in the Blondie to obey the Headmaster's commands—especially ones delivered so forcefully—that Iason was almost tempted to obey. He clutched the triangular arms of the steering wheel with resolve, though his entire body was shaking.

"Did you hear me, Iason? TURN BACK AT ONCE!"

He shook his head. "I can't. Computer, terminate call."

The screen returned to the rotating identification glyph. Iason was breathing hard. "Computer, block all incoming calls, with the exception of Amon Qentu and any calls in that region," he said firmly.

"I cannot block all calls," the computer answered. "You are entering Forbidden airspace. Tanagura Police are requesting confirmation of your identity and the immediate alteration of your flight path."

"Override Alpha-Seven-Seven-Delta-Nine."

Iason waited anxiously, expecting Jupiter to come on-screen next, or perhaps one of the Sentinels. But nothing happened. He sighed, turning his attention to the matter at hand, and wondering how he would be able to get Riki—and himself—out of Amon's grasp alive.

To be continued in
Taming Riki Volume II: A World Divided, Part 2